A GOODE INHERITANCE

A Chief Inspector Sofia Faraday Mystery

PAULA WELCH

ISBN: 978-0-6487655-6-1 (POD)

National Library of Australia NLApp106213

Cover Designer: Donika Mishineva | www.artofdonika.com
Typesetting and e-book design: Emayyam Infotech
                    www.emayyaminfotech.com

Email: pjwelch.author@bigpond.com
Website: www.paulawelch.com.au

Previous Books by Paula Welch

Adult Fiction
River of Fortune
Cloud Piercer

Children's Fiction
The Interlopers

Dedication

I dedicate this novel to all my favourite detective novelists. Especially Agatha Christie who created two amazing sleuths—Miss Marple and Hercule Poirot.

Acknowledgements

Thank you to everyone at Aurora House, your professionalism is greatly appreciated.

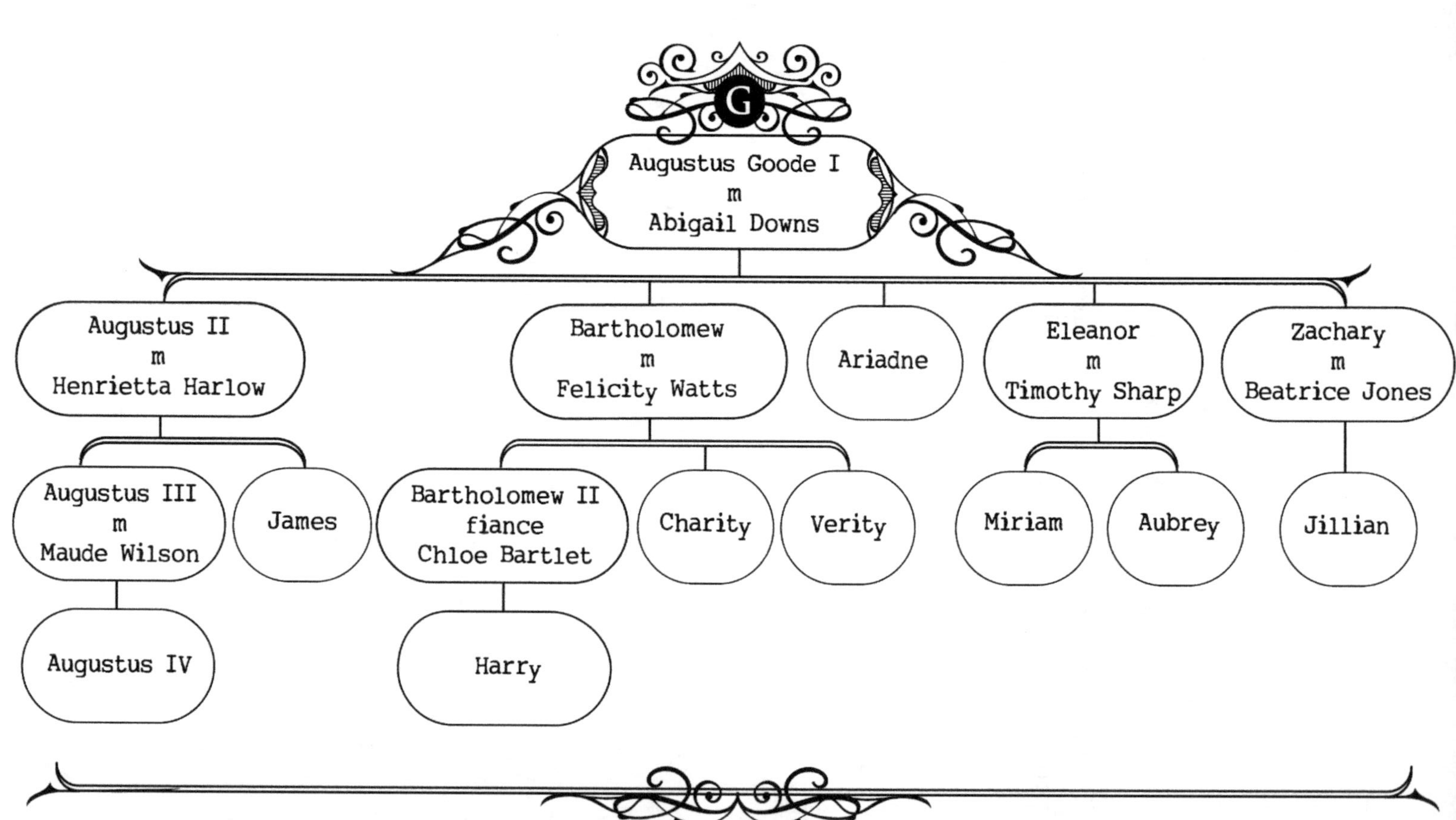

G
Augustus Goode I
m
Abigail Downs
Augustus II
m
Henrietta Harlow
Bartholomew
m
Felicity Watts
Ariadne
Eleanor
m
Timothy Sharp
Zachary
m
Beatrice Jones
Augustus III
m
Maude Wilson
James
Bartholomew II
fiance
Chloe Bartlet
Charity
Verity
Miriam
Aubrey
Jillian
Augustus IV
Harry

Prologue

Some people believe our future is written in the stars, while others believe it's found in the cards that are dealt. Does that mean we should follow a path already paved out for us? No matter where it leads? One single event could set off a ripple effect long into our futures. Do we hitch a ride, sit back and see where fate takes us or actively intervene and, in doing so, change our destiny?

The Goode family were good neither in name nor in virtue. The monarch of the family was Sir Augustus Goode I. The 'I' was added after he was knighted. However, his knighthood was not through exceptional achievements or for services to his country, far from it. Instead, it was in lieu of a debt.

Augustus I had five children.

Augustus II was the heir. He endeavoured to follow his father's footsteps by hook or by crook. He was followed shortly after by Bartholomew, the spare. His razor-sharp mind told all who knew him he would far exceed his father and brother, legitimately or otherwise.

Next came Ariadne, followed two years later by Eleanor. Their dreams and ideals were of little consequence to a father who looked upon them as incidentals. Ariadne wanted nothing more than to paint the world and everything beautiful in it, and Eleanor, whose intelligence far surpassed all her siblings, was left feeling bitter and resentful. She worked twice as hard as her brothers and was given little recognition for her efforts.

Bringing up the rear was Zachary, the baby of the family. His true bloodline was never spoken of. Neither was the fact that he looked nothing like his father or fellow siblings. All in all, he was their mother's favourite.

Augustus I believed strongly in tradition and planted many seeds of prosperity, which he intended to enable his first-born son and heir to reap the rewards for many generations to come. Whether he was up to it or not.

It only took one generation to bring it all crashing down.

THE FOOL

The first card of the major arcana

The Fool is someone who is about to begin an important journey. Blissfully ignorant, he heads off into the unknown. Sometimes, he is thought of as an innocent adventurer, a dreamer and risk taker.
With his head full of dreams and ideas, he is led by his own desires. But, if he is not careful, he will encounter a journey too far to travel and take one too many risks.

1

Bartholomew Goode

A Monday in October

'It's inoperable.'

Bart stared at his doctor in disbelief, unsure if he heard him correctly.

'You better get your affairs in order, old chap,' the doctor added, showing as much compassion as Judas supping with his friend.

Bartholomew Goode stood up abruptly and exited the doctor's surgery. Like most people, he thought cancer only happened to other people.

Fucking hell! was his only thought.

2

Cricklewood Hall, Allington, Kent

Later That Same Day

'Welcome back, sir.' George Fox stood aside to let Bartholomew into his house. He could tell the news wasn't good.

George followed Bart into his study. Bart's ashen face told George all he needed to know. He was truly remorseful about Bart's situation. He walked up to the drinks trolley and fixed Bart a scotch. After adding ice, he handed it to his friend. Bart's dogs ran into the room to greet their master. But George could see Bart was in no mood to accommodate them. He called for Laurel and Hardy to follow him as he left Bart to his thoughts. George knew Bart would talk when he was ready.

George had known Bart all his life, first growing up together at Ashburton Manor, where his father was the estate manager, then later when he came to work for Bart on his own estate, Cricklewood Hall. George was loyal and regarded as a friend before servant. He had been grateful when Bart took him on as his driver. His drinking had cost him his previous jobs. Now, he was Bart's estate manager and all-rounder at the Hall, a sprawling estate in Kent, which Bart purchased shortly after his divorce.

George spent the afternoon tending to estate business. Eventually, he was summoned back to the study. When he entered the room, Bart was standing in front of one of the four giant windows that fanned out along the expanse of the room, gazing out at the resplendent landscaped gardens. The Hall was perched on top of a hill. Manicured gardens circumnavigated the entire estate. It was as worthy as any award-winning garden. Down by the lake, a garden folly overlooked a small waterfall. Fanning out along the lake, trees of every size and colour brought tranquillity to the gardens.

The folly was Bart's favourite place on the entire estate. He liked to walk down there each morning with his dogs. Nestled on the far side of the estate was an old walled garden. Untouched for decades, it was filled with an assortment of wildflowers, which had taken on a life of their own. Ashburton Manor paled in comparison to the beauty of Cricklewood Hall. Bart had spent nearly as much on the restoration of the gardens as he did on the Hall itself. Cricklewood Hall had been run-down with a leaking roof, damp walls, prehistoric plumbing and lighting that dated back to before WWI when he purchased it. Now, it was the jewel of Kent.

Bart had a natural gift for spotting investments. It was this gift of foresight, along with his shrewd business sense, which had made him a millionaire a hundred times over. He was a risk-taker and predicted the Hall's future beauty, even as the wallpaper peeled off the walls.

George walked up to Bart's desk.

'What did the doctor say?'

'It's inoperable,' Bart's reply was said without emotion, while he stared out the window.

'Poppycock! You're as tough as nails. You need a second opinion.'

Bart turned to face George.

'I was told to get my affairs in order, George. Time's run out. I can't fucking believe it. I'm not even fifty yet.'

'Don't act defeated, it doesn't suit you.'

Only George could get away with speaking to him that way. Bart looked at his friend and thought, *Why me, and not him?* However, he said nothing. Jealousy was a trait he didn't like to express openly.

'I changed my will after the divorce, when I first bought this place.' Bart looked around the room at what he had accomplished. 'My children are adults now and loathe being in my presence, thanks to my vixen of an ex-wife. My son despises my success and lack of attentiveness. Which by the way, paid for his education. And my two daughters barely share a single thought for me, unless it's to ask for more money. As for the rest of my family. Well...' He gave George a pointed look.

'They're not all half bad, sir,' George remonstrated. 'I know you love your children and Ariadne.'

'Of course I do. But Ariadne's always been needy, and my children should know better. When has hard work ever been a crime?'

George allowed the rebuff to go unanswered.

'As for the rest of them, egotistical, arrogant and thoughtless. I own more of the Ashburton estate now than Augustus does, and he still thinks it's his.'

George knew not to comment when it came to the two brothers. They were chalk and cheese, each tolerating the other for family sake. Always competitive. Appearance-wise, they were loving brothers, but behind closed doors their loathing was palpable.

Bart had spent the afternoon reflecting on his many achievements. He wasn't done yet. Down on the desk was a piece of paper with the Hall's crest on it where Bart had written out the names of his siblings and children. Beside their names he wrote down a single word that best described each of them. There wasn't one name that had a flattering analogy beside it. 'She Devil', was next to his ex-wife, Felicity. She obviously needed two words.

'You'll know what to do when the time comes,' George reassured him.

'Will I?' Bart mused.

'George.' Bart walked back to his desk and picked up the piece of notepaper. He stretched out his hand, offering it to George. 'Can you please send an invitation to the names on this list? Ask them to join me this weekend. It's best I get it over with.' George took the note; he knew everyone on the list all too well.

'Of course, sir.'

'I'm going to London for a few days to visit Sam and Hugo. I'll stay at my club.'

'Yes sir, I'll make the arrangements. I'll also make an appointment with another oncologist, while you're in London.'

Bart smirked, 'It won't do any good, George.'

'It won't do any harm either,' he replied, as he walked out of the room, muttering something about Bart's idiot doctor.

George entered his office below stairs and began making calls. The first one to an oncologist in London, the second to Bart's club.

George paused before he began calling Bart's family. George liked to envision them as chess pieces, cleverly positioning themselves on the board in readiness for when the king fell. The only exception was Ariadne, she was nothing like the others. But nothing drew the Goode family together like money. Whatever the outcome, George knew the months ahead were going to be very challenging indeed.

In regard to his own future, George wondered if his days at the Hall were numbered. Maybe it was time to put old ghosts to bed and move on with his life.

The thought terrified him. He needed a drink.

3

Ariadne Goode, Rose Cottage

'Why on earth does Bart want all the family together, George?' Ariadne asked, as she used the end of her paintbrush to scratch through her already tangled hair.

'I can't say, Ariadne. Bart will explain once everyone has arrived.'

'All right, I'll be there, but it won't be pretty.'

After hanging up on George, Ariadne had an uneasy thought. She knew it wasn't Bart's birthday, or anyone else's in the family. *Why on earth would Bart want the whole family together? He knows it never ends well.* He was up to something.

At forty-five, Ariadne had no children and lived alone in Rose Cottage on Bart's estate. Originally, she had rented a cottage on Augustus's estate, Ashburton Manor. Unfortunately, the more debt her brother got into the more he increased the rent.

Bart had thrown Ariadne a lifeline—Rose Cottage at Cricklewood Hall. Bart had promised Ariadne she could stay there indefinitely. This she accepted with gratitude. The gardens were far superior to walk through and paint in than the Manor's. It was a relief to Ariadne to get away from her childhood home. Bart was the only one of her siblings to understand and accept her neuroses.

Ariadne regarded herself as an artist, although she had never sold a single painting. She hated to part with them, except to present them as gifts to her family on birthdays and at Christmas. The word 'bohemian' best fit Ariadne's lifestyle.

Beautiful was an overstatement, but unattractive was underplaying it. She was slender with long scraggly auburn hair with hints of copper running through it. She liked to wear a scarf to keep her wayward hair out of the paint. One of her eccentricities was her collection of glasses, which she changed each day to reflect her mood.

On their father's death, Bart, Ariadne, Eleanor and Zachary had each received a respectable inheritance from the family estate. This covered Ariadne's rent and expenses, which allowed her to indulge in her passion. On rare occasions, Ariadne agreed to teach art classes at the local community centre.

George had always encouraged her to spread her wings. He was afraid she would become a recluse.

The phone call had made Ariadne anxious.

As always when in one of her moods, she called her friend Angeline Toussaint for guidance. Angeline was a friend and talented clairvoyant and cartomancer, who offered Ariadne guidance through her readings and insights. This was part of the reason Ariadne was concerned about Bart's announcement.

At Ariadne's last reading, Angeline warned of dark days ahead. However, she did often warn of dark days ahead. Only, last time, she sounded sincere, if a little standoffish. In Ariadne's three-card spread, *The Fool* talked of a new journey she was about to take, while *The Hierophant* indicated Ariadne should look deeper into herself and find the emotional endurance needed to commence her journey. The final card was *Strength*. Ariadne often wondered why she turned this card over more than any other, it was one of the character traits she lacked. Obviously, the cards were trying to tell her something.

Ariadne was often prone to panic attacks, so she relied on Angeline's cards for direction during those uncertain times. Angeline often told her the cards were only a guide to her subconscious. They would protect her if she saw the good in what they represented. But it was ultimately up to her to seek out and embrace the good in her life.

Ariadne had met Angeline during one of her infrequent art classes in Maidstone. They struck up an immediate friendship and had been close friends ever since. Bart told Ariadne not to trust her, he often said *'we're in charge of our own futures and not via fortune cards'*. Bart made sense, as usual, but Ariadne found comfort in what Angeline said.

Ariadne tried to get back to her painting. But her thoughts kept drifting to Bart. What was he up to? She was tempted to go over and ask him. But his indirect invitation for the weekend told her he didn't want company until then.

It was no good, Ariadne couldn't concentrate. She made herself a hot chocolate and sat in her little garden at the back of the cottage, contemplating Bart's announcement. Whatever it was, no good was going to come of it.

4

Potts & Billingsworth Partners, London

The Next Day

'Good to see you, old friend,' Hugo Billingsworth said as he approached Bart with an outstretched hand and a slap on the back. 'What brings you to London?'

Samuel Potts entered his partner's office through a connecting door between their respective rooms and gave Bartholomew the same warm welcome. Being schoolboys together had cemented their friendship for life. They were also the spares-not-the-heirs, which had required them to seek out their own fortunes, in whatever dubious manner they saw fit. Samuel and Hugo had become lawyers.

'I've got cancer,' Bart said, not waiting on ceremony. 'My doctor has given me six months, give or take. He didn't like to commit.'

'Fuck, Bart... how did that happen?' Sam interjected.

'How the fuck do I know? I was fine one day and not the next.'

'Sorry, mate, I mean hadn't you felt unwell?'

'No. I just felt off this last month.'

'How can we help?' Hugo said.

'I need to change my will.'

'Of course,' Hugo said. 'Just let us know who gets what, and we'll take care of the rest.'

'George has organised for me to see another doctor. I don't want to hear the same thing twice, it'll be like a second nail in my coffin. But he wouldn't take no for an answer.'

'He's a good man, Bart,' Hugo said.

'I know. But my current will is outdated, and I need to make changes. It's going to be messy. My only consolation is I won't be alive to see everyone fight over it.'

'Don't worry, we'll make it as watertight as a duck's arse,' Sam said.

'I know you will,' Bart replied, solemnly. Talk of wills was depressing him. 'I feel like I've been robbed of time.'

Neither friend knew what to say to him, so the room remained quiet until the ice broke.

'What are you going to do with the time you have left?' Hugo asked, sincerely. 'I can't imagine you want to spend it in the bosom of your family.'

'Fuck that. I'm going on holiday for as long as I can. Then I'll return and spend my final days at the Hall.'

'That's the spirit, Bart,' Sam said, trying to sound optimistic.

'Do you know who the lucky benefactors are?' Hugo asked.

'I've got to leave it to someone but fuck if any of them deserve it. At least Felicity can't get her hands on it. I always hoped I'd outlive that bitch.'

'Pity you can't bump her off on your way out,' Sam joked. 'It's not like they can give you a life sentence.' They all chuckled at the idea. Bart looked off in the distance as he contemplated the astute thought.

'So, what do you want to do? Sell, pass it down the line, or divide it up?' Hugo asked, returning the conversation to a more serious note.

'I haven't gotten that far yet. I've invited everyone to the Hall this weekend. I want to gauge their reactions to my misfortune. Once it's played out, I'll give you my final instructions. While I'm away, I want you to keep an eye on my brother's estate. If Ashburton Manor forecloses during my absence, I want you to buy it.'

'You got it. It won't be pretty evicting Augustus,' Hugo said, with a smirk.

'That's an understatement,' Sam said.

'I want him out. He's had me over a barrel for too long. Not anymore.' Both men nodded, they understood why.

'Would you like us to join you this weekend?' Sam asked. 'I've always wanted to be an umpire.'

'That's not a bad idea. I'm going to need friends around me while I endure my family's insincere condolences and scheming.'

'That's sorted then, we're coming,' Hugo said.

'Bring Jane and Harriet with you, if you think they could stand it.'

'I think not, we never mix business with pleasure,' Hugo said.

'Besides,' said Sam, 'with all your family there, sparks will fly, and your wife uses too much hairspray.'

All three men chuckled.

'Thank you, you've been good friends over the years.' Bart was sounding resigned. All three friends felt uncomfortable. Emotion wasn't a strong quality any of them aspired to well.

'Fuck it, let's go to the pub,' Sam said.

'Why not! The Prospect of Whitby, my shout,' Hugo offered, as he stood up.

Now you're talking, thought Bart as all three friends stood up to leave. Hugo gathered his jacket from the coat stand and they walked out of his office.

'Keys!' yelled Alyson, sticking her right hand out in Hugo's direction, wiggling her fingers back and forth. Hugo obeyed her command and handed over his keys with a wink before heading out the door.

Bart's driver took them to the riverside pub where they stayed until last orders.

The next day Bart paid a visit to the oncologist George insisted he see.

THE MAGICIAN

The second card of the major arcana

The Magician is on a journey, one he believes he can traverse with conviction and confidence. Unlike The Fool, who blissfully heads into the unknown, ignorant of what lies ahead, the Magician is driven by self-assurance in each endeavour he undertakes.
But the reversed Magician can turn trickster. He will lead you astray. So be wary of him and do not stray from your chosen path.

5

Cricklewood Hall, Allington, Kent

Four Days Later

As the cars arrived at the Hall early Saturday afternoon, George was there to welcome everyone and see them to their rooms. Sam and Hugo were already present and relaxing privately in the library, enjoying cigars. Something their wives discouraged.

Bart watched from an upstairs window as his family arrived. He didn't want to see any of them until dinner was served. He still felt angry and resentful. *Why me?* kept ringing in his ears. *I'm not done yet*!

In business, Bart's confidence had always ensured his success, but his life choices had left him wanting. Everyone says, *if I could go back, I'd change this or that*. But he wasn't a man to dwell on past misgivings. Money was tearing his family apart. But it was also the only thing keeping them together.

Bart kept hold of his maudlin thoughts as he dressed for dinner. Laurel and Hardy were lying on his bed. Two constants he could depend on. All they wanted was companionship and a pat of acknowledgement.

After they arrived, Bart's family meandered into the sitting room for afternoon tea. They made polite small talk, while enjoying canapés and drinks. *So far so good*, thought Ariadne, although they hadn't been in each other's company for more than half an hour.

Bart's children, Bartholomew Junior, or Bartie to his family, was twenty-five, while the twins, Charity and Verity, were twenty-three. Bartie felt uncomfortable about being summoned to the Hall. Gossip was his father was about to announce his retirement. Bartie didn't believe that for a moment, he knew his father was too obsessed with his work to simply walk away from it in his prime.

Chloe, Bartie's fiancée had agreed to join him this weekend. He reached out and gently squeezed her hand. He hoped the rumours were false. He was concerned his father would ask him to take over the business. Something Bartie wouldn't consider. He wanted to make his own way in the world. Chloe had told him before they arrived to stand fast, no matter what. Bartie wasn't his father.

Bartie didn't know his father as well as he should, but he knew the type of man his father was. Bart would never just pass his estate on down the line of succession. He despised that tradition. Bart had worked too hard to see his business run aground under someone else's steerage. He had endured frustration after frustration watching Augustus destroy his own father's business. Bart knew his son was clever, but his resentment ran deep, thanks to his mother. Bart refused to be like his own father. Lineage meant nothing to him. He would have handed over the business to any one of his children if they held the slightest interest and ability in running it.

Charity and Verity cared less about why they were summoned to the Hall. He knew, like always, their only task this weekend was to persuade him to increase their allowance. They would have been well coached by their mother before their arrival. And would undoubtedly inform her of everything that transpired during the weekend.

Bart's children had gone to the finest schools money could buy. However, the twins didn't seem interested in lasting careers.

Bart blamed his ex-wife for their behaviour, but, in reality, he could have stopped their indulgences. He instead opted for a peaceful existence, anything to keep Felicity off his back.

Bart often envisioned that, if his father had let him run the family business, their lives would be very different. But his father had been a traditional man, who always stated "The heir inherits". The consequence of that tradition had seen Augustus II sell off acre after acre of the family estate to Bart over the last ten years. The more of Ashburton Manor Bart purchased, the more resentful Augustus became.

The brothers' distaste for each other could be sensed in the air around them. After the family business collapsed, Augustus II relied on the rents from the estate cottages. When he realised the potential for selling the cottages to 'townies' from London, he sold the lot. Believing himself to be shrewd, he had relieved himself of all the maintenance costs and landlord responsibilities. Then, the money ran out, again. As it stood, there wasn't much left for Augustus III and his children to inherit. Regrettably, Bart's brother never thought that far ahead.

Watching them all from a distance, Bart knew he would have to make a decision soon as to who should inherit his fortune. But damn if any of them deserved it. His only gnawing thought was to make sure Felicity never got her sharp claws into any of it.

In the evening, they gathered in the sitting room before dinner was served, where George prepared their cocktails.

Bart paused before opening the door to the sitting room, deliberating over when he should inform everyone of his news. Before their after-dinner mints or after. Should he let them enjoy dinner or watch them squirm uncomfortably at the dining table? It would certainly give them something to talk about all evening.

Fuck it! Bart decided to spoil their appetites.

Bart entered the sitting room to find everyone clustered in small groups. Chloe was sitting with Ariadne on the settee. Bartie and Chloe's son Harry was with Chloe's parents for the weekend away from the volatility that was sure to erupt over the weekend.

Eleanor and Beatrice (Zachary's wife) were sitting together talking about inconsequential matters, for appearances' sake. While Zachary and Timothy (Eleanor's husband) had secreted themselves away in the corner of the room. Being business partners for nearly four years didn't stop Timothy thrusting his finger into Zachary's chest. Charity and Verity were oblivious to everyone as they were on their phones. Augustus and Henrietta were huddled together by the window talking with their eldest son Augustus III, and his wife, Maude.

Hugo and Sam were sitting across from each other beside the fireplace, waiting for Bart to make his appearance.

Once more unto the breach, dear friends. Bart walked into the room.

He picked up a drink from the drinks trolley and stood in the middle of the room.

'Can I have everyone's attention,' he said, raising his voice over the chatter.

The Goode family quietened down as Bartholomew cleared his throat. He had the room, all eyes were on him.

'I have something I need to tell you all.' But before he could continue, Augustus interrupted him.

'Save the speeches, Bart. We're starving, and I'm not in the mood for your dramatics. It can wait.' He believed he was speaking for everyone as head of the family. Henrietta shuffled a little farther away from her husband.

'No, it can't,' Bart said, sneering at his brother. Predictable as ever. *Why me and not him?* Bart thought again.

'Well, what is it?' Augustus snapped.

'I'm sorry to say I have cancer… My doctor has given me six months to live.'

There was a long pause. Everyone remained silent. They stopped drinking, posting across social media, and fidgeting. All waiting for the punchline. None was forthcoming. The only one who took Bart seriously was Ariadne. Tears started to well up, but she would never dare to show her grief, not in this room.

'That isn't very funny, Dad,' said Bartie.

'I'm not laughing, son.'

This was followed by a flurry of 'Oh my gods' and 'Oh, poor Bart'.

Bart thought he saw a wry look pass fleetingly over Zachary's face. But it was gone as quickly as it arrived.

'There must be treatment?' Bartie said, genuinely shocked.

'Not at this late stage,' his father replied, noting his son's concern.

No one knew which way to look. This was not what they expected when they received their invitations.

'Of course, we'll come and look after you, won't we Charity?' Verity said, nudging her twin, who looked a little taken aback by her sister's hollow suggestion.

'Oh, yeah… of course.'

'Thank you, my darlings, but that won't be necessary. I'm going abroad for as long as possible. Somewhere where the sun always shines. Then I'll return and enjoy my final days at the Hall.' This remark was followed with more, 'Ohs' and 'that's a good ideas', one 'well, why not, you should enjoy yourself' and a silent 'for fuck's sake'.

As it turned out, dinner was unusually sombre and strangely polite. Bart sat at the head of the table, king on the board, looking out over his subjects. Hugo and Sam were on either side of him, like two steadfast bishops. Bart could rely on them to propel conversation forward throughout dinner. He managed to catch a few whispered conversations but couldn't hear what was said. He only knew the chatter was about him.

Once dinner was over, everyone withdrew to either the sitting room or the billiards room. Throughout the night, everyone paid their deepest respects and sympathy. The outpouring of sympathy was nauseating. *Why me?* kept creeping into Bart's thoughts as he accepted their platitudes. But he accepted their empathy with graciousness all the same.

'That didn't go too badly,' Sam said, smoking one of Bart's expensive cigars while sitting on the terrace later that evening with Hugo and Bart.

'You're right. I studied them all through dinner,' Bart said. 'Most could barely look at me. When they did, they grinned sheepishly. God knows what they're all whispering now.'

'They're scared of showing emotion. That's the upper class for you. But I did hear a few interesting snippets of conversation,' Hugo said.

'What?' Bart asked.

'Timothy and Zachary for one. If looks could kill… and I don't mean you, Bart. Their partnership is starting to unravel.'

'Let it. It will be interesting to see what Zachary does.'

'Do you want us to have a quiet word with Timothy?' Sam asked.

Bart thought for a moment, 'No… let it ride.'

'Why didn't you tell them what the other oncologist said?' Sam asked, eyeing Bart through the haze of thick cigar smoke, before the breeze took it away.

'Because I want to see how they behave over the next few months.'

'You're playing with fire, Bart. Someone's going to get burnt,' Sam replied. 'Don't be foolish.'

'No one's ever accused me of being a fool, Sam. I'm a risk taker, always have been. That's why I'm successful. I'm about to undertake the most arduous journey of my life, and I'm taking my family along for the ride.'

'Be careful, especially where Augustus is concerned,' Hugo warned, agreeing with Sam.

'I can handle him. Whatever happens, I'm going to have the last laugh,' smirked Bart as he slowly exhaled his own cigar smoke.

The three friends stayed up until the early morning discussing Bart's predicament.

The family innuendos, plotting and scheming didn't start showing themselves until the following morning at breakfast.

6

Breakfast

Eleanor joined Timothy at the breakfast table. Her husband had been unusually quiet since last night. Eleanor didn't believe it was due to Bart's news. They weren't that close.

Already present at the table were Augustus, Henrietta, Ariadne, Zachary and his wife Beatrice, who was wishing the weekend was already over. The third generation of Goodes was still in bed. Hugo and Sam ate their breakfast in their respective rooms. A luxury they were never afforded at home.

At forty-one, Zachary had been blissfully married for fifteen years. He believed Beatrice didn't know about his affairs. They had one daughter who was away at school. Being the youngest of the five siblings, Zachary had been his mother's favourite. He was sired by a man she actually loved. His handsome good looks never failed to secure him privileges. He had a face that made most women go weak at the knees. It served him well over the years. However, old habits die hard in the Goode family, and his extramarital affairs were now about to impact his marriage.

Zachary was a hedge fund manager in a small but prestigious finance firm in London, which he co-owned with his brother-in-law, Timothy. Unfortunately, Zachary thought being a hedge fund manager, meant hedging one's bets.

Timothy, who sat at the opposite end of the table from Zachary this morning, learnt this the hard way. Timothy had relied on the Goode family name and connections to bring in lucrative clients. Business had been profitable until discrepancies started to appear on the balance sheets. Timothy cursed himself for not dealing with Zachary sooner. Glaring at Zachary down the table, Timothy regretted ever going into business with him. He was grateful Eleanor didn't know anything about his predicament. Timothy still believed he could resolve the matter on his own.

Eleanor, at forty-three, was the fourth sibling. She had become a successful marketing executive. Married to Timothy Sharp for nineteen years, they had two daughters, Miriam, eighteen, and Aubrey, sixteen. Unfortunately, Eleanor had lost sight of her own good fortune as jealousy and bitterness had never forsaken her. She detested the traditional hierarchy and everything it stood for. Mainly because in the Goode family, it never included women. Even if she had been the oldest sibling, Augustus, Bart or Zachary would have inherited before her. Eleanor's resentment was like a tick, dug in deep that sucked the benevolence out of her. Although, thanks to a flourishing career, she earned more than Augustus and Zachary combined. But that didn't stop her acrimony towards her brothers, especially Augustus who squandered everything he had been given and Zachary, who only had to ask to get what he wanted.

Eleanor was itching for a confrontation, so she decided to have a little fun at breakfast. Ariadne wouldn't bite, but she knew she could get a rise out of Henrietta. She took a sip of coffee and cleaned her teeth before commencing.

'I wouldn't be surprised if Felicity already knows about Bart's condition, thanks to Charity and Verity,' she said to no one in particular at the table. She waited for a response as she put more butter on her toast.

'Well why wouldn't they,' Henrietta replied on cue. 'She's their mother.'

'I'm sure she's already made an appointment with her lawyers to ensure she… sorry, I mean her children, get the bulk of Bart's money.' Eleanor watched for anxious faces around the table.

'I saw Felicity at the theatre last week,' said Beatrice. 'She looks smashing for her age.' She looked at Eleanor when she made the last remark, knowing Eleanor could never compete with Felicity in looks or style.

Eleanor eyed Beatrice, wondering if the stories around town about Zachary's philandering were true.

'How about you, Ariadne, seen anything of your sister-in-law recently?' asked Beatrice, knowing Felicity was a raw subject with her.

'No, and I don't intend to,' replied Ariadne, who was losing her appetite. She knew where the conversation was headed.

'Felicity has no claim on Bart's estate anymore,' Henrietta said. 'I don't know why you feel the need to bait everyone.' She took another sip of her tea.

'You know Felicity. That bitch will find a way,' Eleanor replied.

'Bart's lawyers will take care of any disputes,' Augustus II said, finally entering the conversation. 'Those three are as thick as thieves. The last thing Bart would want is Felicity getting her hands on his money.'

'True, but if she challenges the will it could be years before anyone gets anything. That might put you in a bit of a pickle, Augustus,' continued Eleanor, with a snide grin.

'I don't know what you're talking about,' Augustus replied, eyeing his sister with contempt.

'No… really? I thought Bart had been buying up the Manor, acre by acre? He owns more of it than you now, doesn't he?' she said mischievously.

'That's between him and me. Mind your own business,' he snapped.

'You're sounding bitter again, Eleanor,' Beatrice chimed in. 'Not a good colour on you.'

Henrietta wanted to get up and leave. But she knew it was just what Eleanor expected her to do. Augustus's family had dubbed her the family neurotic because it felt to her like that the sky was always falling down. Mind you, she was neither neurotic nor anxious before she married Augustus. Henrietta had endured their declining years with dignity. Her inheritance depleted years before and her marriage a disappointment, but Henrietta was still lady of the Manor. But the Manor was falling down around her ankles. Just like last year's knickers. She knew Bart would eventually own all of the Manor. That was too much to bear.

Once Bart owned Ashburton Estate in its entirety, they would be out on their ears. Not that Bart had anything to be jealous about. In a way, Henrietta felt relief. It would all finally be over with. She knew the brothers' resentment ran deep. She often heard Augustus talk in his sleep. She chose to remain silent, for now—what was the point in dwelling on anything now, Bart would be dead in six months. But she feared the trouble had only just begun.

Henrietta's thoughts were interrupted by Eleanor.

'I guess you'll have to foreclose soon, if Bart doesn't bail you out, again?'

'Why wouldn't he, Eleanor?' Henrietta remarked. 'They're brothers.'

'Be quiet!' admonished Augustus to his wife.

Henrietta looked at her contemptable husband. She hated it when he spoke down to her.

'Don't panic, Henny.' Eleanor smirked as she put more toast in her mouth.

'Stop calling me that! It only belittles you.'

'Maybe you can move into one of your own estate cottages. Oh, hang on, you can't, you sold them all.' Eleanor winked at her brother with satisfaction before forking the last of her scrambled egg into her mouth.

'Enough!' Ariadne yelled. 'Bart will leave his fortune to his children.' She didn't know what was wrong with her sister this morning.

'Ashburton Manor has been in our family for four generations. It's his duty to keep it that way,' Augustus retorted.

'Four, ha! You mean two,' scoffed Eleanor.

'Our father's legacy will continue.'

'What legacy, you mean the one started with our father cheating in a poker game? *That* legacy?' laughed Eleanor.

'Stop fretting, Augustus,' interrupted Zachary. 'Bart won't embarrass the family name. I'm sure he'll leave us all a little something.' Wishful thinking on Zachary's part.

'You better hope so,' Timothy barked. Eleanor gave her husband a curious look.

'Bart will do whatever he chooses. It's his money,' Ariadne admonished.

'Of course it is,' Eleanor replied. 'I'm sure Bart's children will squander their father's inheritance, just like you did ours, Augustus.' Eleanor had saved her bacon for last.

'You've always been a spiteful bitch, haven't you?' Augustus snapped.

'Not by choice,' she replied. 'I'm sure you'll get exactly what you deserve, Augustus.'

'If not,' Zachary said, 'you'll just have to get a job like the rest of us.'

Zachary had never forgotten Augustus' reply when he had asked him recently for a loan.

Ariadne excused herself from the table and went for a walk, just as the rest of the family started to come down for breakfast. She didn't want to hear anymore. Ariadne knew Bart would be generous, he always was. God only knew why—they didn't deserve it. Was everyone else's family as dysfunctional as hers? Ariadne's siblings had been rivals since they were young. She often wondered why her parents encouraged it.

Their jealousy ran deep. She hated all the petty squabbles. Bart was dying and all they could talk about was his money. Life was too short to worry about petty things. She knew it would only get worse over the next few months. She felt depressed and wanted to go home. There was a half-finished painting there that needed her attention.

Ariadne walked down to the folly where she found Bart sitting on a bench with Laurel and Hardy by his side. They were rolling on the grass trying to dry off.

'Aren't you hungry?'

'I had something in my room, earlier,' Bart said, as he moved aside to let her slide down next to him. Laurel and Hardy sat up on Ariadne's arrival and waited for their customary pats on the head.

'They're already at it!'

'I thought they might be,' he replied, smiling.

'What are you up to?'

'I'm not sure yet.'

'Think positive, Bart. I think you should get a second opinion.'

'George thought the same thing.'

Ariadne turned and hugged her brother for what felt like a millennium, she thought he needed it.

Bart was nearly tempted to tell Ariadne his news, but he stopped short. He allowed her to comfort him, he thought she needed it. She had always been overemotional.

Bart watched on as his family departed down the long country driveway. They had all behaved as he expected, pre-judgemental, fake, empathetic and conceited. He was contemplating his predicament. A plan began to form.

As Zachary drove away, he was grinding his teeth. Something Beatrice hated. He needed an injection of funds, and soon.

Timothy and Eleanor remained quiet for most of their drive back to London. Timothy was weighing up his options. Fight or flight came to mind. Although… he wanted to kill Zachary. Eleanor, who had amused herself earlier at breakfast, now felt ashamed. She flicked away a tear as she reflected on how bitter she had been then. Her only thought was *why do they always make me behave that way?*

Eleanor had barely spoken to Ariadne all weekend. They were sisters, supposed to be best friends. Eleanor couldn't understand why it bothered her so much to see Ariadne so happy with so little. Ariadne always appeared content with her life.

Verity and Charity drove back to London in Charity's Mercedes-Benz. Verity was calculating what she thought should be her share of her father's estate. She would finally be able to buy her own apartment and move out of the shadow of her sister and mother. Charity, who vexed her sister by driving under the speed limit, knew everything was going to change now. The thought terrified her. All she kept thinking was her family was getting smaller and smaller. She felt even more alone.

Augustus drove home in stony silence. He was in no mood for conversation. His family decided to stay clear of him for the next few days.

7

One week later

Bart's bags were packed. He had learned a shocking lesson, life really was too short. The only two people who knew Bart's true destination were Hugo and Sam. They were sworn to secrecy. He knew he could trust them; they were more like brothers to him than Augustus and Zachary could ever be.

Hugo had given Bart the heads up that word about town was Felicity had already paid a visit to her lawyers. Bart laughed at the thought and promised himself that, over the next few months, no matter how challenging, he would put his time to good use.

Bart took a walk through the gardens of Cricklewood Hall before George drove him to his club in London. He had arranged to spend the night with Hugo and Sam at their club.

As he climbed into his car, Bart turned around and looked solemnly up at Cricklewood Hall. He was going to miss her. A sudden chill ran down his spine. He turned away quickly, determined all would go well.

On their arrival outside the club, Bart turned to George. 'Take care of the Hall and Laurel and Hardy. Don't over feed them, will you?'

'Of course not. I'll also look in on Ariadne.'

'Of course you will.'

They shook hands before Bart entered the club. George was relieved to see Bart's demeanour had improved of late. He wasn't sure how Bart would act on his return. George knew Bart could have a spiteful side to him.

That evening, the three friends toasted to life and happiness. Their drinking continued until the early hours. By mid-morning, Hugo had dropped Bart off at the airport terminal where they exchanged their final goodbyes.

Once comfortable in his first-class seat, Bart took a quiet moment to reflect on his life's choices. Past and present. Regarding his past business affairs, he wouldn't change a thing. Regarding his private life... he should have ran a mile when he first clapped eyes on Felicity. He pondered even longer on one more regret. He never should have gone into the woods.

He shook the melancholy away. He needed to resolve his relationships with his children. That would be a priority on his return.

Bart hadn't been a bad son, husband or father. But he certainly hadn't been a good one either. Building an empire had been hard work. He hadn't left much time for family commitments. He was driven by the need to prove his father wrong in his choice of Augustus to run the family business. Nevertheless, by the time Bart made his fortune, his father was dead, and his marriage was on the edge of a precipice.

Felicity appeared to be the perfect wife, from outward appearances she was sophisticated, charming, and elegant, everything Henrietta wasn't. Gradually, Bart discovered her inner qualities as well: vindictive, greedy and completely void of empathy. Towards him anyway. Their children were her weapons against him. So, she was handsomely rewarded in the divorce. Felicity kept their house in Pimlico, plus a sizable alimony. Although, since his diagnosis, he had stopped all payments to Felicity. She couldn't touch him now. None of them could.

As the plane accelerated down the runway, Bart felt the velocity of its engines thrust against his chest forcing him backwards in his chair. He felt afraid, but his only chance was to move forward.

As he rested his head back, he remembered the flurry of visitors that came to the Hall in the few days leading up to his departure. All paying their last respects in the old Goode family tradition.

By the time his plane landed in Switzerland, Bart had every single detail of his plan mapped out. He just needed to get over this malignant inconvenience first.

THE HIGH PRIESTESS

The third card of the major arcana

*The High Priestess is desperate to seek out her
inner knowledge and spiritual side. Her gifts are
her wisdom. Unlike the Fool or the Magician,
the High Priestess is on a spiritual journey of
enlightenment.
But think twice, when reversed the High Priestess is
heading down the wrong path. Someone is giving her
bad advice and will try to make her go against her own
intuition.
Beware of Greeks bearing gifts.*

8

Ashburton Manor

Three days before Bart's departure

'Did you speak to him?' Henrietta asked, as she climbed into bed next to her husband.

'Yes, I did,' Augustus replied.

'*And?*'

'How do you think it went?' Augustus belligerently recounted his conversation with Bart, leaving out certain discretionary details that his wife didn't need to know.

Cricklewood Hall

Earlier that day

'Your brother Augustus is here to see you, sir.'

'Send him through, thanks, George.'

'Refreshments?'

'He won't be here that long.'

Bart was sitting in his favourite worn out leather chair in the library, reading. He placed it on the side table beside his cigar and picked up his Scotch whisky. There were a few opened letters that needed his attention scattered on the small table. A rug was spread out in front of the fireplace where Laurel and Hardy slept soundly.

Augustus was shown in and sat down in the seat across from his brother. There was a moment's silence.

'We need a serious talk about your will,' Augustus said, cutting to the chase.

'Go on.'

'I've no revenue coming in now that I've sold the last of the estate cottages. If I don't get an injection of funds, I'll have to sell the Manor, and you wouldn't want that.'

Bart studied his brother's disposition, carefully. This was where they always ended up.

'If the wrong people learned about your little secret, you'd be spending your last days in prison.'

'I hardly think so, Augustus. Let's not forget, you're complicit for concealing it and extorting money from me ever since. You're the one that will go to prison, I'd be dead, remember?'

Augustus eyed his brother carefully; he knew he was right.

'No one wants to dredge up the past. I've been left with our father's failures, and as we can't all be as perfect as you, I need help repairing it. We need a fresh start. Before it's too late.'

'A fresh start for who?'

'Family takes care of family,' Augustus reminded Bart.

'Like you did Ariadne?'

'That was business. She could have bought the cottage off me, if she really wanted it.'

'That would have taken all her savings. What she had left of it, considering how generous she's been over the years towards her siblings and their children.'

'Look, this needs to be sorted in case...' Augustus left the last part of his sentence hang in the air. 'I know you'll give most of your estate to your children. I'm simply asking that you allocate funds for the Manor. It was your home too once, don't forget.'

'I've never forgotten. You've made sure of that. You'll know my answer when my will is read.'

'I'd rather have the funds before you depart.'

'By depart, do you mean on holiday or my death?' he asked sarcastically.

'You know what the upkeep of these estates is. I need an injection of funds before you leave. Then we can call it quits.'

'That's generous of you, Augustus. Don't worry so much. Everyone will get what is coming to them.'

'What does that mean?'

'If you have to foreclose before my death, I'll put in a good offer.'

'You fucker.'

'Ditto. You shouldn't have told her.'

Augustus paused for a moment. 'I... I was drunk, and it slipped out. How was I supposed to know she'd use it against you?'

'Because you're two of a kind.'

Ashburton Manor

Later that night

'Well, that wasn't too hard was it?' Henrietta said, as she continued to rub hand lotion vigorously over her hands and arms. Her face and neck already well covered.

Augustus ceremonially pecked his wife on the cheek. He cringed internally. *Like kissing a soggy Lady Finger biscuit*, he thought. He was left with the taste of lemongrass and lavender in his mouth. Augustus turned over and feigned sleep. He was fuming. Bart would not stop until he bought Ashburton Manor out from under him. *If Bart dies, his secret dies with him. But, then again, there wouldn't be anyone to contradict my version of events.* Augustus wondered if Bart's children would pay to keep their father's secret. He doubted they would.

His resentment towards his brother had morphed into anger by the time he finally fell asleep.

Henrietta continued to sit up in bed, she couldn't concentrate on her book, so she watched her husband feign sleep. She knew his visit didn't go well. Not that her opinion mattered in the slightest. A wasted degree from Cambridge was the least of her regrets. Marriage to Augustus Goode had been deemed prudent by both families. In the early days, she often wondered if she had married the wrong brother. However, over the years, she'd come to learn she had married into the wrong family. Her only accomplishments were her two sons, Augustus III and James. She prayed each night that her children would not turn out like their vindictive father and cruel grandfather.

Her saving grace was her charity work. She was highly respected by her peers for her services to charities in Kent, which had become quite successful under her watchful eye. It was a crying shame that Augustus had never contemplated asking Henrietta for her advice regarding the Manor.

Henrietta turned over and thought about her future. She was hit with a stark realisation. Augustus and the Manor would not be a part of it for much longer. With that blissful thought floating through her mind, she fell into a deep and restful sleep. She had Bartholomew to thank for that. Whether he knew it or not.

9

Two days before Bart's departure

'Your brother Zachary is here to see you, sir,' George said, raising his eyebrows.

'I thought he might come. Show him in, thanks George.'

Zachary sat down in the same seat his brother Augustus had the day before. Bart knew why he was here.

'I'm sure you know why I'm here,' Zachary began. Bart smiled and nodded. 'I'm grateful for the funds you gave me, but they weren't enough. I was hoping you could help your little brother out one final time. You're the only one I can ask. Augustus isn't exactly a great role model.'

'I didn't give you the funds, it was Ariadne. I told her not to. I told her she was only attempting to plug a sinking ship.'

Zachary was taken aback. 'I'm not sinking, Bart. I just have a cash flow problem.'

'Is that what you're calling it? Does Timothy know the full extent of your "cash flow problem"?'

Zachary looked long and hard at his brother. He was no fool. Zachary held no doubts Hugo and Sam would have dug into his business affairs on Bart's behalf. 'I've put my life savings into that firm. I just need a little help until I'm back on my feet again. I should never have gone into business with Timothy.'

'So you're blaming him now?' replied Bart, who waited for a reply. None was forthcoming.

'What about your house?'

'What about it?'

'It's worth a fair bit. Use that as collateral.'

'Fuck, Bea would kill me if she found out.'

'What makes you think she doesn't already know? She's a smart woman.'

'Are you going to help me or not?' Zachary was becoming impatient with his brother's nit-picking.

'I'll tell you what I told Augustus. Once I'm gone, everyone will get what they deserve.'

Zachary knew not to push his brother. It would only prolong his humiliation.

He stood up and walked out of the room. But before Zachary disappeared from view, Bart yelled out one last riposte.

'Be sure to thank Ariadne for the loan.'

Zachary was gone. Without even offering his brother a remorseful goodbye.

Cricklewood Hall

One day before Bart's departure

'Your daughters have arrived sir,' George announced.

'Wonderful.' Bart finished dressing and headed downstairs to meet all his children. Bart felt privileged to have so many family members arrive at the Hall to see him off.

Bartie, Chloe and their son Harry had arrived earlier in the day. They were currently taking a stroll around the gardens. Harry had found amusement chasing a squirrel. On their return, Chloe put Harry down for a nap.

Bart did love his children, but every time he met with them, he felt his ex-wife's vindictiveness boring into him. Especially Verity, who was her mother's daughter. However, he wished Charity would show some gumption and follow her own path. She was timid and always on edge. He hated that weakness in her.

Bart remembered what Sam had said about bumping Felicity off. It was still a tempting thought. Bart's main regret was not being honest with his children. He should have told them the truth years ago. Maybe they wouldn't have despised him so much. But then again, the risk would have been too great.

Bart hated self-loathing. But that was all he was left, lately. All that would have to change on his return. Providing all went well.

Everyone gathered on the terrace, where refreshments were waiting for them.

'How are you feeling, Daddy?' Verity asked.

'Not bad, thank you, sweetheart. What brought you all out here on this unexpected, but not unpleasant, visit?'

'We're concerned about you, Dad,' Bartie said, genuinely.

Bart had learned to his detriment that his son believed every man should stand on his own two feet. So, it was no surprise Bartie had little time for his sisters, who showed no talent or passion for anything except their own self-gratification.

Bartie knew his sisters were intelligent, but they never used it to their advantage. He tolerated his mother, out of respect, but always left her presence feeling dejected and emotionally torn apart. But most of all, he was angry at his father for not putting up a stronger fight during the divorce. It made him feel he wasn't worth the effort. To make matters worse, his father bought Cricklewood Hall shortly after the divorce and put all his time and energy into it, leaving none for his children. Bartie was too proud to ask why. As a child he used all his pent up energy on hate and resentment. But as an adult he no longer cared and put all his energy into his career and his own family.

As a small act of rebellion against his father, and the whole Goode family, he called his son Harry and broke with tradition. Bartie had always detested the class system in England and rebelled against it frequently. Little did he know, Bart was secretly pleased his son had mettle.

The only significant similarities between Bart and his son were their sharp minds and fierce heads for business. Bartie wanted his independence and not to be tied down to someone else's dream. In fact, Bart knew if Bartie inherited his business and estate, he would sell it all tomorrow.

Looking over at his father, Bartie did feel for his father's predicament. *To know you're going to die can't be easy.* Bartie did love his father, he just found it hard to like him.

'You don't need to go' Bartie said. 'If you stay, we can spend more time together.'

'I would have liked that, but I have to go. We can spend time together when I return. I'm sorry we haven't been a close family. But I am proud of you all.'

'Then stay,' Bartie urged. His emotions were starting to well up.

'I have to go.'

Bart had a moment's regret for what he was doing. But he allowed it to pass by.

'Why don't I stay here and look after everything for you?' Verity said.

'George will take care of Laurel and Hardy and the estate,' Bart replied.

'Who?' She asked.

'My dogs.'

'Oh.'

'I'll be gone for only a few months, when I'm back, we can spend time together.'

Bart's children stopped protesting. However, Verity's emotions could have been construed in one of two ways. A: she was sad her father was going and wouldn't get to see him until the end, or B: she was relieved he was going and wouldn't have to see him again until the end. It was hard to tell the difference.

Charity had remained silent throughout the conversation. She was torn between loyalty to her mother and sadness for her estranged father. She was becoming agitated and needed something to take the edge off.

Later that same day

'I did!' Verity yelled into her mobile. She was walking around the garden for privacy.

The voice on the other end of the call was inflexible and demanding.

'I need to know what the estate is worth, do you understand? Not just the house and grounds, but the contents as well. I need to know which paintings are originals, excluding your dizzy aunts. What furnishings are antique? If I'm to lay claim on anything, I need to know its worth.' Felicity was losing her patience.

'Fine, but I can't just come out and ask him, can I?'

'You can do it once he's gone.'

'He doesn't want me to stay at the Hall. George is looking after it.'

'It's your father's estate, you can do what you want—once he's gone.'

Verity hung up on her mother. She was fuming and wanted nothing more than to distance herself from both her parents. She was impatient to get her hands on her share of her father's estate. She knew why her mother had chosen her to valuate her father's estate. She was afraid Charity wouldn't know a Constable from a Monet. As Verity walked briskly back into the Hall, she knew one thing for sure. She had no intention of sharing her share of the inheritance with her mother.

Verity hated her mother. But she despised her father more. Verity cursed her father for being a cheat and a liar. She cursed her mother for making him that way.

A short time later

Charity was having her own phone battle with the same inflexible voice 'I will try, but Dad said George would look after the estate.'

The line went dead. Charity knew why her mother asked her to stay at the Hall and valuate her father's estate. She didn't trust Verity to do it. She would hawk everything of value.

Charity hated her mother's vindictiveness. But she loathed her father more. Why did he have to ruin everything with his lies and deceit? Charity trudged back into the Hall. All the while thinking, *I could disappear with my share of the inheritance. Go somewhere where nobody could disappoint me.* But the thought of being alone terrified her. She wanted to go to her Aunt Ariadne.

Bartholomew watched Charity enter the Hall from a sitting room window. He knew who she had been talking to. He felt sorry for both his daughters; his wife was a manipulative bitch.

He smiled at the thought of what Felicity would do when she eventually found out the truth.

THE EMPRESS

The fourth card of the major arcana

Her gift is abundance, she provides emotional support, generosity, security and comfort in times of need. Her goal is to foster harmonious relationships.
Although, when in reverse, she is a disruptive influence and causes strife in the home.

10

Cricklewood Hall

The day of Bart's departure

'Hello Bart,' Ariadne said, as she entered the sitting room.

'Come in and sit down. Pour yourself a drink,' he said. 'Everyone's come to see me off, literally. Except Eleanor, of course.'

'Knock it off. Pity doesn't become you,' she replied, as she took a seat across from him.

'Cheers,' Bart said, raising his glass to her. 'I would have thought I'd get more sympathy from you.'

'You've always used money as a weapon. Just like Dad.'

'I'm nothing like him,' Bart was clearly offended by the remark.

'Yes, you are. More than you know.'

'I've always been better than him, and you know it.'

Ariadne didn't want to argue with Bart.

'Don't go. Spend the time you have left with Bartie, Charity and Verity. They're going to need you. Charity came to see me yesterday. She's confused and angry.'

Bart wished he could, but he stopped short of telling her his plan. He couldn't trust her. She was too self-righteous.

'It's about time you told Bartie and the girls why you didn't fight for custody of them during the divorce. Before it's too late. They deserve to know the truth.'

'I can't. Not now, anyway.'

'When then? It might be too late when you return.'

'I need you to trust me, Ariadne. All will be well in the end.'

'You don't know that!' She always hated her brother's assuredness.

Bart watched as a tear ran down Ariadne's face. She always believed in worse case scenarios. Niggling regret crept in. So he took another swig of whisky to numb the pestilent feeling. He was touched that she cared. Bart couldn't tell her about his visit to the second oncologist, not until he knew the final outcome. He still had his doubts.

11

Two weeks later

George watched quietly from the hallway as Verity and Charity walked around the living room. Verity brazenly took photos of the paintings that graced the walls of the Hall. Then she took pictures of the furniture. Not knowing or caring if it was antique or not.

They had arrived the night before. After dinner, they began photographing the grand foyer, then the library, music room and study. Today, they were cataloguing the living room.

George kept his distance. Bart had told him, if his children arrived while he was away, he was to make them welcome. It was obvious to George what they were up to. But he did as Bart requested and kept an eye on them.

Verity and Charity headed down into the cellar. They didn't know a claret from a merlot, so Verity videoed everything on the shelves. On their return upstairs, George was there to greet them.

'If it makes it any easier, I have a full stock list of the wine cellar.'

'May I remind you, this is our father's estate and will be ours soon. *He* may tolerate you, but *I* will not,' snapped Verity. At least he thought it was Verity. He was unable to tell them apart.

'But until then, I'm accountable for everything in it. If your mother needs a catalogue of the estate's assets, I suggest she ask Bart on his return. Not that it's any of her business.'

'Why don't you go drink yourself into a stupor,' replied Verity. 'We all know you want to.'

George was sure which sister he was addressing now. He imagined shoving her face into the wall. But he chose instead to remain silent.

After a long pause, Charity interceded.

'Let's just go, Verity?' She wasn't in the mood for her sister's provocations.

'Will you not stay for dinner?' George asked. 'The cook is serving tripe. You know all about that, don't you, Verity?'

'Don't get too comfortable, George,' Verity replied. 'Your days here are numbered.'

The twins walked off. Only Charity did so with her head down. She hated what her mother was making her do, and she was ashamed that she needed her father's money. Initially, she had just smoked pot to calm her nerves from time to time. It helped numb her emotions. But it gradually became an addiction. Sleeping pills helped put her to sleep, while others kept her awake. She didn't care what she took anymore, as long as it numbed her emotionally. She felt she was losing control of her life. She wanted to get away from her mother's control. None of her family cared for her, least of all, her sister whom she shared an apartment with in London. The only one she could truly rely on was Ariadne.

George watched them from a second-floor window as they sped off. He pulled out his mobile and called Bart.

Bart didn't seem surprised. He knew who had put them up to it. But he was still disappointed in his daughters.

Bart laughed at George's retort about the stock list. Replying it would have been even funnier if Felicity had been there herself. George asked after Bart's health. His only reply was, 'as well as can be expected'.

George looked out over the great estate; the gardens were the only thing that kept him sane. They had a calming effect on him. A serenity, which he was going to miss. He called for Laurel and Hardy to join him outside. He took them down to the folly. He really needed a drink.

What are you up to, Bart?

THE EMPEROR

The fifth card of the major arcana

He is a protector, a man of maturity and wisdom, but he also demands power and respect in return. He keeps his emotions under control and uses rational negotiation and respect to protect what is his. With self-confidence, he controls his life, home and work and keeps everything in balance.
But when in reverse, The Emperor can be power-hungry. He can present as demanding and aggressive. He has no boundaries in what he will do.

12

Cricklewood Hall

Five Months Later

Monday, A dark and rainy afternoon in March

'Thank you everyone, I know it's been a wet and sad day,' Hugo Billingsworth said as he stood up and addressed everyone in the dining room.

No one appeared to care about the weather, so Hugo continued. 'Bartholomew Goode's ashes are now resting peacefully in his favourite part of the garden. Down by the folly. It's a shame he deteriorated so quickly at the end and couldn't return home to his beloved Hall.' Again, nobody appeared overly emotional except Ariadne and Bartie. Chloe sat next to Bartie, resting her hand on his in a small display of affection.

After a short memorial service, the meagre amount of guests had filtered into the sitting room for a light supper and drinks. As instructed by Bart before he died, it was a small family affair, with only a few close friends in attendance. Everyone was cordial and polite as condolences were offered up to his siblings and children. Once the guests had left, his family made their way anxiously in the dining room for the will to be read. The only exception to the rule about family was George Fox, Bart had requested George be present at the reading. Hugo and Sam had set up a television and linked their computer to it in preparation.

Verity entered the room, glaring at George as she passed him. A smile crept across her face.

'Start packing,' she whispered, as she walked past him. Charity had followed shortly behind her, eyes darting around the room. Ariadne witnessed her unkempt appearance—her bloodshot eyes and bitten-down nails—and could see immediately that it wasn't only due to remorse, but her worsening drug addiction. Her niece clearly needed help.

'Can we just get on with it?' Augustus said, already seated and impatient.

'Dear Augustus, I'm afraid it will take as long as it takes,' Sam said. 'This is Bart's will reading, not yours, so it should take more than two minutes.'

Henrietta took a seat next to her husband. She was looking forward to today's proceedings. She wondered how her husband would react.

'Everything that happens now is on the explicit instructions of Bartholomew Goode,' Hugo began.

Sam pressed enter on his laptop, then sat beside Hugo.

'This is Bartholomew Goode's last will and testament,' Hugo continued. 'Bart will be reading his own will, and I have printed copies, should anyone wish to review the transcript later.'

Ariadne turned ashen faced when she realised what her dead brother was about to do. She looked around the room to see an assortment of expressions ranging from distasteful to irate. She lowered her head.

But before Hugo could press play, he felt a sudden chill run down his spine. He thought a window had just opened. He quickly looked around him. Then he saw Felicity standing by the door.

She removed her coat, gloves and hat and strutted herself into the room, making sure every pair of eyes was upon her. Everyone sat motionless as she moved across the room. She had not been invited to the funeral and was not mentioned in Bart's will. Nevertheless, ferrel, ravenous dogs couldn't keep her from attending her ex-husband's will reading.

Hugo and Sam had been pre-warned, should Felicity try to interfere with Bart's will, as he knew she would, they were to fight her tooth and nail, until there was no money left. Her presence, though unnerving, was not unexpected.

Murmurings and hissing sounds came from under bated breaths as she stealthily placed herself between Charity and Verity. Her steely green eyes zeroed in on Hugo as he let out a cough and played with his tie before continuing. He now felt strangely hot around the collar.

No one was brave enough to tell her to leave. Not even Eleanor, who held her tongue for the sake of her nieces and nephew.

Once the room settled down, Hugo continued.

'As I said before, this is Bartholomew Goode's last will and testament. If his will is contested, no party shall receive their bequest until all disputes are resolved.'

'This is absurd,' protested Augustus.

'Be quiet, Augustus,' ordered Zachary, who was anxiously waiting to learn how much his possible good fortune would be.

Bartholomew Goode's image appeared on the screen. He was wearing a cream short-sleeved linen shirt, and a straw sun hat which hid what little dark hair remained on his head. The room was brightly lit by sunlight streaming in through a window. A keen observer would have noticed that he looked a little tanned.

'Good afternoon, everyone. By the time you are watching this video, I'll be dead. Please do not distress yourselves by this video. I'm sure there are only dry eyes in the room. I have lived a full and rich life. I'm proud of my success and the decisions I've made throughout my life. My only regret was not getting to know my children better than I did. For that, I am sorry.'

Bart gave a moment's pause to allow his children to reminisce on what could have been. But only a moment.

'Felicity, I knew you couldn't keep away.'

Felicity was clearly vexed, but she nodded graciously at her dead ex-husband. Bart rested back in his chair, satisfied with himself, now that he had everyone's attention.

'I thought long and hard about my will and who I should leave my fortune to. My children, whom I love, have shown little regard for me over the years. I've always felt regret for that. But I had my reasons. Bartie, I am proud of you and your success, but you have shown contempt for my wealth over the years and have chosen to seek your fortune elsewhere. You accepted no money from me, in your endeavours, for that I commend you. However, my contemptible hard work paid for your education. If I left you my estate, you would sell it off shortly after, with little regard to how hard I worked to achieve it. Verity and Charity, I should have paid you more attention, I'm sure you wouldn't have been as disreputable and thoughtless as your mother if I had. Unfortunately, your insincerity and lack of empathy were inherited from

her, no doubt. You received first-rate educations and squandered them. Money holds no value for you; it simply gets you what you want. I can't leave either of you my business, as you have no business sense.'

Bartholomew paused. All eyes flicked excitedly to Bart's children, who sat stunned by his remarks. Verity was scarlet and wanted blood for her father's comments. Charity lowered her head to hide her tears. She knew her father was right but despised him all the same.

These remarks gave Bart's siblings hope that they might receive a greater portion than previously expected.

'Augustus, I have bailed you out time and again, but never once did you seek my advice or help in running the family business. If you had, it may have survived you. You will have no say whatsoever, regarding my business affairs or estate.'

'Eleanor, it couldn't have been easy knowing you were inconsequential to a father you admired. Your drive for success was at the cost of your relationship with your family, who you chose to ridicule and despise at every opportunity. My only insight about you is that you dislike me less than Augustus but more than Zachary. You even showed contempt for Ariadne, who has helped you more than you know.'

'Zachary; you were always Mother's favourite—we all know why. But being the third son of a father who only valued the first has left you ignoble. You've charmed and schemed your way through success and failure, at your family's expense. You know what I'm talking about. Could I trust you with my business affairs? I think not. Which is why I sold my business while in the Bahamas. Lock, stock and barrel.'

Bart paused again to allow everyone time to absorb what he said. The twins were looking to their mother to intervene. It took all her strength not to react to her husband's performance. Bartie was a little surprised but chuckled at his father's overall predictability.

The only person he hadn't addressed directly yet was Ariadne, who anxiously awaited her turn. She kept fiddling with her necklace. It was about to come apart any minute, like her nerves.

'Lastly, Ariadne, you were dealt a shitty hand. But instead of living with the cards you've been dealt, you've chosen to wallow in self-pity. Stop living in the past and get on with your life, before it's too late. Regret is a cruel bedfellow. We've both had sleepless nights over the years. Get over it and move on.'

Ariadne was flushed and uncomfortable, everyone was looking at her. Bart had no right to bring up the past like that. George could see Ariadne's discomfort. He wanted to go over to her. That's all he had ever wanted to do. But he remained fixed in his seat as Bart's voice engulfed the room once more. George didn't like where this was going.

'To that end, I have decided to give you all nothing... You don't deserve my fortune. Your contempt and laziness have soured my good opinion of you all.'

'But, in the spirit of fair play, if you want my money, you'll have to earn it. So, I have set up a little game for you to play, with the help of Sam and Hugo, the two people in the room I trust most. Three tasks must be completed. The first person to complete them all will win the prize. You may work alone and, in doing so, pocket all the reward. Or you may work in teams and share the prize. Once you've solved the first clue, you will be privy to the second, and so on. If you fail to solve these three clues within one week, my fortune will go to someone more deserving. Namely George Fox.'

Oh Shit! thought George. It was now his turn to turn red in the face, he hadn't expected that. *What the hell are you playing at, Bart?* Bart paused again to allow everyone to settle down, as he had known all eyes would be on George, the poor bastard. Bart allowed himself an agreeable smile before continuing.

'*If you do not wish to play my game, advise Hugo and Sam before leaving this room. You are free to go and live your lives in the same contemptible manner as you did before. If you choose to play, Hugo and Sam will give you your first clue.*'

'*Thank you and good night.*'

The television clicked off and the room fell silent. For about five seconds. Then it exploded in an uproar. George wanted to dart for the exit, but when he saw the state Ariadne was in, he remained seated. Even in death, Bart was a cunning prick. George had only learned about Bart's game a few days ago, when Hugo and Sam arrived to set it up. He hadn't known the full extent of the game or his part in it until now. George sighed, dreading what the following week was going to be like. *Whatever happens, it will be sensational.*

Above the clamour, Hugo heard Zachary ask, 'How much is the estate worth now?'

'It is now worth an estimated, £70 million.'

'Fucking hell,' he replied.

'Holy fuck,' Verity, said under her breath. Whistles and sighs were heard reverberating around the room as everyone took in Bart's net worth.

'We'll have our lawyers onto you by morning, Hugo,' Augustus said.

'As you wish,' Sam replied. 'But remember, if you don't solve the clues within the week, George gets the lot.'

'You may contact Sam or myself at any time to receive the second and third clue, except Saturday night, as we have previous engagements. We wouldn't want to charge Bart penalty rates,' Hugo laughed, although no one else found his wit amusing.

'Remember, only when you give us the correct answer will we give you the second clue,' Sam reiterated.

'This is outrageous. Bart assured me he would bequeath me a financial sum. Just give me the money,' demanded Augustus.

'No can do, mate,' Sam said, enjoying Augustus' irritation. 'Bart's instructions were explicit.'

'What if I don't solve them first? The Manor is lost?'

'The quicker you solve the three clues, the sooner you'll win the prize,' Sam said.

Hugo stood up, 'Your week will start tomorrow morning at 8.00 am.'

'What if I contest the will?' Felicity said, speaking for the first time.

'This is none of your business, Felicity. You shouldn't even be here,' interjected Eleanor, finally standing up, ready to pair-off against her ex-sister-in-law. Eleanor's contempt for her brothers was only out-pipped by her contempt for Felicity.

'Don't talk to my mother that way,' snapped Verity, rising from her chair.

'If any of you contest the will,' Hugo interrupted, 'all funds will be blocked to everyone until each claim has been resolved. May I remind you, Bart instructed Sam and me to contest every claim made against his will. No matter the cost. The only ones who will benefit will be Sam and me.'

'And if we walk away now, we get nothing, is that correct?' Bartie asked.

'Correct,' Sam said.

'Fine, I'm out. I'll say goodnight to you all,' Bartie turned his back on his family and walked out of the room. Chloe followed quickly behind him, proud that Bartie wouldn't play his father's game. Although, £70 million was no small change.

Stupid boy, Felicity thought, knowing he was as pigheaded as his father. She wasn't going to let anyone else inherit Bart's fortune except her children and, by extension, herself. *If Bart wants to play games*, Felicity decided, *I'll play along*. She was going to wipe that smirk off his face one way or another.

'Give me the first clue,' Felicity demanded of Hugo, stretching out her hand.

'I'm sorry, Felicity, you're not named in the will, so I can give you nothing. I'm sure you'll be kept well informed,' he said, turning to Verity and Charity. He could never tell one from the other, except today one sister looked more dishevelled than the other.

On that note, Felicity spoke quietly to her daughters, then picked up her hat, coat and gloves and walked out of the room in a dignified manner. She had business with her son.

Those who remained in the dining room waited patiently for the first clue.

Sam retrieved his briefcase and extracted a folder containing the first clue. He handed out envelopes to the rest of the Goode family.

Augustus seized his envelope and stormed out of the room. He needed to speak with his lawyers. Henrietta followed quietly behind her husband. She found it difficult to hide her smile, which was growing by the minute. She nodded politely to Sam, Hugo and Ariadne before taking her leave. She knew things had taken a strange turn for the worse… or better, depending on how you looked at it.

Zachary took his envelope with a wink, trying to show indifference. Beatrice knew it was all for show. His demeanour didn't fool her. She knew he was in financial strife and needed his brother's money.

Zachary was still offended by Bart's earlier comments. *Trust—what did Bart know about trust*? He would wipe that sanctimonious look off Bart's face. *How sweet would it be,* he thought, *if the youngest child inherited the family's largest fortune?* Zachary left the dining room, pondering only whether he should work alone or collaborate with someone else.

Eleanor was tempted to walk out like Bartie. She didn't need the money. But it was the principle of the thing. *How ironic if I won the prize.*

The idea of bettering her brothers made playing the game all the more worthwhile. She could end up owning both estates. Damned if she was going to let Felicity get her hands on it. Eleanor took her envelope from Sam and, with rigid dignity, walked out of the room. Timothy followed behind her, he hadn't said anything during the reading. His heart sank in his chest when he heard Bart say Eleanor and Zachary would get nothing. *Goddamn Bart!*

Verity and Charity each took their envelope with the first clue then left the room in search of their mother. Verity knew if anyone could solve these stupid clues it would be her, by hook or by crook. She would insist on getting a share. A share didn't mean half.

Charity was shaking. Her dreams were dashed. She wasn't going anywhere for the time being. She desperately needed something to take the edge off. Ariadne had finally persuaded her to check herself into a clinic. Charity had agreed, as long as she told nobody. Once she was clean and sober, Ariadne insisted she stay with her at Rose Cottage.

Ariadne was the only family member left in the room. George walked up to Sam and took her envelope. He sat down next to Ariadne and handed it to her.

'It's anyone's game. Why don't you play along?'

'He said I had to stop living in the past. That I was full of self-pity. Do you think that?' she asked, still fiddling with her necklace.

'Bart was a very confident and challenging man. Used to getting what he wanted. He was robbed of time. That would have angered him. Neither of us want to see you live in the past. You have so much to give, Ariadne. You're got more talent in your little finger than all your family has put together.' Nodding his head towards the door her family had exited from.

Ariadne saw George's sincerity. Smiling back, she squeezed his hand and agreed to play. The thought of leaving Rose Cottage terrified her.

She stood up and walked over to Hugo and Sam, who were packing up.

'He gave me Rose Cottage, but there isn't anything written down on paper that I know of. Do you think I will be able to keep it, even with this new will?'

'I'm sorry, Ariadne, if there's nothing on paper it will belong to whoever wins the prize. I'm sure whoever wins will allow you to continue living there,' Hugo said, feeling regret for the first time that afternoon.

'Let's hope no one solves the clues in time, then you can keep the Cottage,' replied George.

'You knew Bart better than anyone, Ariadne,' Hugo said, putting his hand on her shoulder. 'Play the game. You never know, you may inherit the entire estate.'

'I'll help you, as best I can,' George said. 'I didn't set up the game, Bart obviously didn't trust me to... So there's no reason why I can't help you.'

'You know where our office is, if you have any questions,' Hugo offered.

George walked Ariadne back to her cottage. No one chose to stay at the Hall that night. They were either too angry or had too much to get on with. The question on everyone's mind was: *do I work alone or strike up an alliance, and with who*? Trust was not a word the Goode family embodied, especially not when it came to each other.

No one solved the first clue on Monday; they all spent the remainder of the day trying to absorb what Bartholomew had done. The scheming only commenced once everyone had time to gather their thoughts. Phone calls were made, deals broken or, rather, made. Suffice to say, nobody trusted anybody.

To no one's surprise, not one person thought to speak to Ariadne.

CLUE ONE

POTTS & BILLINGSWORTH

To solve your first clue, you must first solve the riddle in the poem. You will find a key within the poem that will help you solve the cipher and lead you to your first clue.

Once there, the answer will present itself to you. Only on completion of the first clue, will you receive the second clue.

Beware! Oh fools, in this game of chance
A game of clues, will send you on a merry dance
Remember, as you struggle to solve
Time is of the essence, seek and behold

<u>Single Column Transposition Cipher</u>

HIII	OOOW	VSPT	PLOA	THUA	ETIA	AFUT	ROSR
MIPH	RNOO	YBLE	ISAU	EIID	ODEU	SSEI	OOLA
LNTN	SBNE	MPYS	PTUO	TSNE	STPI	EASN	TPSS
TIPB	FETK	AGTT	NL				

CONTACT DETAILS: (0) 20 7249 8000 – INFO@PBLAW.CO.UK
POTTS & BILLINGSWORTH PARTNERS
35th Floor, 40 Bank Street, Canary Wharf, LONDON E14 5NR

13

Potts & Billingsworth

Day One, Tuesday Morning

'Mrs Goode is here to see you, Mr Billingsworth,' Alyson announced.

'Argh, send her in, I've been expecting her.'

By the time Felicity Goode was escorted into Hugo's office, Sam had arrived from his own office and sat down on Hugo's sofa. He wasn't going to miss this.

'Tea, coffee, scotch?' Alyson asked.

'Leave,' Felicity demanded. Hugo nodded east to west, so Alyson curtsied and made a discreet exit, making sure Felicity didn't see the expression on her face.

'Felicity,' Hugo said, extending his hand.

'Cut the bullshit, Hugo. I know you're both enjoying every bit of this.'

Felicity perched herself down in the chair directly in front of Hugo. Her dark hair was neatly pulled back in a bun, emphasising her large pearl earrings and deep-red lipstick. Hugo could see why Bart married her; her beauty had not diminished in all the years he had known her. She was a striking woman. It was a shame her beauty was only skin deep, inwardly she had venom in her veins. Her sharp grey eyes needed little makeup, outside of mascara, as they bore into him.

'Now, now, Felicity, all's fair in love and war. I've often described your divorce like the battle of Waterloo. You've had Bart on the run for years, now he's on the counterattack.'

'Bart's fortune belongs to my children. Not a fucking chauffeur.'

'Bart doesn't see it that way,' Sam said.

'Don't mess with me. It won't go well for either of you. I've spoken with my lawyers.'

'We're just following Bart's *very explicit* instructions,' Hugo said. 'We shouldn't even be discussing this with you, Felicity. You're not a beneficiary in his will.'

'But my children should be.'

'Only if they win Bart's game,' Sam said.

'What'll it cost?' she asked.

'I'm not sure we understand your meaning,' Hugo said, raising an eyebrow.

'Yes, you do, one, two million? Name it?'

'Sorry, Felicity, we've been instructed, if any Goode family member offers us a bribe or incentive during the game, we're to double it and add it to our fees.' Hugo couldn't help but smile.

'Would you care to offer us three?' Sam said.

'Fucker…' Felicity was sitting up even straighter than she was before. Ready to pounce. 'My lawyers said I could contest Bart's will on behalf of my children, on the grounds of a diminished mind. Which Bart clearly had.'

'That may be true. However, Bart met with two psychologists before his death, who signed affidavits to his competence. Good luck with that angle of attack,' Sam said.

'May I remind you,' prompted Hugo, 'if the three clues are not solved within the week, George Fox shall be declared the winner. The longer you challenge Bart's will, the less time you have to solve the clues.'

Felicity snarled at him. Hugo felt like a canary trapped in a room with a finely manicured Persian.

After a brief, hostile staring match, in which Hugo and Sam felt somehow outnumbered, she rose abruptly and left Hugo's office without another word.

Sam stood up and closed Hugo's office door. 'Do you think she'll tell the others?' Already knowing the answer.

'I doubt it,' Hugo replied, 'she's too vindictive. She'll allow the others to waste their time paying us a visit.'

Sam chuckled, 'Augustus will probably offer us five. He's more desperate than greedy.'

'I hope Bart knows what he's doing,' Hugo said.

Out on the street, Felicity wrapped her scarf around her neck as she waited for her driver to take her back to Pimlico. She had spent yesterday studying the clue but realised she would need professional help to solve them. So, she had invited a retired analyst from the Government Communications Headquarters, commonly known as GCHQ, for lunch. GCHQ provided security and signals intelligence to the government and armed forces of the United Kingdom, so Felicity was sure the analyst would be able to crack Bart's code. His hourly rate was higher than her lawyer's.

After the will reading, Felicity had caught up with Bartie and convinced him to participate in the game, no matter how distasteful he thought it was. Felicity reminded her son of family loyalty. Four chances of winning were better than three. Felicity was including herself in the game, unofficially of course.

After the reading, Felicity could have killed Bart, if he weren't already dead. While he was alive, she'd had him over a barrel. But dead, she had lost the upper hand and a lucrative income. She had an irritable feeling Bart's game was created especially for her and Augustus. Bart's warped way of getting back at them.

I will prevail, Felicity promised herself as she climbed into her Rolls Royce. *All's fair in love and war*, she thought as the black car stole her away from Canary Wharf.

Bartie had to explain to Chloe that he only agreed to play out of loyalty to his whole family. He knew if Verity and Charity won, his mother would see to it that nobody else benefited. He cared about his Aunt Ariadne and didn't want to see her lose Rose Cottage. Not after everything she had done for his sisters.

Bartie knew money was the cause of the underlining current that pulsed around his family every time they were together. Distrust was rancid. The only exceptions were Ariadne and his cousin James, who had attended the same boarding school as Bartie. They had managed to remain close friends despite their family's in-fighting. He never found that same closeness with James's brother Augustus III, though. He always seemed to have the weight of the world on his shoulders. Bartie was pleased the bitterness between siblings didn't extend to their children. He wanted the past to remain where it belonged.

Bartie knew something was wrong with Charity. She'd been fidgety at the will reading and looked hung over. He knew she drank too much, that was evident whenever she came for dinner. But after speaking with Ariadne, he was now concerned about her drug problem as well. In the Goode old family way, personal problems were never aired in public. But he was grateful to Ariadne for agreeing to help her.

14

Potts & Billingsworth

Day One, Tuesday Mid-Morning

'Mr Augustus Goode II and Mrs Henrietta Goode to see you Mr Billingsworth,' announced Alyson.

'Argh, send them in, I've been expecting him.'

After a short interlude, Augustus and Henrietta entered Hugo's office. He offered them a seat, which Augustus took without a word spoken.

'Thank you,' Henrietta said.

'Coffee, tea, Alka Seltzer?' Alyson asked.

Hugo gave Alyson a disapproving look that was all for show before she left the room.

'How may I help you today?'

'There's no point challenging Bart's will. Nevertheless, we all want this over with, one way or the other. If you give me the solutions to the clues, I will give you a reasonable reward for your efforts. You can be assured I will take care of Bart's children.'

'That's good of you, Augustus. How much?'

Henrietta rolled her eyes upwards; she knew what was coming. She had warned Augustus not to come. But, as usual, he refused to listen.

'I'm sorry?'

'How much do you intend to give Sam and myself?'

Augustus pondered Hugo's question a moment. Uneasy for the first time since arriving. 'Argh… let's say three million pounds.'

'That's very generous of you. Felicity only offered us two.'

Augustus instantly loathed Hugo. He enjoyed mocking him.

'What did you say to her?' Henrietta asked, trying to recover some dignity in the situation.

'The same thing I'm going to tell you. Bart has instructed Sam and me to double whatever anyone offers us and add it to our bill. We cannot be bought.'

'Son-of-a-bitch,' hissed Augustus, under his breath.

'That's the end of it, then,' Henrietta remarked, as she stood up to leave.

Hugo stood promptly and nodded to Henrietta, then he turned to Augustus and said, 'Solve the clues, and you'll win.'

'What if I can't?' Augustus whined.

'He was your brother. You only have to know him to solve the clues. Have you been *that* self-absorbed that you don't know your own brother?'

'I knew him well enough. In fact, well enough to keep his dirty little secret all these years. As have you.'

Hugo eyed him, coldly. 'Yes, and it cost him dearly.'

'What secret?' Henrietta turned from the door.

Hugo glared at Augustus. Neither of them needed to say anymore. Hugo's expression told Augustus *Be very careful.*

Augustus marched out of Hugo's office. He remained silent until he and Henrietta were back on the street.

'You'll need to hire someone to help you,' she said. 'There was nothing in the rules that said you couldn't. You can bet Felicity will. We'll speak with Augustus and James, I'm sure they'll know someone that can help.'

Augustus knew his wife was right. She was always right. It was what he hated most about her. They climbed into the Bentley. Augustus pulled out his mobile and searched for a number.

'Dirty little secret?' Henrietta asked, peering sideways at him.

Augustus cursed himself for being indiscreet, 'Forget I ever mentioned it. None of your business anyway.' But, Henrietta wasn't the type of woman to forget anything. She knew more than she cared to reveal at this moment.

'We need Bart's money if we ever want to repair that bloody roof,' she said. 'We only just managed to pay those exterminators. If James hadn't helped us, they would have sued us for payment.'

'You're the one who kept complaining about hearing giant rats scurrying around in the attic,' admonished Augustus, annoyed by his wife's infirmities.

'How could I sleep knowing they were up there running around?' Henrietta mumbled the last few words under her breath as she looked away from Augustus and out the window of the Bentley. She felt trapped inside the car, as she often did at the Manor.

Augustus had received a call from Zachary last night suggesting they pool their resources and share the money. Augustus told him he would consider an alliance. He wasn't inclined to share, but he needed to win. His bribe had failed, and two heads were better than one. Augustus dialled his brother's number.

'It didn't work.'
'I told you it wouldn't. So… are we in agreement?'
'Yes.'

15

Prospect of Whitby

Day One, Tuesday Afternoon

'You were right, Felicity and Augustus came in to see us this morning,' Hugo said.

'I thought they would,' laughed Bart, before finishing his pint. He was wearing a grey cap as his thick dark hair hadn't grown back yet. His raincoat was slung over the back of his chair.

Sam returned to their table with a fresh round of drinks.

Bart knew Eleanor would be too proud to visit Sam and Hugo. Ariadne would never consider it, and Zachary would be too busy scheming to waste his time on a fool's errand.

Hugo relayed the events of the morning's visits, along with a cautionary word to Bart that he was playing with fire. Bart only laughed and shrugged off Hugo's concerns. He was too excited at the thought of seeing everyone's expressions when they discovered he was still alive.

Bart's near-death episode had taught him a timely lesson in mortality. He'd worked hard all his life and what did he have to show for it? He had a lovely house, but no one to share it with, children who despised him and an ex-wife who clung to him like a monkey on his back.

His children would inherit his fortune, of course they would. However, Bart's reprieve from death stirred up old sentiments. He wanted to have a little fun. He wanted his family to appreciate him. He wanted them to appreciate his money. Past deeds also needed to be put to rest.

Bart's game was designed to challenge his siblings and see who was the most deserving of his respect. He also knew once everyone learned of his resurrection, old ghosts would drift out of the past to haunt him. He would have to deal with Felicity and Augustus once and for all. He would not allow them to blackmail him any longer. Life was going to change. But for now, he simply wanted to have a little fun.

'Good on George for organising the second oncologist,' Bart said, raising his second pint in the air. Hugo and Sam saluted also.

'Hear-hear,' they chanted.

Apparently, Bart's second oncologist's diagnosis wasn't as dire as the first. While his family thought he was in the Bahamas enjoying his last healthy months, Bart had been in Switzerland receiving treatment for his cancer.

Once the tumour had reduced in size, it was successfully removed. Chemotherapy and then radiotherapy ensured it would not return, at least not for the foreseeable future. With renewed vigour, Bart did eventually head to the Bahamas for his recuperation. It was during his convalescence that he conjured up the inheritance game. Like a cartomancer, Bart believed he had the ability to control and empower all those around him. He would lead them all down a challenging path he had orchestrated himself.

Unfortunately, like the Magician, if upended, his actions could turn against him. But for now, Bart was untouchable. Fate would have nothing to do with it.

'You should have told Ariadne and George. They actually care for you,' Sam said.

'I couldn't risk Ariadne blabbing to everyone that I was still alive. George has always had a soft spot for her, he would have told her.'

'You've deceived George into believing he'll inherit if no one solves your clues. That wasn't very nice,' Hugo said.

'He'll understand,' Bart said, a little too offhandedly. 'Let him dream he could become a multi-millionaire for a week.'

'You can be a right prick at times,' Sam said.

'Can't we all?' replied Bart, taking another gulp of his beer.

'When will you come into the office and sign your new will?' Hugo asked.

'I'll sign it once the game is over, next Monday.'

'See that you do,' Hugo said, finishing off his pint. 'More importantly, how long are you staying at my weekender?'

'I thought I'd move into one of the cottages on my estate tomorrow. Someone should have solved the first clue by then. I want to be there when they arrive. Don't worry, I'll be discreet, no one will see me. The cottage is at the far end of the estate.'

'You're on a fool's journey, Bart,' Sam warned, shaking his head and downing the last of his own pint.

'I know what I'm doing, Sam.'

'You know, your family are probably still deciding who to collaborate with,' Hugo grinned.

'So, who do you think will win? My money's on Felicity, she's the most ruthless,' Bart wagered.

'Mine's on Eleanor, she's the smartest,' Sam said.

'Well then, I'm going for Ariadne,' declared Hugo. 'I'll wager a £100 she'll outfox the lot of them.'

'You're on,' replied Bart and Sam, simultaneously. They shook hands on it.

'Mind you, I think Bartie will do well, as long as he breaks free of his mother,' Bart added, glad his son had agreed to play.

After they departed, Hugo and Sam hailed a cab and headed back to their office. Bart stayed a little longer, watching the river go by. He was looking forward to going home tomorrow, if only to a cottage on his estate. He missed his gardens.

He would have blamed himself for his children's behaviour, and his own, come to that, if he was accustomed to dwelling on past transgressions. Luckily for Bart, he wasn't. During his treatment and recuperation, though, Bart had reflected on his past. He only had one profound regret. No matter how deeply or shallowly they were buried.

Bart's game would last one week. That was long enough to see what his family was made of. He learnt, during his treatment in Switzerland, that Verity and Charity had stayed at the Hall. George kept him informed of the estate's comings and goings throughout his absence. He had predicted his wife's first move and had ordered George to remove the most expensive paintings and take them below stairs. He replaced them with lesser valued ones. He wouldn't put it past his daughters to remove them altogether on duress from their mother.

Bart's gift had always been the ability to predict a profitable outcome on his investments. His only misjudgement was marrying Felicity. In her, he had met his match in cunning and ferocity. Unfortunately, Felicity's claws were sharper than even his and often dipped in poison.

Bart smiled at the thought of Felicity's vexation. She had a lot to answer for. He made himself a promise, *Once the game is over, there are going to be some stark changes.*

He did feel a pang of guilt for George. He had been a loyal friend. But decided he would make it up to him on his return. Then he brushed that thought aside. Bart knew George had a soft spot for Ariadne. It could never amount to anything, though, and he certainly wouldn't want to encourage it.

Bart finished his pint and left the pub. He pulled his cap down and buttoned up his raincoat. The street was empty except for a woman on her mobile across the street. She stayed long enough to watch Bart walk down Wapping Wall and turn right onto the Thames Path.

Then, she followed him.

THE HIEROPHANT

The sixth card of the major arcana

The Hierophant brings unity between the body and soul.
He is also an educator. He will show you support, help
you realise your potential and allow you to grow.
He represents good judgement and fairness.
But, in reverse, the Hierophant can show poor
judgement—in yourself and in others. Don't be misled by
him, trust in your own judgement and decision making.

16

Rose Cottage

Day One, Late Tuesday Afternoon

'Thank you for coming, Angeline,' Ariadne stood aside to let her friend and confidante in.

'You sounded most urgent, *mon cher*.' Angeline entered the old cottage and took off her coat and hat, then headed straight for the fireplace.

Ariadne made them a hot chocolate. With a drop of Bailey's in Angeline's. While they drank, Ariadne explained what occurred at the will reading. She ended her account by confessing, 'So, if I can't solve the clues before the rest of my family, I could lose Rose Cottage.

'I was in shock yesterday, I tried to read the first clue, but I couldn't focus,' she said.

Ariadne gave Angeline the letter from Potts & Billingsworth which contained the first clue. Angeline cursed Bart for what he was doing, 'He's a thoughtless bastard, your brother!'.

'Let's see what the cards say. But I think you already know their answer, Ariadne. You must play your brother's game.' Angeline retrieved her Tarot cards from her handbag. She unwrapped them from their lavender velvet cloth and placed them on the table.

'We shall do the week ahead, *mon amie.*'

Ariadne quickly came to the table and sat down on the chair opposite Angeline. She shuffled the cards then gave them back to Angeline, who spread them out in an arch in front of Ariadne. Ariadne chose eight cards then handed them to Angeline. Today, Angeline used all 72 cards of the major and minor arcana. She knew Ariadne needed a more precise reading. Angeline still held hope that Ariadne would one day learn to trust her own instincts. She knew the cards reassured Ariadne, but she couldn't rely on them for ever. A day would come when Ariadne would need to trust in herself.

The first card Angeline turned over was the signifier. The *Five of Cups*. It denoted, upset and loss. Along with her sadness over the death of her brother, Ariadne was filled with trepidation about the possibility of losing her home. But, as Angeline turned over the other cards one at a time, they revealed a long overdue journey Ariadne needed to take.

It was only a few weeks before that Ariadne had finally opened up to Angeline about her troubled past, the reason for her neuroses. An attack at such a young age had left Ariadne with panic attacks and anxiety. But Angeline could sense there was something else Ariadne still wasn't able to confide in her about. The weight of it was a heavy burden for Ariadne to carry. Angeline would have to take her time with Ariadne. She would reveal everything to her in her own good time. Watching her friend now, as she turned over the cards, Angeline saw a woman trapped in the past, unable to free herself of its grip. Until she did, her life would never be fulfilled.

Angeline had told Ariadne that she could not move forward in life until past deeds had been resolved. But Ariadne had only said it wasn't her secret to tell.

Finally, to Ariadne's relief, the *Ten of Pentacles* appeared, which represented an inheritance, generosity or a relationship that would bring with it wealth and happiness. This perked her up a little, until *The Hanged Man* appeared. It told of sacrifice and enlightenment.

'Fear not, *mon cher*, all will be well.' Angeline reassured Ariadne. Angeline knew Ariadne wasn't the family fool her siblings believed her to be.

Ariadne gripped Angeline's hand and thanked her. These sessions always calmed her. Both women studied the clue together for a while longer before Angeline departed. Ariadne offered Angeline one of her paintings in lieu of payment. Angeline accepted with gratitude. Unlike Ariadne's family, she knew talent when she saw it.

Ariadne's last painting, in lieu of payment, had sold for £500 to a private collector. However, Angeline kept her two remaining paintings; she knew their value would one day surpass everyone's expectations.

To Ariadne, Angeline was a mysterious woman. She held a confidence that told anyone in her presence that she loved the way she looked with every year that she slid away from forty. She was confident and charismatic. The very opposite of Ariadne. She always walked with the air and grace of someone untouched by vanity.

Since childhood, Angeline had been taught about the spiritual world and the art of cartomancy, by her mother and grandmother. The Cards had always played an important part in her life. She graduated from Burgundy University with a degree in psychology. But found the interpretation of the cards far more fascinating, especially when getting a client to open up to her. The art of superstition, myth and persuasion can have profound effects on people's lives. If represented correctly.

Angeline had been a frequent visitor to England over the years. Though she always returned to her hometown outside Burgundy. But her latest visit had seen her reside solely in Kent. Soon, it would be time for her to go home. But she needed to help Ariadne before she departed.

Angeline had a very diverse clientele, both in England and in France. Some clients she regarded as friends. Her greatest challenge was Ariadne. She hadn't yet unlocked all of Ariadne's secrets. Only when she did, would Ariadne finally be released from her past. Then, Angeline could go home.

'Call me if you need help with your game. Remember, you knew Bart better than anyone, *mon amie.*'

'Thank you, Angeline, I will.'

Ariadne waved goodbye and closed the door behind her. Everything was happening too fast. The reading was positive, so why did she feel so on edge again? Ariadne made herself another hot chocolate and found a Flake for extra support, before sitting down by the fire to reread the first clue.

The key was in the poem. Ariadne re-read the poem repeatedly between sips of chocolate. She didn't need Bart's estate. Just Rose Cottage and a reasonable annuity. She had left Eleanor a phone message asking her if she would like to work together. But Eleanor still hadn't returned her call. In fact, nobody called Ariadne asking her if she wanted to work with them. She knew what her family thought of her. *No one believes I can contribute anything worthwhile to this game.*

George had always been the only one to encourage and believe in her. Her paintings could be found displayed proudly on George's office and bedroom walls, while they were left to moulder in obscure cupboards and attics of Cricklewood Hall and Ashburton Manor.

Ariadne cared for all her siblings, but her family temperament caused them to be cruel, bitter and jealous towards each other and at times herself.

She chose long ago to keep them at arms-length. It was safer that way. But she truly loved her nieces and nephews and hoped the bitterness had skipped a generation.

Ariadne decided to call Eleanor's number once again. She waited for the line to connect. She listened to the familiar voicemail greeting before speaking.

'Oh hi, it's me again... Just wanted to know if you would like to solve these clues together... Right then, I look forward to hearing from you.' Ariadne was outwardly disappointed as she hung up, she knew her sister wouldn't call her back.

She decided not to call anyone else. She couldn't handle the rejection. She wondered if the rest of her family were going it alone. It would be just like them to be alienated and suspicious of each other.

On second thought, she decided to call Bartie. The call didn't go to voice mail this time.

'Hi, Aunt Ariadne. How are you?'

'Good, sweetheart. Are you playing your father's game?'

'Yes. But not because my mother asked me to. She's livid, by the way. I'm not sure what Dad was up to with this game, but whatever happens, I wanted to reassure you that you will keep Rose Cottage.'

Ariadne wanted to cry.

'Did you want to work together?'

There was a moment's hesitation before Bartie answered.

'I would love to, but Mum is in a vile mood. I can't antagonise her any more than she already is. She's hired some code breaker to help solve the clue. If we win, then I'll be able to help you.'

'I understand. Thanks, Bartie. Good luck to you,' she said, before hanging up.

Ariadne re-read the poem again. What was the key?

Beware! Oh fools, in this game of chance
A game of clues, will send you on a merry dance
Remember, as you struggle to solve
Time is of the essence, seek and behold

She wondered if it was about Felicity. Ariadne went to her desk drawer and retrieved a pen and paper. *Damn it, I'm going to solve this on my own.* She knew she wasn't the fool her family believed her to be.

Ariadne opened her computer and searched the internet on how to solve a single column transposition cipher. After finding what she was looking for, she returned to the poem to find the key. She first thought it was Felicity. She drew up a grid table and used Felicity's first name, but it made no sense. Then she tried her full name, which made even less sense.

She went back to the poem and wrote down everything Bart loved in his life, Cricklewood Hall, Laurel and Hardy, his wealth, his children. Finally, Ariadne realised it. *Bart loved himself most of all.* She cursed herself for not seeing what was right in front of her. The first letter of each line of the poem spelt out Bart's name - BART.

BARTHOLOMEW GOODE

Ariadne wrote out Bart's name on a new piece of paper. As before, she drew a line underneath his name, then down between each letter. Finally, she drew several lines across the page until it represented a grid. Ariadne counted the number of letters in the cipher. There were 110. She then divided them by the number of letters in Bart's name, sixteen. She knew she needed six full rows plus one row of fourteen. To solve the cipher, she first wrote down the numbers one to sixteen in alphabetical order below each letter of Bart's name. Starting from the As, then the Bs and so on. Once she completed all sixteen, she took the four-letter codes from each block and wrote them down in the columns, starting from column one, through to sixteen.

It was very late in the night when Ariadne finished transposing the cipher, she sat back and read the clue out loud.

WHAT YOU SEEK IS NOT VISIBLE BUT APPEARS IN PLAIN SIGHT—STOP—IT BELIES A TRUTH—STOP—FIND ME AT NO PURPOSE—STOP—IF NOT I AM LOST AND YOU LOSE

Ariadne smiled at her own ingenuity. She knew the clue would be at Cricklewood Hall somewhere. *Find me at no purpose. What has no purpose?*

It was 2.00 am. Ariadne took that thought to bed with her. By morning, she knew the answer.

THE LOVERS

The seventh card of the major arcana

Archangel Raphael, the angel of love and healing, presides over the lovers' union. He helps guide the lovers through a union or decision that needs to be made. His advice: lead by your heart not your head.
But, whatever you choose, do not make it lightly.
When upended, the Lovers are in crisis and may need to question the decisions they have made.

17

Cricklewood Hall

Day Two, Wednesday

George watched Ariadne walk through the gardens from a ground floor window at the Hall. She headed straight for the lake. He smiled at her resourcefulness; he knew she would solve it. Unfortunately, she wasn't the only one who had walked down to the lake that morning. Felicity had beaten her to it and had left an hour later. He wondered how long it would take Ariadne to find what she was looking for. As he headed outside, he whistled for Laurel and Hardy to follow him. He knew the answer was down by the lake, but as he wasn't privy to the clue, he didn't know what it could be. George decided to keep his distance. He knew Ariadne would solve it herself.

The dogs' tails wagged as they followed George across the garden. Bart left no instruction in his will regarding the care of Laurel and Hardy. *They must stay together*, George thought. He doubted if any of Bart's family would take them. Except Ariadne and possibly Bartie. But Bartie lived in an apartment where two large dogs wouldn't be practical. *Whatever happens or wherever I end up, I'll take them with me.* He doubted if any of the Goodes would even notice.

A place that serves no purpose. A folly.

Ariadne would have arrived earlier, but the cold morning made her lie in bed longer than she anticipated. The folly was Bart's favourite spot in the entire gardens.

Bart's body had been cremated before being returned to England. He insisted on it. His family and only a few close friends gathered at the folly to say their farewells as his ashes were scattered over the lake. Ariadne wandered around the site until she found a small tombstone. It wasn't there on the day of Bart's funeral. Ariadne walked up to it and studied it.

Then the penny dropped. Ariadne smiled at the birthdate on Bart's tombstone. It was incorrect. *It 'belied a truth', could it be that simple?* It couldn't be, there was still a part of the clue that she hadn't solved. *What you seek is not visible but appears in plain sight.* There had to be something behind that sentence that Ariadne hadn't figured out yet. She sat looking out over the lake for a while longer as she thought about the clue's message.

It was always peaceful here. She could still feel Bart's presence. She wished she could stay all day, but she needed to call Hugo and Sam.

From the bushes on the other side of the lake, Bart had watched Ariadne arrive through his binoculars. She must have realised the date on the tombstone was wrong. She never missed his birthday. She just sat on his seat, staring blindly out over the lake, as if in a trance.

Earlier, Bart had watched Felicity arrive with a man he didn't recognise. He chuckled at the thought of claiming his £200 prize from Hugo and Sam. Obviously, his children hadn't bothered to join their mother. But then again, they would only get in her way.

Bart stayed until Ariadne finally walked off. Then he headed back to his little cottage, he was hungry. He believed the game would be well over by the weekend.

'Hello, Ariadne,' Sam said when her call was put through.

'Is the first clue the first of August?' she asked.

'Very good. Come to my office, and I'll give you the second clue.'

Ariadne hung up the phone. Was it that simple?

What you seek is not visible but appears in plain sight.

The incorrect birthdate was clearly visible on the gravestone. Maybe that was it. The correct birthdate was not visible.

Ariadne looked around the lake. Whatever that niggling feeling was no longer mattered as she had solved the first clue. She enjoyed the solitude of the folly for a few more minutes before heading back to her cottage to change for her journey to London.

Walking across the grounds, Laurel and Hardy joined her. She patted and played with them, sensing George would be close by.

When he finally caught up to the dogs, they stood apart from one another.

'Congratulations. I believe you're the second to solve the first clue.'

Ariadne only smiled at him. Then she walked up to George and kissed him on the lips. She winked at him and walked off in what almost appeared to be a skip.

George called the dogs to follow him back to the Hall. It was turning into a surprisingly good day. He hoped no one else would turn up today to solve the first clue.

Once Ariadne had changed her clothes, she headed for the station to catch the train to London. She hated travelling into the city. *Far too many people confined in the one place,* she often thought. But she knew she would have to suck it up if she wanted to see the game through to its end. She was proud of herself for solving the first clue so quickly; however, she still had a niggling feeling something was amiss.

On Ariadne's arrival at 40 Bank Street, Canary Wharf, she took the elevator up to the 35th floor and entered the offices of Potts & Billingsworth.

She was shown into Sam's office, where Sam and Hugo were waiting for her. Ariadne repeated Bart's correct birthdate.

Hugo gave her a wink and handed her a large box. It was gift wrapped with a red bow. Ariadne thanked them and turned to leave. Before she walked out of his office, she turned around and asked.

'George said someone else had solved the clue this morning.'

'Charity and Verity were here two hours ago, along with their brother.'

'Really!' Ariadne was surprised, she loved her nieces dearly, but she never saw any aspiring qualities in them, it must have been Bartie who solved it. No, on second thoughts…

'Felicity solved it, didn't she?'

'You can have help, too. But I don't think you need it,' Hugo said, smiling at her. He was looking forward to winning the bet.

'When will you rectify Bart's birthdate on his grave?'

They were both surprised by her last question.

'Oh… once the game is over, it will be rectified, Ariadne,' Sam promised.

'Thank you.'

Ariadne walked out of the building carrying the box under her arm. She opened her umbrella as a light rain started to fall. She always loved the rain, but only when it fell in the countryside. The lush green fields and woodlands lived and breathed under the droplets as all lifeforms fed off its life force. The tiny rain drops made everything glisten and shine with their touch. The city rain was cold and depressing. It made everything look and feel bleak and miserable. She was looking forward to returning home to her cosy fireplace.

Deep down, Ariadne was pleased Bart's children had solved the first clue. They deserved the inheritance. Bartie promised her Rose Cottage… She hoped rather than believed he would keep that promise. But, if Felicity had anything to do with it, she might end up out on her ear. Ariadne never understood what Bart saw in her. For a shrewd businessman, Felicity had taken him to the cleaners. She had been upset for Bart when he lost custody of his children. He had been protecting a secret. Ariadne often wondered if Bart had confided in Felicity about their past. Although, it was possible he talked in his sleep. It was a family trait. If he had, it would explain a great deal. Bart was no fool. He would never have told Felicity, consciously.

Ariadne walked to the nearest tube station. She was tempted to open the box while on the journey home but chose instead to look out the window and watch the countryside go by.

Hearing a chime, Ariadne opened her mobile to see a text message from Bartie. It read, *Go to the folly. Look on the grave.* She texted her nephew back with a thumbs up emoji and told him she already had the second clue. Ariadne looked out the window, proud of her nephew. Relieved the mistrust and contempt had obviously skipped a generation.

Augustus, Eleanor and Zachary, meanwhile, were still struggling to solve the first clue!

Eleanor had been of two minds whether to continue the ridiculous game. But, for once, Timothy had stepped in and made up her mind for her. Eleanor was already on compassionate leave because of Bart's death. Not that she really needed it. So she decided to spend the rest of the week solving Bart's game. She understood how to solve the cipher, but she didn't yet know what the key was. The cipher could be solved without a key but the combinations were far too many for Eleanor to go through with the limited time she had. Timothy insisted she call Ariadne back, saying 'Two heads are better than one'. But Eleanor, in her single-mindedness, decided to go it alone.

Meanwhile, Augustus had called a family meeting. Once James arrived, everyone was instructed to help solve Bart's clues. Ashburton Manor was in turmoil. Augustus II finally came clean on the position of their debt. Augustus III was fuming. He hadn't known the extent of his family's situation until his mother had enlightened him the night before. He had no intention of ending up like his father.

James couldn't stop laughing; he knew his father had relied on his uncle's generosity in buying parcels of the estate to keep them afloat. James once suggested selling

Ashburton entire, but the yelling match that followed put a swift end to that discussion. He didn't envy his older brother. James was free to live his life, while Augustus III was tied to the Manor forever, just like their father.

The family agreed to work together. Now wasn't the time to challenge their father. But it wasn't until lunchtime on Thursday that they finally solved the first clue.

Zachary Goode spent Monday evening and all of Tuesday trying to solve the first clue with his wife Beatrice by his side. She didn't do it out of allegiance or greed, but out of desperation. If they solved the clue, she could file for divorce and actually leave with money in her purse.

Zachary had formed a coalition with Augustus, but he didn't trust his brother. So he formed another alliance, one out of necessity rather than loyalty. It wasn't until Friday that Zachary finally solved the first clue. Well, *he* didn't, but his collaborator had given him the answer.

THE CHARIOT

The eighth card of the major arcana

*The Charioteer will guide you on your new journey.
You must draw on your past experiences to succeed
in your quest. The Charioteer imparts a strength that
enables you to take charge of your life and, in doing so,
find victory.
Be wary though, in reverse, the Charioteer reveals an
arrogance and egotistical approach to life. Poor judgement
and selfishness will come before the greater good.*

18

Offices of Potts & Billingsworth

Day Three, Thursday, 02.00 am

A lone figure entered the law offices using a stolen key card. The thief walked stealthily through the office until they found what they were looking for. Wearing a black tracksuit, mask and hoodie, the figure picked the lock and entered Sam Potts's office. Finding nothing of interest in there, the figure entered Hugo's office via the internal door. The thief had no chance of getting into the company safe. But instead had to content themselves with rummaging through the desk drawers and filing cabinets in Hugo's office, hoping to find the information they were after. The intruder was about to come away empty handed, when they noticed something of interest shoved down the back of one of Hugo's desk drawers. The figure had a quick scan of the document before taking a photo and hastily putting the papers back in the desk drawer.

The trespasser left the same way they arrived, via the elevator. They were in and out within ten minutes. Unfortunately, the offices' motion sensors triggered a silent alarm.

The prowler left Canary Wharf moments before the police arrived.

Hugo Billingsworth's Residence

Day Three, Thursday, Too bloody early in the morning

'Do you know what the fucking time is?' grumbled Hugo after leaning over and looking at the clock on his bedside table.

'Sorry, sir,' replied Jeremy, the firm's office manager. 'We had a break-in at the office.'

Hugo was instantly alert. He switched on the light and sat up in bed.

'What was taken?'

'Nothing that I can see. I'm in the office now. The alarm was triggered around 2.00 am. I'm here with the police. Some documents have been disturbed and a filing cabinet was busted open, so was your desk drawer. Did you have anything important in it?'

Hugo knew exactly what was in it: Bartholomew Goode's current unsigned will. Hugo had left it there, waiting Bart's signature. Bart's original will was secure in the firm's safe.

'Which filing cabinet was opened?' Hugo asked.

'Filing cabinet 'E to G,' Jeremy replied. Hugo allowed himself a moment's reprieve at the thought that it was probably a member of the Goode family, foolishly attempting to steal the answers to the clues.

'I'm on my way,' he said as he climbed out of bed and hung up the phone. Hugo would never get back to sleep now. The last thing Hugo and Sam wanted was the police snooping around. God forbid any of their clients should find out they had a break-in. It wasn't good for business. Potts & Billingsworth had very distinguished clientele.

There was no way anyone could get into the vault without both keys, which Sam and Hugo both held onto tighter than their wives. However, less sensitive documents were locked in filing cabinets. Hugo was confident it was someone connected to the Goode family. Obviously desperate to win. Felicity popped into his mind. Then Augustus and Zachary.

Hugo was annoyed with Bart. The last thing he or Sam wanted was undue attention brought to the firm. He was starting to have second thoughts as to the merits of Bart's game.

Hugo walked into his office at little after 4.00 am. He walked past the two police officers without saying a word. He walked up to Jeremy and said, 'Next time call Sam, he suffers from insomnia.'

Hugo, grossly underdressed for the office in a ten year old pair of faded jeans and a tracksuit jacket, walked in and closed the door. Several minutes later, he re-emerged to address the police.

'I can't see anything missing, it was probably kids,' he said.

'We'll have to record it anyway, but if you're *sure* nothing was stolen...?' asked PC Hubbard.

'I'm sure.'

'We'll need to take a look at your video surveillance.'

'Of course, when our security officer arrives in the morning, I'll have him go through the tapes and send you a copy.'

'Thank you, Mr Billingsworth,' said the PC, making notes. As she and her partner walked towards the elevator, she stopped and turned to face the two men, who seemed far too eager to see the backs of them.

'Wouldn't they need a security card to get into your office?' she asked, before pressing the button for the elevator to return.

Good point, thought Hugo, who didn't have an answer for the constable.

'You'd better check that none of your staff are missing their access card,' PC Hubbard said, as she entered the elevator. 'I'll await your call, then.' She gave them a warm smile as the door closed between them.

'If it was one of the Goode family members, how the fuck did they get in?' Hugo demanded.

'I don't know, I'll check which access card was used and then the security cameras,' replied Jeremy.

'I want to know before anyone else. Understood?'

'Sure thing, Hugo.'

THE STRENGTH

The ninth card of the major arcana

Strength represents courage. A woman holds open the mouth of a lion. Her calm nature implies a moral victory. You must trust your higher self, as it will always guide you to victory. Show patience and sensitivity, and through your leadership you will find resilience and vitality.
Only when reversed will Strength imply you have ignored your instincts. Weakness will prevail and hinder you from making decisions, thus preventing you from finding the strength you need in yourself.

19

Rose Cottage

Day Three, Thursday, around 8.00 am

Ariadne sat in her sitting room with the contents of the box scattered across the table. Yesterday had been an eventful day. When she arrived home, she undid the ribbon and opened the box as carefully as a bomb disposal expert.

Ariadne felt guilty, Eleanor had finally called and offered to join forces. Ariadne hadn't returned her call. She wondered if Eleanor knew she had solved the first clue and was too proud to ask her brothers for help.

With renewed *joie de vivre*, Ariadne was determined to solve the clues by herself. If she won, she would help everyone, just like she always had, but she wanted to prove something to herself and to the rest of her family.

But this morning Ariadne was no closer to solving the second clue than she was the night before.

Sitting at her table, Ariadne read the second clue again with a fresh pair of eyes.

CLUE TWO

POTTS & BILLINGSWORTH

CLUE 2

Inside this box are 25 cubes. Each side of the cubes displays a letter.

Unscrambling the letters will show you the way. What lies beneath will lead you to your second clue.

Present what you find to our office to receive the final clue.

A small poem to help you along the way

Good luck!

What Lies Beneath

A ray of light shines the way
Blink and it is gone
I change my appearance every day
I am old as the day is long

The second clue required Ariadne to unscramble the twenty-five cubes. She had written down all 150 letters, numbers and punctuation marks on each side of every cube and tried making words out of them. She had given up after 1.00 am and gone to bed, but she couldn't sleep. This morning, she conceded that she needed help. She called the one person she could rely on.

One hour later, Angeline was sitting at Ariadne's table cutting squares from pieces of paper and writing a single digit on each piece of paper until they had all 150.

'So these,' Ariadne said while moving two more squares in front of them, 'two numbers 15 and 27 might represent a quantity or date,' scratching her head with a pencil. Then she realised she already had a pencil stuck in her hair and removed it.

'Did anything significant happen on any of these dates, personally for Bart or your family?' Angeline added.

Ariadne had to admit the dates didn't stand out to her either. They weren't birthdays, deaths or anything significant to her. They tried adding the numbers together, one plus five = six, two plus seven = nine. Could six or nine represent June and September? Just in case she'd misremembered, Ariadne spent some time looking up and writing down the birthdates, deathdates and anniversaries of her immediate family members, moving on to more and more distant relatives as she struck out.

Thirty minutes later, Ariadne sighed and agreed to try another avenue. She spent another half hour searching for a website that had an algorithm which could transpose all the letters into words, but gave up on that also.

Looking at all the letters in front of them, Angeline rearranged them in alphabetical order, leaving the full-stops, colon and numbers to one side. There were two Zs.

'We have two options,' she said, 'First to search for all words with a Z in them, or to search for words with two Zs in them.'

As she was speaking, Ariadne moved the two Z's down into the middle of the table. They both smiled when Angeline said, 'This *puzzle* isn't as hard as I thought it would be.'

Relieved to have found one confirmed word in the puzzle, Ariadne picked up a P, U, L and E and placed the letters next to the two Zs. Now she only had 144 letters to go.

They agreed to pick out T, H and E, as it was a common word. Angeline knew the key to the letters was in the numbers, so while Ariadne played around with the letters, she googled the numbers in numerous formations. Eventually she used 15:27, and a Proverb appeared. They quickly collected all letters contained in the quote, then laughed at Bart's sense of humour.

Proverbs 15:27 – *The greedy bring ruin to their households, but the one who hates bribes will live.*

With the quote secured, and their two words selected, Ariadne had sixty-two letters left to play with. But it wasn't as easy as they first thought.

They spent the rest of the day unscrambling the remaining letters.

During their time together, Angeline prompted Ariadne to open up more about her past. To Angeline's relief, she did. Ariadne found a strength within herself that had been buried for too long. Bart was dead—their secret couldn't hurt him now. But George was very much alive, and betraying his secret could leave him vulnerable. But Ariadne trusted Angeline and to her surprise, her own relief was palpable.

But George had struggled with alcohol for many years because of their secret. She was grateful when Bart took him on as a driver, then as the estate manager. Ariadne hoped he might benefit from Angeline's advice, but on second thought, Ariadne wasn't sure if she should tell George that she confided in Angeline. She didn't want to cause him more turmoil. He didn't deserve that. Ariadne knew Angeline would never betray her trust. So, she thought it better to let sleeping dogs lie.

By 3.00 pm on the third day of the game, Ariadne and Angeline had unscrambled all the letters and were ready to move on to the next phase of the clue. The remaining letters spelt out the below note.

Behind my words will lead the way to solving the second puzzle. Be guided by the light.

Another puzzle within a puzzle, thought Ariadne. Endless hours passed as she re-read the decrypted words until the meaning of Bart's words, from beyond the grave, found its mark.

Behind my words.

20

Offices of Potts & Billingsworth

Day Three, Thursday, early afternoon

Before Alyson could announce Augustus Goode, he stormed into Hugo's office and said only 'The first of August'.

Hugo offered him congratulations before heading to a locked cupboard behind his desk and retrieving a box with a red ribbon tied around it. The cupboard still contained two more gift boxes.

Augustus eyed the inside of the cupboard, 'I take it I'm not the first one to solve the clue?'

'No, but neither are you the last.'

Augustus stormed out without another word said.

Hugo walked into Sam's office and sat down in front of him.

'I don't think it was Augustus that broke in. He would have come to us before now.'

'True. What did the security camera footage show?' Sam asked.

'The person wore a hoodie and a shabby looking black tracksuit. They had a mask over their face, so no I.D.'

'Shape, size… anything?'

'They appeared smaller than average, so I have to rule out Augustus and Zachary. Ariadne and Eleanor might fit the bill, but Ariadne has already solved the first clue, and Eleanor hasn't come in yet.'

'Whose security card was used?'

'It was the cleaner's card. They cleaned the office early yesterday evening and had their card with them then, but Jeremy called them this morning, and now they can't find it. I had Jeremy put someone on it. So far, they appear kosher. They have alibis, but we can't rule out someone paying them for their access card.'

Hugo asked the question, 'What about Felicity?'

'Can you see her wearing a shabby tracksuit?' Sam inquired, with a smirk.

'Point taken. Charity or Verity?'

'Possible, but highly unlikely.'

Sam and Hugo didn't like the idea one little bit. Even though their instincts pointed to a member of the Goode family, they couldn't rule out any involvement by another high-profile client.

'I think we need to have a word with Bart,' Sam said, picking up his mobile.

Bart watched Eleanor as she stood near the folly, looking out over the lake. This was her second visit in as many days. Bart was enjoying watching her struggle with the answer, until a pang of fierce (and best not examined too closely) hurt swept over him. He realised she didn't remember his birthday.

'Serves herself right,' he mumbled.

Augustus had arrived earlier that day. He crossed paths with Eleanor on her return, but they never spoke. *Poor*

Eleanor, he thought, *always the outsider*. She would never ask Augustus for help. But it didn't matter. He would never give it.

21

Goode Family Estate,

Ashburton Manor

Maidstone, Kent

Day Three, Thursday, Late Afternoon

Augustus and Henrietta called another family meeting.

James and his brother, Augustus II, along with his wife, Maude, waited patiently for their father to return home. Their cousins, Verity and Charity, had been unusually quiet on Facebook, Instagram, and TikTok. They also hadn't replied to their cousins' text messages. No doubt their mother's doing. They weren't giving anything away.

Family aside, James and Bartie had been good friends all their lives. After the will reading, James had given Bartie the heads-up that his father was on the war path. It was on James' advice that Bartie played his father's game, if not for himself, then for his sisters and Ariadne.

When Augustus returned from London, everyone was waiting in the dining room, where sparsely hung portraits were the only artefacts of colour and interest. The only valuable item on display was the ornately long dining table, which spanned the length of the room. The missing wall tapestry had been sold five years earlier. There was still a stain on the wall from where it had hung for over a century.

'I've got the second clue,' Augustus said, storming into the room without acknowledging his family. 'I wasn't the first, but I wasn't the last either.' He placed the box on the table. Henrietta immediately opened it and placed its contents on the dining table.

'Who's already solved it?' she asked.

'I don't know or care. But probably Felicity and her lot,' Augustus remarked, offhandedly.

'You mean our cousins,' James corrected him.

Henrietta lost herself in a daydream of having enough money to finally leave Augustus and this rundown manor that she both loved and hated. Her elder brother, who inherited her own family estate, refused to help Henrietta financially, not while Augustus ran the Manor. Her brother believed Augustus would squander any money given. Augustus winning Bart's game was the only hope she could cling to now. Henrietta often dreamed of turning the Manor into a prestigious hotel. But they were only frivolous pipe dreams that would never amount to anything. Not while her husband was still around.

Henrietta's thoughts were interrupted by Augustus' pompous voice reminding his sons that the only way to win Bart's fortune was to solve the clues together. Three heads were better than one.

'You mean four, don't you, Dad?' James said, nodding at his mother.

'You mean *five*,' Maude said, who was finally understanding her mother-in-law's frustration.

'What about Uncle Zachary?' Augustus asked, 'I thought you were a team?'

'I've changed my mind,' his father said. 'If he hasn't solved the first clue yet, then he is of little use to us.'

'How do you know he hasn't?' his son asked.

'I know my brother.'

'What about Uncle Bart's children?' James asked.

'What about them?' replied his brother.

'They're his children, they deserve to win. It wasn't right what Uncle Bart did.'

'Codswallop. Do you think, if the shoe was on the other foot, they would give you the money?' his brother replied.

'*Yes*. At least… Bartie would.'

'Your cousins would sell everything and keep the money,' their father snapped.

James hated where this was going. He despised what his family was turning into, for the sake of their decrepit manor, not least because he had no stake in it.

'Look, if we win, we'll give your cousins some money, all right. We need the money for our future and the future of Ashburton Manor,' Augustus III announced.

Their father scoffed at his son's last remark.

'How generous of you all,' Henrietta drawled.

'What about me, what do I get?' James asked, sounding flippant.

'Of course you'll get some,' replied his father.

'I want an equal share.'

Augustus eyed his youngest son for what appeared to be the first time in a long while.

'Agreed.'

'I want it in writing.'

THE HERMIT

The tenth card of the major arcana

The Hermit is a lonely person who seeks guidance and privacy. He's looking for self-exploration and time to heal in mind, body and soul. The Hermit shows you that it is best you live quietly for a while as your journey is more a spiritual one rather than a physical one.
But, when in reverse, you may feel cut off from everyone and everything, alone and unsupported. This is more an emotional state rather than a physical one.

22

Residence of Eleanor and
Timothy Sharp

Day Four, Friday, Mid-Morning

'Stop being so bloody stubborn and ask Ariadne for help,' Timothy snapped. Eleanor had been pacing the floor for half an hour, and he was getting sick of it. 'You've solved the cipher but still haven't figured out the final answer.'

'She won't help. I left her a message.'

'Because you never called her back. Go and see her. Ask for her help. I heard you and Zachary are the only two who haven't solved it yet.'

'Great.'

'Think of what you could do with the money?'

'I don't need the money. I have everything I want. I earned my money.'

'Yes, but with Bart's money, you could finally start up your own marketing firm.'

Timothy's persistence finally paid off. Eleanor agreed to call her sister again. But it went to voice mail. Eleanor couldn't blame her. She'd never wanted Ariadne's help to begin with. Eleanor hated herself when she acted like this: stubborn, pigheaded and solitary. Always being determined to tackle everything alone had made her lonely and estranged from her family.

'Ariadne knew Bart better than anyone. Go and *see* her,' Timothy pleaded.

Eleanor finally relented and agreed to stop by Ariadne's cottage before going to the Hall one more time. She wasn't sure what she was going to say. She had held a deep resentment towards her brothers for many years, but that was no excuse for being alienated from Ariadne. Her sister never appeared angry or frustrated by their parents' indifference towards them. Eleanor felt Ariadne had accepted their treatment and indifference all too simplistically and just got on with her life. It made Eleanor resentful, and she grew up believing she wasn't good enough.

It wasn't until she met Timothy and had her own children, Miriam and Aubrey, that she finally understood what deep and meaningful love truly was. It only made her bitterness towards her family deeper, especially towards her mother, for depriving her of that love as a child.

Eleanor arrived at Ariadne's cottage unannounced. She was afraid of rejection. Afraid of Ariadne refusing to help. Eleanor walked along the path towards the cottage; she could see a light on in the sitting room. As she neared the window, she saw a table with a number of cubes on it, most of them were built up on top of each other, while the rest were scattered across the table.

A knock at the door startled Ariadne. She peaked through her window and saw Eleanor standing by the front door. Ariadne spent a few moments tidying up before she opened the door.

Eleanor waited a full minute for Ariadne to open the door. The archway above the door and the trellis on either side was intertwined with an abundance of red roses. A subtle fragrance filled the air around her. It was pleasant.

'Eleanor... What a nice surprise. Come on in.'

Eleanor entered and walked into the small sitting room. The cubes on the table were gone.

'I thought I'd come in person.'

'You never have before.'

The two sisters stood in front of one another, not really knowing what to say. Finally, Eleanor broke the ice.

'I'm sorry, I didn't return your call when you first rang. As always, I wanted to solve the clues alone.'

'I know.'

'At first, I scoffed at Bart's game, thinking him thoughtless as usual. But now I'm angrier than ever. He was my brother, I should be mourning him, but instead I'm just angry all the time at what he's done. We were never close, and we should have been. Like you were.'

'We weren't that close, Eleanor. He felt sorry for me. But I'm tired of being pitied and ridiculed by everyone.'

'Then I'm sorry for that, too.' Eleanor paused before speaking again. 'Why are sons so much more important to a father than a daughter?'

'Not all. Just our father. He wanted to play at being an aristocrat in a decaying society. He schemed his way in, and our family has been paying for it ever since. But I know one thing, Miriam and Aubrey will want for nothing with a mother like you. I can't say the same for Verity and Charity. I don't recognise them anymore. Verity's gambling is getting worse, and Charity is becoming more reclusive each year. Her drug use doesn't help matters. She's so lost.'

'I didn't know. I should have, shouldn't I?'

'I wished Bart had taken them in hand. Money can't buy everything. Certainly not love,' Ariadne said. 'He failed them in that regard.'

'I know the mother usually gets custody, but Bart didn't try very hard during the divorce. I often wondered why. I presumed he didn't care. Maybe they would have turned out better if he'd tried.'

'The past is the past, leave it where it belongs. We can't change it now. Why did you come here today, Eleanor?'

Eleanor gestured vaguely at the two armchairs by the fire and waited until Ariadne nodded before sitting down to continue their conversation. Eleanor spoke openly about her pent-up anger and frustration about their family and Bart's game.

'I know I should be remorseful about how I've behaved. But to be honest, I'm so angry about being ignored. I worked twice as hard to please everyone, and it didn't make one bit of difference.'

'Don't you think I felt the same way? No one cared about my dreams. I became the family joke,' Ariadne replied.

'Timothy says I have to put it behind me and move on. But actions are harder than words.' Eleanor confessed it was Timothy who had persuaded her to finish the game, and to come today.

'I'm humbly asking for your help, Ariadne.'

Ariadne poured them a glass of wine, and, for the first time in their lives, the two sisters enjoyed a deep and meaningful conversation. Eleanor saw another side to her older sister and realised Ariadne was more insightful and intelligent than anyone had ever given her credit for. She hadn't considered the depth of Ariadne's artistic dreams.

Eleanor was embarrassed at her lack of consideration towards her sister.

They shared lunch before Eleanor said it was time for her to leave. As they returned to Ariadne's front door, Ariadne told Eleanor to look closely at Bart's gravestone. The sisters kissed and parted ways. Within ten minutes, Eleanor was standing by the folly looking down at Bart's gravestone. She took a photo on her iPhone and drove straight to Potts & Billingsworth.

'Eleanor Sharp has arrived,' Alyson said flatly.

'Send her in,' replied Hugo, who was overly tired and grumpy this afternoon. He still had no idea who had broken into their office. He hated loose ends.

'Shall I get a caramel macchiato with skim milk, coffee syrup, heavy on the whipped cream, hold the sugar, with five cubes of ice over caramel drizzle, just in case she's parched?'

'Now, now Alyson. I would have thought you'd like Eleanor, she's a self-made woman.'

'Yeah right… the snooty bitch.'

Alyson escorted Eleanor to Hugo's office. She wasn't supposed to know that Bart was still alive, but nothing at Potts & Billingsworth got past her. For all his family's faults, Alyson thought he was a real shit for deceiving them with his game. She wanted to tell them all it was just a scam. But she held her tongue. She wasn't going to lose her job for anyone related to the Goode family.

'The first of August.'

'Well done, Eleanor,' Hugo said, handing her a gift box. Eleanor could see there was one box left in the cupboard.

Once back inside her car, she opened the gift box and found a second letter from Hugo and Sam, plus twenty-five cubes to unscramble.

From what she remembered through Ariadne's window, she needed to build them up, but into what, she didn't know. The cubes only had letters on them. Maybe they spelt something out. She would have to wait until she arrived home.

Later that same day

Ariadne couldn't keep the smile off her face, proud at her own ingenuity. She was standing at the entrance to Bart's walled garden. After Eleanor left, she reassembled the cubes, and once completed, she discovered where she had to go.

She opened the red door to the garden, tentatively hoping the answer would reveal itself to her. The air was chilly but fresh as she took a deep breath and entered. The garden was overgrown but its layout was still visible under the beautiful shrubbery. Wildflowers were in abundance. Spring had returned and was resuscitating them back to life. She believed she was the first one to arrive. Nothing appeared out of place.

Ariadne walked around the garden unsure of what she was looking for. The only part of Bart's message that made sense to Ariadne was:

Behind my words will lead the way to solving the second puzzle. Be guided by the light.

Be guided by the light. There were no lights in the garden. Only a few garden seats and overgrown pathways leading around the garden. A bird bath was near the back wall, while a sundial sat prominently in the centre of the garden. She walked up to it. It revealed nothing, as the afternoon was overcast. *Even if there were sunlight. What could it mean?* Was the sundial even important? Ariadne knew it was only effective if the sun shone onto the dial.

Ariadne re-read the quote to the second clue again. *The answer must be here, somewhere, surely…* She remained in the garden for the remainder of the afternoon but couldn't unravel any more of Bart's message. Reluctantly, she sighed and walked out of the garden, closing the door behind her. She would come back tomorrow morning. Hopefully, after a good night's sleep, the answer would present itself to her. She wondered if she was becoming more like Eleanor, pigheaded as well as a loner. Wouldn't it be wiser to ask for help? Ariadne took that thought to bed with her. Hoping both answers would reveal themselves to her by morning.

Unfortunately, Ariadne had a restless night.

23

Residence of Eleanor and
Timothy Sharp

Day Four, Friday Afternoon

'The cubes were built up to represent something, that's all I know at the moment,' whispered Timothy.

'Good. I've got the second clue now, but I'm going to need more information if I'm going to win,' replied Zachary.

'I'm doing my best. But that's all Eleanor said.'

'Push her harder.'

'I can't, she'll get suspicious. If she finds out I've helped you...'

'We need to work together, Tim. We're both going down if I don't get Bart's money.'

'I know. Just remember, once the money is repaid, we're finished. *Got it?*'

'*Yes.*'

Timothy hung up on his brother-in-law. If Eleanor found out what he was up to, she would never forgive him. He had persuaded Eleanor to ask her sister for help, but Eleanor would never have agreed to work with her brothers.

Timothy deeply regretted the day he went into partnership with Zachary. He thought using the Goode name would secure them a lucrative client portfolio. It had, but he hadn't counted on Zachary being so completely inept. Hedge fund managers needed nerves of steel, not an attractive physique or good family name. Timothy never understood how Zachary graduated from university with a degree in finance.

A hedge fund manager could make a lucrative living with the '2 and 20' rule: managers were paid 2% of the total investment, plus 20% of the profits. Unfortunately, Zachary's analytical skills were non-existent. He relied on his charm and wit to bring in clients, but sold short and gambled on risky ventures, which had a habit of failing.

The final straw for Timothy came when he discovered Zachary had dipped into Timothy's clients' portfolios and transferred cash to cover his own clients loses. Timothy warned Zachary he would not go to prison for him. He made Zachary go cap in hand to his brothers for help. Bart finally agreed to help, but the handout barely covered ten percent of the debt. Timothy's nerves of steel were beginning to cave in under the weight of their calamity.

Timothy agreed to help Zachary with Bart's game on the understanding he paid back all the debt plus interest and gave his sister half. Then, Timothy was out.

Beatrice also agreed to help; she had no intention of divorcing Zachary penniless. His charm had faded over the years. Lacklustre was the word that best described him now. The only success she attributed to their marriage was their daughter, Jillian. Loyalty only went so far with Beatrice. After Timothy had told her what Zachary had done, she had finally washed her hands of him. She only stayed because she had no financial means of her own.

After the game was over, Zachary would be presented with divorce papers, no matter the outcome.

With renewed energy, Eleanor focused on solving the second clue. Working through the rest of the day and night, she finally fell asleep at the table. She had uncovered the meaning behind the letters and now knew where to look on Bart's estate. But she hadn't unscrambled the letters, so she didn't know what to look for. Timothy silently applauded her ingenuity as he placed a blanket over her. Then, he took out his mobile and took a picture of it.

Augustus' family worked through the night trying to unscramble the letters on the cubes. Thanks to Henrietta and James, they had part of the clue spelt out. Henrietta watched her husband throughout the day. Barking orders, acting like a ship's commander. Only their ship was sinking, and his authority was hollow. What kept her going was the thought of bankruptcy, and the humiliation it would entail.

By morning, Henrietta was so dishevelled, exhausted and irate, she threw one of the cubes across the room, narrowly missing a 150 year old portrait of a person she couldn't remember the name of. The cube left a dent in the wall. James picked up the cube and placed it back on the table. He brushed a piece of his mother's hair back behind her ear, then headed to the kitchen to make everyone a fresh cup of coffee. As he did, Henrietta noticed the label on the top left side of the cube had peeled away. She picked at the edge and peeled off the remaining adhesive.

Behind it was an image, albeit a partial image. Henrietta started removing the adhesive from the other five sides of the cube.

Within the hour, Henrietta and Maude had peeled off all the adhesive from the remaining twenty-four cubes. They started to build a picture; each side of each cube held a piece of an image. Which meant there were six pictures in total. They needed to find the correct one. James and his brother Augustus continued to unscramble the remaining letters. The head of the family had fallen asleep hours ago. They thought it best to leave him alone, he hadn't contributed anything since his return from London, and his temper was vile when he was awake. However, for a man who could be bankrupt at any moment, Augustus slept soundly.

By 7.00 am on Saturday, the fifth day of the game, Henrietta and Maude had uncovered the mysterious picture. It revealed a section of garden on Bart's estate with a red door. It was 8.00 am when James and his brother unscrambled all the letters and had the final piece of the quote. They truly believed they were in with a chance.

Henrietta enjoyed a hot bath to soak her weary mind and body. She indulged in the smallest hope they would be the first at Cricklewood Hall with a good chance of solving the second clue before anyone else. She wondered again, not for the first time, what Bartholomew Goode was up to.

She laid back in her bath and smiled.

Felicity, too, had been very busy over the last few days. She had conscripted the same ex-GCHQ analyst to crack the second clue in Bart's game. The letters hadn't been a problem. She had her quote, but it wasn't until Friday afternoon that they discovered the images hidden behind the adhesive tape. Once revealed, it didn't take long before Felicity's team built up the cubes to reveal the location of the second clue. Thanks to her daughter's mobile video footage of their father's estate, they knew the exact location.

The only two people to truly appreciate the first part of Bart's code were Augustus and Felicity.

Proverbs 15:27—The greedy bring ruin to their households, but the one who hates bribes will live.

The irony wasn't lost on Felicity, who threw one of the cubes out a closed window. She loathed her ex-husband; he knew her too well. It almost felt like Bart created this game to spite her.

THE WHEEL OF FORTUNE

The eleventh card of the major arcana

Spinning the wheel of Fortune is a game of fate.
A change in your destiny where anything is possible.
The wheel can show a turn for the better, so believe
in your destiny.
But be warned, if reversed, you may suffer bad luck.
The Wheel is closure and may mark the end of one journey
before the commencement of another.

24

Cricklewood Hall

Day Five, Saturday Morning

Ariadne was up early and back in the walled garden of Cricklewood Hall on Saturday morning, proud no one else in her family had come this far. Only, she was no closer to solving the clue. She walked around the garden for almost an hour before she decided to call her sister.

Eleanor said she would be there in an hour.

When she exited the garden, she caught sight of George walking Laurel and Hardy across the grounds. The dogs, as always, ran up to greet her.

They weren't the only ones who were glad to see her.

Ariadne and George took a stroll down to the folly, talking all the while. George asked her how she was getting on with the clues.

'I know the sundial is the key, and the time of day is important, but what time?' she asked. 'That's what I'm stumped on.'

'The dial needs sunlight to show the time. Bart couldn't predict sunshine on any given day. Especially in England. It must represent something else,' George replied.

'I know. I've come this far. I'll figure it out. Angeline helped me on Thursday. I couldn't have made it this far without her. But I decided to call Eleanor. We had a long talk yesterday and cleared the air about a lot of things.'

'I'm glad for you, Ariadne. But you knew Bart better than anyone. He likes to turn things on their head. I can't say any more than that.' George hadn't asked to see the second clue, but he did know something about its solution. He wanted Ariadne to solve it herself. He believed in her.

George had watched Hugo and Sam, over a week ago, coming out of the walled garden. He knew they were up to something. But he didn't know what. He entered the garden and tried to establish what had changed. It took him a while, but he finally realised what they had done. It wasn't until the will reading that he clocked on to its significance.

Ariadne eyed George closely — had he just given her a clue?

She could have kissed him for that. Even if she didn't know what it meant, yet. They walked back to the Hall together, before parting, George leaned over and kissed Ariadne on the cheek. Her heart warmed at his touch, as it always did.

'Are you going to be okay, George?' she asked.

'I will be. I miss him, you know. For all his faults he took me in and helped me get my life back together.'

'I understand. With Bart, it's a love or hate relationship. No in between. But why didn't you come to me for help?'

'I didn't want to be a burden.'

'You're never that. We've both clung onto the past as if it was a life raft. It's about time we let it go. For good.'

George nodded his agreement, 'I'm sad Bart is gone, but at times I feel relief. It's like the past is finally buried with him.'

'What will you do once the game is over?'

'Move on, I guess.'

Ariadne felt the sting of loss already. She didn't want him to leave. *But I've just told him to let go of the past. How can I ask him to stay?*

They arrived at the servant's entrance. George bid Ariadne goodbye, then headed to his office.

That familiar saying 'life is too short' replayed in her mind. It reminded her that life was for the living. Today, she felt very much alive.

Unbeknownst to Bart, his game had done Ariadne an enormous service.

Once her light-headedness lifted, Ariadne felt her usual spasm of anxiety return. She knew she had to tell George about her confession to Angeline. But he seemed so happy, she couldn't bring herself to do it right now. She decided to tell him when the game was over.

Ariadne pulled out her phone and called Bartie, she needed to return a favour.

Eleanor was as good has her word. After hanging up on Ariadne, she told Timothy where she was going. Her sister had asked for her help. She found herself racing out the front door. Once Timothy watched Eleanor drive away, he pulled out his mobile and made a call.

Ariadne was there to meet Eleanor on her arrival at Cricklewood Hall. They walked back to the walled garden together, explaining along the way what they had each found out about the message. Although, that was as far as Ariadne got. When she re-entered the walled garden, they were not alone.

Felicity and her daughters, along with their entourage, were walking around the garden.

Everyone froze, each group surprised by the presence of the other. It was like a scene from the O.K. Corral. Felicity's expression was feral. She was vexed at being on par with Ariadne, who apparently hadn't needed to solicit professional help.

Still believing the sundial held the key, Ariadne didn't want to head directly for it and risk losing the upper hand. However, time was of the essence, and she needed Eleanor's help to figure out what the clue meant.

Unfortunately, Felicity's team had also figured out the importance of the sundial. They were currently hovering around it. However, they hadn't figured out its significance either. Which meant they were all on an even footing.

Eleanor and Ariadne walked into the centre of the garden and cautiously up to the sundial. Ariadne whispered something to Eleanor as they circled around it.

Polite hellos were reciprocated between Ariadne and her nieces. Felicity gave Ariadne a dressing down with her steely eyes. Eleanor couldn't hold back her contempt any longer.

'I think you and your shark tank should leave, Felicity. You're trespassing.'

'I'm here on behalf of my children,' she replied with a snarl.

'Looking at your professional help,' added Eleanor, 'you've finally accepted your inadequacies at last.'

'I'm playing the Colour Bet, Eleanor. My chips are on both red and black. But I see you've tagged along with Ariadne.'

'We're sisters, of course we stand together. However, you're no longer a part of this family.'

'Lay off, Aunt Eleanor. We're all here for the money,' Verity snapped. 'It should be ours anyway.'

Ariadne put her hand on Eleanor's arm before any more words were said that couldn't be unsaid.

Neither team wanted to continue their search while the other team was present.

'Oh, this is ridiculous,' Charity said, finally speaking up. 'Can't we just solve this together?'

'We could,' Ariadne replied. Charity was about to reply to her aunt, when her mother put a swift end to the suggestion, stating,

'Absolutely not!' Her words brooked no argument.

Charity walked off in a huff, she'd had enough. She felt unwell. She'd had a late night the night before, and her head was still spinning. She began circling the garden in the hope of finding something, anything, even if she had no idea what she was looking for. Anything to get away from her mother.

A few minutes later, Bartie arrived. He spotted his two aunts before clapping his eyes on his mother and sisters and their entourage. His mother had texted him, long before Ariadne had. But he was pleased his aunt thought of him. He wasn't sure who to approach first. The idea of his mother getting control of his father's estate irritated him more than his father's reckless game. He knew one thing for sure, his father would never want his mother getting her hands on his estate. Bartie couldn't understand why his father would create such a foolish game in the first place. He knew it was a test. But for what purpose?

Bartie finally made a choice. He walked over to his aunts and stood beside them before whispering a thank you to Ariadne.

Felicity was clearly vexed by her son's choice. *Stubborn as his father.*

Finally, Ariadne decided to intervene.

'Look! We all know the sundial has something to do with the clue,' she said, taking a gamble. 'Only, I don't know what exactly. Proverbs 15:27 would suggest a time, 3.27 pm, perhaps. But I don't know what day Bart was referring to or even if it's relevant. Plus, we can't rely on there being any sunlight at that specific time on any given day. Maybe it's a false clue. We can all stay in this garden until the week is up trying to figure out the clue, or we can work together.'

'Aunt Ariadne's right. It doesn't make any sense,' Bartie agreed. 'What if the day has already passed? The sundial reveals a time at a slightly different position each day, which makes it unpredictable.'

Charity echoed the need to work together, but her mother flatly refused. If she had had the gumption, Charity would have moved to stand beside her brother. As it was, she remained still and alone.

'Why don't you let them think for themselves, for once?' Bartie spat at his mother.

'They'll thank me one day, when their future is secure. As will you.'

Before the conversation rose in temperature, Augustus, Henrietta, their sons and Maude entered the garden. Their faces dropped when they realised they were not the first to arrive.

Arguments flared up immediately between Felicity and Augustus. He demanded anyone not directly involved in the game should leave the premises. He ordered Henrietta to fetch George Fox. Henrietta did as Augustus instructed. She was secretly pleased Ariadne, Bartie and Eleanor were also present.

Before Henrietta returned, Zachary and Beatrice arrived and entered the walled garden. Zachary had no idea what he was looking for. Timothy's text only stated Eleanor was meeting Ariadne at Cricklewood Hall. He had to assume she had solved the second clue. He was simply going to ride on the coattails of his sisters when he got there. The picture Timothy sent revealed the location but not how to solve the clue. He only found the red door when he saw Henrietta walking through it.

Now the whole Goode family was on an even keel. Whether they liked it or not. Each group squared off against their opponents. All were surprised Zachary had figured it out. They put it down to Beatrice.

When George arrived, he politely informed everyone that he was an official judicator of the game.

'By whose authority?' snapped Augustus.

'Hugo and Sam's. If you have any questions, please call them.'

George announced everyone would have one hour alone in the garden to figure out the second clue. He would draw the names out of a hat to see who went first and so on. If they worked in a team, they would still have only one hour. Anyone who wasn't a player would not be allowed back in the garden today. Although, if they did not solve the puzzle on their first visit, they could return to the garden once everyone else had had their turn. Again at one-hour intervals until they solved it.

Everyone reluctantly agreed to George's rules. Augustus had no intention of working with anyone, especially Zachary. Eleanor asked Ariadne if they wanted to separate to have more time in the garden. Ariadne said no, she was happy to work together.

'Well, are you joining us Bartie?' Felicity asked.

Bartie took a moment before answering. He knew, once he did, his relationship with his mother would never be the same again.

'I'm going to work with Aunt Ariadne and Eleanor, thanks all the same.'

Bartie had finally declared his side. If he won the money, he knew exactly what he would do with it. He couldn't say the same for his sisters.

As Felicity observed her son, a flicker of respect for him passed across her mind. But her balance of power over him had just shifted, and respect quickly turned to infuriation. She knew her daughters would need all the help they could get when they re-entered the walled garden.

Once their teams were confirmed, George wrote down everyone's name on a piece of paper and folded them before putting them in his hat. He drew the names out one at a time. Augustus was to go first, then Zachary, who was going it alone—not by choice, followed by Charity and Verity. Last would be Ariadne, Eleanor and Bartie.

George asked everyone to go up to the Hall, where tea and coffee would be served while they waited their turns. It was going to be a long day. Everyone begrudgingly agreed and headed back to the Hall.

Bart watched in amusement, from a safe distance, as the day unfolded.

He had a camera set up in the walled garden and had enjoyed the theatrics of his family sparring off against one another. He was proud when Bartie stood up to his mother. *That's my boy*, he thought to himself. *Once the game is over*, he promised himself, *things will be very different between us*. Not just with Bartie, but Charity and Verity, also. He hadn't realised just how much they all needed him.

No one spoke to anyone. The atmosphere was even more frigid than at the will reading. Bart's inheritance game was tearing the Goode family apart rather than bringing them together. George wondered if that was what Bart had intended all along. He wished this week would end. Then he could move on with his life. He knew Bart would never leave his estate to him; he wasn't that naïve. But he didn't know Bart's end game. George believed there had to be another will in the wings, waiting to be announced. But he knew Hugo and Sam would never let on.

As the hours trickled by, each team waited impatiently for their turn in the garden. In the lead up to their turn, Felicity's daughters spent their time with their mother's advisors, discussing what to look for. They suggested videoing the entire garden on their phones, just to be on the safe side.

Ariadne sat talking with Bartie, reaffirming his decision to work together. She knew it would come at a cost.

Eleanor's curiosity had gotten the better of her. She was interested in how Zachary had managed to solve the second clue. She hadn't believed he had it in him. She walked over to where he and Beatrice were sitting.

'How did you figure it out?'

'Figure what out?'

'The second clue.'

'Oh… Same as you, it was the blocks.'

'How long did it take you to unscramble the letters?' Zachary began fidgeting in his sister's presence.

'Not long—Beatrice helped.'

Before she could ask him another question, he excused himself and headed to the side table and made himself another coffee. Eleanor knew then that Zachary hadn't solved it. Finally, Beatrice got up and left the room. Eleanor decided to follow her.

Eleanor watched Beatrice enter the guest powder room and bathroom then decided to go in after her. While Beatrice was in the cubicle, Eleanor washed her hands at the sink and touched up her hair in front of the vanity mirror.

'It's good we're all on an even par now, wouldn't you agree, Beatrice?'

'I guess so. But I'm sure you'd have wished otherwise,' she replied waspishly from inside the cubicle.

'Don't you find it unusual that we all descended on the garden at the same time?'

'Luck, I guess.'

'Luck be damned, how did you solve the puzzle, I know it wasn't Zachary?'

'It was actually.'

'Bullshit.' Eleanor stopped playing with her hair. She was making it worse.

'We figured out half of the letters. Then he got a call, and we were out the door.'

'Who from? I thought he was working alone?'

'I don't know.' Beatrice was getting annoyed about her lack of privacy.

'Who was he working with?'

Beatrice flushed the toilet and opened the cubicle.

'I don't know or care. All I know is we need the money, and if we win, I'm out of this fucking family once and for all. Now excuse me, I want to wash my hands.'

Eleanor stood aside. She had no idea her brother's marriage was on the rocks. Before Beatrice could leave the bathroom, Eleanor put her hand on the door to block her exit.

'What time did he get the call?'

'About three hours ago. Now, do you *mind?*'

Eleanor moved aside to allow Beatrice to leave the bathroom. Before she left, Beatrice had one last barb to hurl at Eleanor. 'Why don't you look a little closer to home for your answer?'

Beatrice's remark hit its mark. Eleanor left the bathroom, physically shaken. Not wanting to re-enter the sitting room, she walked instead into the library. She absentmindedly sat down in Bart's favourite chair. A book by Oscar Wilde was still resting on the worn-out armrest. She picked it up and tossed it on the side table unceremoniously. Her body was shivering with the thought of betrayal. For the first time since playing the game, she was frightened. She felt as if her life had just been ripped out from under her.

Zachary knew this was his one chance. He was next to view the walled garden. Once his nieces entered the garden, it wouldn't take long before Felicity and her arsenal solved the clue. He finished his drink, then headed to the bathroom. He wasn't sure what he was looking for, but he knew Ariadne did. He'd find out from Timothy soon enough once Eleanor updated him. He was surprised Bartie had joined them. His nephew had more gumption than he had given him credit for. He whistled all the way to the bathroom. On his return, he saw Eleanor standing by the library door. *If looks could kill...*

Zachary hesitated a moment, then continued through the Hall and outside into the garden. He continued to whistle all the way down to the walled garden, where he met George. He would be ready as soon as his brother's time was up.

Zachary chuckled when Augustus stormed out of the garden, his family was waiting for him outside the walled garden. They quickly followed in his wake. Augustus told George he would return later that day. He had no intention of hanging around until his next turn in the garden. Zachary laughed at his brother's ineptitude then entered the garden.

Inside the Hall, Felicity had kept close to her daughters and specialists in the living room. She had not acknowledged her son once during that time.

After James left, Bartie had joined Ariadne and Chloe on the sofa.

'I'm sorry, Aunt Ariadne, for not visiting you more often. We should have invited you to our new home long before now.' His anger towards his father had extended indiscriminately towards the rest of his family, and he was sorry for that.

'It's all right Bartie, you both have busy lives.'

'That's no excuse,' said Chloe. 'You've always been good to us.'

'Once this stupid game is over, you're coming over for dinner,' Bartie announced.

'Thank you, I'd like that.' Ariadne also felt regret for not being a better aunt. She could see Bart's children struggled with relationships, in and outside of the family. She promised herself she would show more gumption in affairs of the heart from now on.

They spent the rest of their time talking about Bartie's son, Harry.

After Felicity and her troupe left the sitting room, it became very quiet. Not long after, Eleanor re-entered the sitting room looking drained and tired. The hours had passed slowly for Ariadne. She had been the first one in the walled garden that morning, but now would be the last to re-enter.

Finally, it was Ariadne, Eleanor and Bartie's turn to enter the walled garden. Ariadne asked Bartie to keep track of time. They couldn't afford to waste one single minute of their allotted sixty. Eleanor appeared distracted and wasn't focused on the task at hand. Something had shifted in her sister's demeanour since that morning. Ariadne wondered what was wrong but decided not to pry. Now wasn't the time.

They walked up to the sundial and gazed at it for some time, willing it to tell them something. It was a large brass globe, resting on a column. Rings wrapped around it with an arrow piercing through the centre. Then, Ariadne remembered what George had said to her earlier that day. *Bart liked to turn things on their head.*

'Bartie, which way is the arrow supposed to point on the sundial?'

He wasn't entirely sure, he pulled out his iPhone and googled it.

'True north.'

'Which way is it pointing now?'

Bart found a compass app on his phone and used it to find true north.

'It's pointing north-east.'

Ariadne stepped up to the sundial and marked the arrow's current position. Then, she removed the arrow and placed it at exactly true north. The arrow now pointed towards the far corner of the garden. There was nothing there, except a brick wall. They walked up to it and started looking carefully at every brick. Ariadne eventually found a small inscription on one of the bricks. It was loose, so she pried it out of the wall. Inside the cavity was a piece of paper with a quote written on it. Bartie laughed when Ariadne read out the proverb. They were still laughing as they headed out of the garden. But not before putting the piece of paper back behind the brick and returning the arrow to its original position.

Outside the red door, Ariadne pecked George on the cheek before leaving the estate. It was early afternoon, so they still had time to call Hugo and meet him at Potts & Billingsworth to receive their final clue.

Augustus, Zachary and Felicity's daughters waited their turn to enter the garden for a second time. They remained until it was too dark to see.

25

Offices of Potts & Billingsworth

Day Five, Saturday Mid-Afternoon

Bartie drove Ariadne into London. Eleanor said she would meet them there and left the Hall in her own car. She had been quiet all afternoon and had lost interest in the game.

Hugo had been at a luncheon at his club in London and agreed to meet Bartie, Ariadne and Eleanor outside his office at 3.30 pm.

When they arrived at Canary Wharf, Hugo was there to meet them in the square. They waited for Eleanor to arrive before giving him the answer to the second clue. When she arrived, it looked to Ariadne as though she had been crying.

Ariadne recited the quote that had been written on the piece of paper, hidden behind the brick in the walled garden.

'*An inheritance claimed too soon will not be blessed at the end. Proverbs 20:21.*'

Hugo congratulated them, then opened his coat and retrieved three envelopes and handed one to each of them.

'You're the first again, Ariadne.'

'I'm rather enjoying this, Hugo.'

'Easiest £200 I ever made.'

'Come again?' she asked.

'Nothing, I'll tell you later.'

Bartie thanked Hugo, but Eleanor only took the envelope and said she needed to go home. Ariadne and Bartie caught up with her and asked her what was wrong.

'I don't want to talk about it now. But could I come and stay with you for a few nights, Ariadne? At least until the game is over?'

'Of course you can,' she replied. Eleanor looked haggard with dark bags under her eyes. Ariadne didn't press her and knew they could talk when she arrived at the cottage. Eleanor thanked her and left.

Ariadne and Bartie decided to take a walk through Jubilee Park, which was situated across the road from Hugo's office building. Bartie bought them a hot drink and found a seat. They agreed they would go home and work on the final clue separately, but as soon as either one solved it or needed help, they would contact the other.

While they sat in the park, Bartie pressed Ariadne about his father. He wanted to know what type of man he really was. Bartie was hoping his aunt would give him an honest reply for once.

Ariadne could sense the regret and sadness in her nephew's voice. She knew he deserved the truth. Bartie wanted to think well of his father, but he had no foundation on which to base that sentiment.

'Your father was a complex man, Bartie. I know he loved you and your sisters very much.'

'Then why didn't he try harder after the divorce to make time for us? If he truly cared about us, he would have.'

'It's complicated.'

'Nothing's complicated unless you want it to be. I'm not a child, Aunt Ariadne. Don't treat me like one. I know there had to be a reason for my dad's behaviour. It had to be bad, otherwise he surely would have fought harder for us. Please. You must know something.'

'You're right, I'm sorry.' Ariadne knew the time for secrets and lies was coming to an end. Strangely, the truth didn't frighten her as it had done in the past. Enough was enough.

'Before I tell you anything, I need your word that what I say will go no further. It's not just my secret I'm going to tell.'

'I give you my word,' Bartie promised, wondering what was so secretive.

'A crime was committed a long time ago, when your father and I were young. It was a moment in time we wished we could re-live again and change for the better. I believe your mother found out about it. I don't know how. I can't imagine your father telling her. But he must have, and she used it against him during the divorce.'

'*What?*'

'Once this silly game is over, I'll tell you everything in more detail. But your father helped cover up a crime. Not a malicious or calculated crime, but one to save me. He protected George Fox and covered it up. But I need to speak with him first. Warn him about what I'm going to tell you. It's his secret too. I believe your mother has been blackmailing your father ever since. That's why your father couldn't fight for custody of you during the divorce and why he kept paying her large sums of money, more than what she was entitled to after the divorce.'

Bartie was stunned but not silent. 'Christ, I know she can be vindictive, but I didn't know she was capable of something like that. Didn't she realise it hurt us as much as it hurt Dad?'

'I can't answer that. Both your parents are complicated individuals. Too hot-headed for their own good. That's what drew them together in the first place. Neither likes to lose.'

Ariadne put her arm around her nephew. They sat together in the park a while longer, then Bartie dropped Ariadne off at the train station. Ariadne wasn't sure if she had done the right thing in telling Bartie about the blackmail.

But she was sick of all the lies and secrets told by her family for the sake of a brother no longer alive. She wanted to be free from it all. But she had to protect George. Their secret had been slowly killing him, but if it came out now, she wasn't sure how he would react.

After saying goodbye, instead of going home, Eleanor walked towards the river. She was afraid to go home. Afraid to face the truth. Instead, she watched the river race quickly past her, hoping it wasn't Timothy that betrayed her.

Once inside her car, she sat numbly thinking about what to do when she got home. She was too deflated to scream.

Sharp Family Home

One Hour Later

'You back already?' Timothy asked when Eleanor closed the front door.

'Yes.'

'How did it go?'

'Well.'

'Did you solve the second clue?'

'Yes.'

'I knew you could. Well, don't keep me in suspense.' He didn't like the one-word answers.

'You wouldn't believe me if I told you. Bart buried a small box in the garden, at the southern end of the wall, next to some wild daffodils.'

'You don't say!'

Eleanor said the first thing that came into her head. From what she could remember seeing in the garden, the daffodils stood out the most, they were her favourite flower.

'I'll get dinner started,' he said.

'You do that. I'm going to lie down.'

Timothy watched Eleanor climb the stairs, then he walked into the kitchen to prepare dinner. He picked up his phone and texted Zachary. He felt like a fink.

Eleanor lay on the bed, shaking. *How could Timothy betray me?* She cared not why he did it, only that he was capable of doing it. He was the one person she thought she could always trust. Timothy knew how she felt about her brothers. Her feelings weren't exactly hatred, but more along the lines of jealousy. It was the idea of not being treated as an equal by her parents, no matter how hard she worked or tried to impress them. Regrettably, her jealously often disguised itself as hate.

Eleanor feigned a headache and didn't come down to dinner. Her only thoughts were of an uncertain future with Timothy. The game never crossed her mind once.

When Ariadne arrived home, Angeline was waiting for her. In the midst of the game, Ariadne had completely forgotten about her card reading. But for once, she didn't want to know how her future was going to impact her. Her future was in her own hands now. *Whatever will be, will be.*

Notwithstanding that, she apologised to Angeline and invited her in. She put the kettle on while Angeline retrieved her Tarot Cards and set them on the table. They went through the usual ritual, and Ariadne chose three cards and handed them back to Angeline to put in front of her.

The first card Angeline turned over represented the Past—*The Chariot*, which symbolised a traveller who was on a victorious journey of discovery. Ariadne liked that card; she took it as a sign she was going to win the game. The second card represented the Present—it revealed the *Magician*, but he was reversed. Ariadne had never seen him upside down before. Angeline told her to be wary of trickery and said she could be misled by someone close to her. Someone would deceive her before the game was over. Ariadne immediately thought of Eleanor. *Would she betray me, is our renewed friendship a lie?*

Ariadne tried to erase her new baseless misgivings about her sister. Her confidence was already starting to deteriorate. Now she wasn't sure who to trust.

Finally, Angeline turned over the third card, the Future—*Death*. Angeline appeared more shocked than Ariadne. But she reassured her friend that *Death* didn't always mean the death of a loved one. It could mean the bringer of change or the swift end of something. She reassured Ariadne that, for new beginnings to take shape, swift change must happen.

Ariadne had to agree, so much in her life had changed this week. Maybe it was a sign that she would win the game, or possibly lose it, along with her home. Was this a test? Could she start over somewhere else?

Either way, Bart's game signified a swift change in her life. Ariadne wondered if she could finally stand on her own two feet without fear of falling. Or did this change have to do with her new closeness with Eleanor and her subsequent betrayal? Ariadne's mind was racing with too many possible outcomes. Who was the trickster? Only minutes before, she had been confident about her life and future.

For the first time since meeting Angeline, she regretted having her emotions guided by the turning of Tarot Cards. She didn't want to see what was coming.

Angeline reassured Ariadne all would be well. It was never her intention to distress her friend. Angelina was proud of her for taking control of her life and future. Maybe now was the time to walk away from the cards and their guidance.

Ariadne had a lot to consider. Angeline bade farewell to Ariadne as she had another appointment. She kissed Ariadne on the cheek and held her tightly, something she had never done before. It was almost as if Angeline were saying goodbye.

'*Fais attention*, Ariadne.'

'Of course, I'll be careful. *Au revoir.*'

Ariadne wondered if Angeline sensed she no longer needed her. Yet she valued Angeline as a dear friend and didn't want to lose that. Ariadne's friends could be counted on one hand—with digits to spare.

'I'll call you later in the week, once this game is over,' she said, as Angeline walked away from her cottage.

Ariadne needed to speak with George. She had to warn him about her conversation with Bartie. Only, he didn't answer when she rang him. She left him a message, asking to meet.

While she waited for George to return her call, Ariadne re-opened the Potts & Billingsworth envelope and read the final clue. She had read it on the train and tried to answer some of the clues during the train ride back into Kent.

Inside the envelope were two sheets of paper, one was on the company letterhead with instructions on how to solve the final clue. Including another poem.

The second sheet was a crossword. Each word across the page contained a shaded letter. All the shaded letters, once unscrambled, would reveal where Ariadne needed to go. But first she had to fill in the correct answers on Bart's crossword.

CLUE THREE

For your third and final clue, solve the crossword on the attached sheet of paper and follow the instructions highlighted in the answer.

The below poem will guide you in the right direction.

As before, you may work as a team or individually.

Behold all, the lover, the warrior and prince
Delve into their cunning but droll importance
Words follow words of wit and sarcasm
I'm only a meagre being of little circumstance
At the end, I'm earnest to start all over again.

CONTACT DETAILS: (0) 20 7249 8000 – INFO@PBLAW.CO.UK
POTTS & BILLINGSWORTH PARTNERS
35th Floor, 40 Bank Street, Canary Wharf, LONDON E14 5NR

Kinship
Take control
Life threatening illness
Business person
Moral quality
Withheld until death
A vision or revelation
Abode
Deceiver
Payment of penitence
Selfish desire
A difficult time
Omen
Garden decoration
Presentation of a subject
Time teller
Change and development
Games end

'It's not fucking there!' Zachary yelled into his mobile.

'It has to be. I got it directly from Eleanor. Keep digging,' Timothy whispered, not wanting Eleanor to hear even his side of the conversation.

Zachary dug up the wild daffodils, then he started on the snapdragons and violets. His mobile was on the ground beside him, so he could use both hands to dig in the earth. He was getting blisters.

'I'm telling you it isn't here.'

Before their conversation went any further, Felicity entered the walled garden, accompanied by Verity and Charity. She looked at Zachary with disdain, then began laughing as she walked up to him.

'What the hell are you doing digging up the wildflowers?'

'None of your business.'

'Please yourself, but your hour is up, and we would like the garden to ourselves before it gets dark.'

Zachary looked up at her with scorn but held his tongue as his nieces were present. He picked up his shovel and headed for the red door with what was left of his dignity.

'Don't worry, there's always tomorrow,' Verity said, smirking.

This time Charity spoke, 'My dad loved this garden. He would never plant a clue in his flower beds for someone to dig up and destroy. What on earth gave you the idea to do that?'

Zachary didn't turn around as he walked through the red door, angry he had been deceived.

Timothy remained quiet during Zachary's conversation with Felicity. Zachary hadn't hung up the phone. Fear gripped him, Eleanor had deliberately given him the wrong information. *Fucking hell, she knows. How?* He thought. *I guess it explains her behaviour since arriving home.* He slumped himself into a chair, realising the enormity of what he'd done.

Goddamn Zachary. He had ruined his business, career and now his marriage. With regret, Timothy knew it was finally time to tell Eleanor the truth. No more secrets. *Goddamn Bart, if he had just given us the funds we needed, none of this would have been necessary.*

Felicity replaced the arrow onto the sundial before leaving the garden. Although, she screwed up the piece of paper she found behind the brick in the wall and put it in her pocket. She spotted George talking to Augustus as she left. On seeing her exit, Augustus headed to the garden. *Good luck*, she thought. He was going to need it. The sun was going down, and there were no lights in the walled garden.

'Has my son returned today?' she asked George.

'No, Felicity.'

Contemptable man, she thought. She hated when the help called her by her first name.

'Have Ariadne and Eleanor returned today?'

'No, Felicity,' George repeated, offering her a warm smile at her obvious displeasure. He whistled for Laurel and Hardy to come to him. Instead, they charged up to Felicity and jumped up at her before she could shush them away. They had just enjoyed a swim in the pond. She hated animals, especially the pet kind. She brushed soggy pond residue from her cashmere sweater and Ralph Lauren trousers. Charity gave them a pat before leaving, but she knew her mother was in no mood to be delayed.

George patted the dogs on their heads.

'Well done.'

Bartholomew Goode had watched his family all day from the safety of his estate cottage. He watched them fumble around the walled garden one after the other. He had a computer set up in the cottage with a live video feed linked to security cameras he had placed inside the walled garden.

He was pleased Bartie had joined his aunts. Knowing how much that would have pissed Felicity off, he was thoroughly enjoying himself. But, as darkness started to descend over the garden, it put a halt to anyone searching the garden after dark. He watched Zachary leave in a temper after Felicity and his daughters arrived. He observed Felicity remove the note from behind the brick in the wall, he also watched her screw it up and put it in her pocket. He loved Felicity's sportsmanship.

It was getting late, and Bart had finally had enough of watching his family's antics unfold on the screen and decided to head out across the grounds to see for himself what was happening. He caught sight of Augustus and Zachary in a heated argument. Bart couldn't stop laughing, knowing they would be back tomorrow without any success.

He watched from behind a tree as Laurel and Hardy jumped up at Felicity. *Well done them*, he thought. They deserved a treat. But, before Felicity drove off, she turned and looked in his direction. He quickly darted behind the tree, confident she couldn't have seen him, not from where she was standing. But still, Felicity had the eyes of a feline.

Felicity drove off at speed, gravel spitting up in her wake. Bart never regretted his divorce, but strangely at times he did miss her. No one challenged him like she did.

Bart recovered quickly from his delirium and headed towards the Hall. The game would be over tomorrow. Then, he could get back to his life and loves. Tomorrow was going to be the first day in his new life.

He watched as George walked the dogs back into the Hall. Bart wished he could have trusted George with the truth about of his existence. Then, he wouldn't have had to stay in a cottage. But he knew George was loyal to Ariadne. Bart had been touched when Hugo told him how deeply upset Ariadne and George were on hearing of his death. George had wholeheartedly believed the treatment would work. *Well, he was right about that*, thought Bart.

Hugo had called Bart earlier that afternoon to confirm that Eleanor, Ariadne and his son had just collected the final clue. Bart was surprised Eleanor had joined them, he had her down as an all-for-one competitor. The thought that his son cared enough to participate, and was winning, made the whole game worthwhile. After Sunday, once the game was over, Bart would put everything right. Then, he could repair his relationship with his children and develop a lasting relationship with his grandson, Harry. *To hell with the past*, he thought. He had a brand-new future to look forward to. First thing Monday morning, he would head into London, sign his new will and then begin proceedings to buy the remainder of Ashburton Manor. Then he could put that old chapter of his life to bed.

Poor Augustus, he thought. He wouldn't want to be him for all the riches in the world. There was something to be said for the second sons of this world. They had everything to prove without the responsibilities of past and present generations bearing down at them.

Bart's game was turning out to be quite entertaining. He was able to see what his family was actually made of. But now, watching the last of them leave, Bart was looking forward to returning. He believed there must be change before new beginnings can commence.

Bartholomew stood outside the terrace doors. He watched Tina, the housekeeper, clean up the afternoon tea service. She would be leaving soon, and Sunday was her day off. He wouldn't have to skulk around anymore. Bart waited until she left the room, then he went back to the cottage and retrieved his belongings. He turned off the video feed and packed up his computer.

He returned to the Hall a short while later. It felt good to be back home. His little estate cottage was comfortable, but there was no place like home. He made his way downstairs and found a light on in George's office. Before he could open the door, Laurel and Hardy started to bark from behind the door. He entered.

'Hello, George!'

JUSTICE

The twelfth card of the major arcana

The scales of Justice express you are deserving,
while the sword symbolises retribution for
past wrongs.
Justice will show you can be the judge of your own life,
so trust in your decision-making when you safeguard
your future.
However, Justice is clear. Redress your past errors and
you will attain a positive outcome. But you must be
accountable and deserving.
But, when in reverse, your life will be out of balance,
and any decisions may go against you. Either through
misfortune or corruption.

26

Sharp Family Residence

Day Five, Evening

Eleanor came downstairs to find Timothy in the drawing room. She was carrying an overnight bag. He had his back to her, facing the fireplace. He was stooping over it as he gently kicked at the logs burning in the grate. His usual confident demeanour had been replaced by a defeated hunch. He turned when he sensed her watching him.

'I'm going to stay with Ariadne for a few days, at least until the game is over.'

'Please don't go,' he said.

'I can't look at you right now.'

'Please just give me a chance to explain. Just a minute.'

'I already know what you did. How could you?' Eleanor couldn't hold back the flow of tears, they would stick around like an evening shower. *Damn him*, she thought. She hated showing weakness.

'I love you. I did it for us. Please let me explain before you leave.'

'People who love each other don't betray one another. Not you, of all people. How could you?'

'I'm fortune's fool.'

'You're not a fool, you're a liar.'

'I had no choice!'

'We always have choices. Did Zachary put a gun to your head?'

'In a manner of speaking… yes.'

Again, Timothy begged Eleanor to let him explain. His hands were shaking, and his voice was cracking under the strain. Eleanor didn't have the energy to fight. She reluctantly sat down on the sofa and listened to his excuses.

Timothy breathed a brief sigh of relief. He had one chance to come clean. He told Eleanor about Zachary's embezzlement. How much he stole from Timothy's clients' portfolios to cover his own clients' losses. If word got out what he'd done, they would both be arrested. At the very least, his career in the city would be over, no one would ever trust him again.

'I was fortunate enough to have generated enough revenue for my own client's portfolios, that nobody has noticed the loss yet. But they will. I've been racing against time to generate as much new investment as I can and putting my own profits back into the company before the auditors come knocking. But I haven't generated enough to save us.'

Eleanor was speechless.

'Your brother's put me right in it, I'm afraid. If I can't generate enough funds, I'll have to fill-in the short fall, which still won't be enough. We would lose this house.'

Eleanor couldn't believe what she was hearing. 'What the *hell* was he thinking?'

'That's the point. He doesn't think. Zachary sees life like a game of chance and damn the consequences.

'I helped him with the game because I thought two chances of winning were better than one. If you win, I can cover the losses, if Zachary wins, ditto.'

'He's always been a charlatan.'

'He's desperate to win. That's the only reason I helped him.'

'Why didn't he go to Bart?'

'He did, at first Bart refused to help. But then he agreed. It wasn't anywhere near enough to bail us out. I thought Bart was mocking us. He knew the debt we were in, and what he gave us barely covered ten percent.

'Now, I'm going to lose everything, including you.'

Eleanor had never seen Timothy this scared before. She couldn't believe her brother could be so thoughtless and irresponsible. But then again…

No amount of charm could help Zachary now. She understood Timothy's predicament, but she couldn't forgive him, not yet. His betrayal cut deep.

'Why didn't you just tell me?'

'I was ashamed and embarrassed.'

'I'm going to stay with Ariadne. I'll finish this bloody game and save your firm and our home. But it'll take more than that to save our marriage and for me to forgive you.'

Timothy's fear gave way to relief when he realised he still had a glimmer of hope with Eleanor. It was enough for now.

Eleanor stood up to leave.

'Good luck. You'll win. You're smarter than all of them.'

'I thought so once,' she sounded dejected. 'But Ariadne has outfoxed everyone.'

Eleanor left the house without saying goodbye and drove to Ariadne's. Her head was spinning, throbbing, she had to pull the car over to calm her thoughts. For the second time that day, she let go of her emotions. Only this time she screamed as loud as she could, expelling every gasp of air left in her lungs. Then she pulled herself together and continued on to Kent.

Eleanor arrived at Ariadne's cottage around 9.00 pm. When Ariadne opened the door, Eleanor burst into tears again. She recounted Timothy's story and laid her heart open to Ariadne, who felt privileged that her sister finally trusted her enough to confide in her. Although Ariadne knew more than she had let on earlier.

'I already knew about the embezzlement.'

'What! How do you know?'

'I was the one that gave Zachary the money, not Bart. Bart told me what Zachary had done and that he'd refused to give Zachary any more money. So, I offered to help. Unfortunately, it was nowhere near enough. Zachary has always been short-sighted about his own talents. I knew it would hurt you, Timothy and the girls if anyone found out.'

Eleanor didn't know what to say, she just sobbed even more and asked for a tissue because her nose was running.

'Why don't we finish the game together?' Ariadne consoled Eleanor. 'Tomorrow will be the end of it, one way or another.'

'Sounds good to me,' was Eleanor's reply before blowing her nose.

Eleanor and Ariadne spent the remainder of the night answering the crossword questions over a bottle of red wine. The sisters were reunited. *At least Bart did something right with his stupid game*, thought Ariadne, who was confident enough to believe no one else had solved the second clue yet.

But self-doubt crept in, and Ariadne couldn't contain herself any longer. She apologetically called Hugo to enquire if anyone else had solved the second clue. He said no. But Felicity had left him an obnoxious voicemail to call her back immediately. He went on to say, quite cheerily, that he and Sam didn't work Saturday nights. But had instead agreed to meet with Felicity at 10.00 am in the morning.

Ariadne and Eleanor now had until tomorrow morning to solve the final clue without anyone breathing down their necks. They spent another hour completing the crossword puzzle. They wrote out the letters of the shaded squares on small pieces of paper, as before, and started to re-arrange them.

But they weren't making any sense. Some of their solutions had to be wrong. They called Bartie and video-chatted with him to confirm their answers. Once they all agreed they had the correct ones, they worked together to unscramble the shaded letters. Which were:

L M N E I H N I T Y D R B F E A R I

By midnight, Ariadne, Eleanor and Bartie had the answer to the final clue.

The shaded letters were re-arranged to reveal the following message.

Find me in the library

'Read the poem again, Ariadne,' Eleanor encouraged.

Behold all, the lover, the warrior and prince
Delve into their cunning but droll importance
Words follow words of wit and sarcasm
I'm only a meagre being of little circumstance
At the end, I'm earnest to start all over again

They all agreed that the final answer would be found in a particular book in Bart's library. But Bart owned thousands of books. They needed to know which one. The poem was the link in finding the correct one.

Bartie said he would come over first thing in the morning.

'It would have to be a book that held significance for Bart,' Ariadne said.

'Who were his favourite authors?' Eleanor asked.

'I'm not sure,' she replied. Bart read extensively, but Ariadne honestly didn't know who his favourite authors were.

A memory stirred in Eleanor—from when she was last in Bart's library. If felt like weeks ago, but in fact it was only that morning. She had been crying in Bart's old chair. There had been a book resting on the armrest. *What was it?*

Then she remembered. It was an Oscar Wilde book. Taking another look at the poem, she smiled when she realised specific words appeared on each line, revealing the answer.

Eleanor was relieved she was finally able to contribute to the game.

THE HANGED MAN

The thirteenth card of the major arcana

Patience is required.
The Hanged Man is content to wait out his fate. But he feels frustrated as events tick slowly by.
You must be patient and try to see things from a new angle.
But, when reversed, your life may not be as calm as you once thought. You may need to rethink your position before it is too late.

27

Cricklewood Hall

Day Five, Saturday evening

Bart poured himself a whiskey and treated himself to a cigar. He hadn't smoked one since he began his treatment. He picked up his favourite book and began reading. Laurel and Hardy were lying on the rug by the fire.

Today, was the first day in Bartholomew Goodes new life. He was finally home and surrounded by his favourite things. Although, his reunion with George hadn't turned out as he expected. He hoped his family would behave better tomorrow.

One hour earlier

Bart opened the door to George's office and stepped inside. George's face went white.

Bart simply raised his arms high and said, 'I'm back.'

He expected his friend to be shocked, then relieved. To jump out of his chair and hug him. But George's shock turned to anger. He did jump out of his chair, but not with excitement. Anger swept through the normally calm man.

George started yelling at Bart's thoughtlessness. To do what he had done to his family and even his own children. He called Bart a selfish bastard.

This tirade continued until Bart snapped and told George to remember who he was talking to. At which point, George responded by punching Bart on the jaw. George stormed out of the Hall in a temper. He needed a drink and possibly a new job.

Now, sitting by the fire in the library, sporting a bruise on his cheek, Bart wondered how the rest of his family was going to react. For the first time since his return to England, Bart had second thoughts about what he had done and wondered if he should put an end to it now and come clean.

Bart lit his cigar and took a long slow drag and then took a sip of his Scotch whisky. He decided to enjoy the rest of the night in peace. If a storm were coming, let it come tomorrow. He read his book in solitude with his trusty dogs by his side. Tomorrow was going to be a very traumatic day for everyone.

George had driven out the main gate and headed to Maidstone to get drunk. He cursed himself for being taken for a fool. He cursed Bart for being a prick.

George stopped the car and got out. He was pacing. Then he realised he wasn't far from Ariadne's cottage and decided to let her know the truth.

When he walked past her window, he saw Eleanor was with her. They were sitting side by side at the table, laughing. Ariadne looked happy; she had her sister back. George's heart ached for her. He didn't want to spoil her evening, Ariadne deserved tonight. He turned away from the cottage and walked back to his car. She would know soon enough.

After downing his third beer, George finally realised it was time to move on. Cricklewood Hall wasn't his home. He had no home; he would have no life while he remained there. Trapped in the past, thanks to Bart. Always waiting on the day when the police would come knocking on his door.

As the night slowly passed, George was too drunk to drive anywhere, so he caught a cab back to the Hall. He would pack his bags and leave in the morning.

George's only regret was leaving Ariadne.

Damn Bart to hell!

28

The Home of Hugo Billingsworth

Day Six, Sunday, 9.00 am

'There is a Felicity Goode here to see you sir, shall I invite her in?' enquired Hugo's butler. Hugo often wondered why Alyson couldn't introduce visitors to the office in the same polite manner.

As it stood, she would have said 'Felicity Goode, as was, accompanied by her insipid offspring, to see you sir.' Hugo laughed to himself. Hugo was tempted to let Felicity wait considering she was an hour early but decided better of it. He wanted a pleasant Sunday morning.

'Show them in, will you, Markham?' he said.

Felicity marched into Hugo's drawing room, followed shortly thereafter by Verity and Charity, who clung to either side of their mother. Before Hugo could say, 'Sorry I was unreachable last night,' Felicity spoke.

'An inheritance claimed too soon will not be blessed at the end. Proverbs 20:21.'

'Well done, Felicity.'

'Just give me the final clue.'

'Sorry, no can do, you're not a legitimate player,' smiled Hugo, showing as much sympathy as the cat who had just caught the canary.

'Fucker.'

'Now, now.'

'An inheritance claimed too soon will not be blessed at the end. Proverbs 20:21,' said Verity, thrusting out her hand for the final clue. She was never up this early on a Sunday morning. Not for anyone.

Hugo turned his back on them, retrieved two envelopes from his briefcase then handed them to Verity and Charity.

'I take it you already gave Ariadne, Eleanor and my son the third clue yesterday afternoon?'

'Correct. I'm sorry Sam and I were unavailable until now.'

'I bet you are.'

'Did you remember to put the note back in the brick wall, Felicity?' Hugo asked, as an afterthought. Bart had called Hugo yesterday afternoon advising him no one else would be coming with an answer to the second clue.

'What do you think?' Removing the piece of paper from her pocket and throwing it at him.

Felicity walked to the door but stopped. After her girls had left the room, she turned to Hugo.

'I know, Hugo. He's going to fucking pay this time.'

Hugo looked on after Felicity and her daughters had gone. He had to warn Bart. He dialled Bart's mobile, but there was no answer. He left his friend a stern message on his voicemail.

'Your fucking game better be over today. Felicity was just here. If looks could kill, mate... By the way, she knows.'

Hugo had predicted that if anyone suspected Bart was still alive, it would be Felicity. She was as cunning as she was ruthless. It was a pity she didn't put her considerable talents into a productive career; although that would mean working, something Felicity felt was beneath her.

Hugo was relieved no one else would be contacting him today, as he picked up his Sunday paper. Felicity had put an end to that. But his money was still on Ariadne.

DEATH

The fourteenth card of the major arcana

Death is the card of transformation and rebirth. It reminds us of our frailty and is the bringer of change, but this change can be sudden and shocking, if its recipient is caught unawares.
There can be no transformation without this change, so be careful what you wish for! Swift change will bring new beginnings. But at what cost?
There is no difference in Death's meaning when reversed, only in your reaction to it.

29

Ariadne's Cottage

Sunday, 09.05 am

Bartie arrived at Ariadne's shortly after 9.00 am. Ariadne insisted he have some breakfast before the three of them walked over to the Hall. When they arrived a little past 9.30 am, they rang the doorbell, but no one answered. Ariadne had a spare key, so they walked around to the servant's entrance and let themselves in.

They walked through the silent, empty house. Ariadne expected Laurel and Hardy to come running up to greet them at any moment, but the house was still. She wondered where George was. She opened his office door, but he wasn't there. Ariadne knew he was an early riser and thought he must have taken the dogs down to the pond for a swim. She had left George another message last night, telling him they would arrive in the morning with the answer to the final clue. But, as yet, Ariadne had no reply.

As they approached the library, they heard one of the dogs howling from inside the room. They heard a scraping sound against the door; it was trying to get out. An eerie shudder crept over the three of them as they looked questioningly at each other.

Bartie walked up to the door and opened it. Laurel came up to him and whimpered. Hardy sat dutifully by Bartholomew's favourite reading chair. He had his head on the lap of someone sitting in it.

Eleanor said, 'It must be George. Who else would be here to declare us the winners?'

But, as the chair was facing away from the door towards the fireplace, they had to walk all the way into the room to confront him. All they could see was an arm draped over the armrest. They inched closer.

Eleanor's screams echoed through the lifeless Hall. She became hysterical.

Bartie had turned away in shock, he couldn't comprehend what he was looking at. He couldn't look again.

Only Ariadne stood there staring at the dead body of her brother, Bartholomew Goode.

Bartie was numb but calm. His father had been alive all this time. But now he was truly dead.

Bartholomew Goode had been stabbed.

Within a minute of Eleanor's screams, a dishevelled George arrived. He walked into the room and found himself looking down at Bart's dead body. He had trouble registering what he was looking at. A letter opener was protruding from Bart's chest. His eyes were still open, but his face was strained and rigid. Almost like he was frozen in a shocked state.

George made no sound and showed no emotion towards his long-time friend. His only thought was to comfort Ariadne. He went to her and held her tightly he felt her shaking in his embrace. He was sporting a major hangover. Then, he noticed the bruise on Bart's face and wanted to throw up.

Bartie pulled out his mobile and called the police.

TEMPERANCE

The fifteenth card of the major arcana

Temperance always acts in moderation. She beseeches you to find peace and reconciliation in a volatile situation. Her task is to find harmony between two opposing forces.
Be mindful, when in reverse, Temperance will throw these forces into imbalance. You will struggle with change and unfairness and allow the past to interfere with your present and future healing.

30

Scotland Yard

Sunday, 11.00 am

Chief Inspector Sofia Faraday sat in her office sipping a short black. It should have been her day off, and she had initially planned on spending it with her ten year old daughter, Francesca, but a colleague had asked her to fill in for him, so she was on call should anything arise.

This would be her first assignment as chief inspector, and she needed to impress. When her promotion came through, she had personally chosen her homicide team at the Yard. They may not have been the most experienced, but Sofia saw potential in each of them. More importantly, they were eager and openly pleased to have been chosen to be a part of her team. They all respected the sharp analytical mind that had guaranteed her a fast-tracked career at the Met.

Sofia's mind was elsewhere when a constable entered her office.

'Sergeant Brooks has arrived, ma'am,' he said, waking her out of her trance. 'And congratulations on your promotion to chief inspector.'

'Thanks, Jesse. What have we got?'

'There's been a murder at Cricklewood Hall. You've been assigned the case.'

'Where the hell is Cricklewood Hall?'

'It's in Allington, Kent, ma'am.'

'Is forensics already down there?'

'Yes, ma'am.'

Sofia headed off in search of her protégé, Sergeant Carl Brooks. She found him chatting to a detective constable near a drinks machine. By his stance, he was about to ask her out.

'Carl, my office.'

As always, the DCI's timing was impeccable. Carl straightened up his tie and grudgingly apologised to the constable before following his boss into her new office.

Carl liked to regard himself as a modern-day Errol Flynn, who happened to be his favourite actor. At twenty-eight he had it all: charm, tick. Flawless manners, tick. Respectable job, tick. Handsome, tick, tick. He had recently been promoted to sergeant alongside Inspector Faraday. He could already see that she was a brilliant detective. She had a manner about her that always conveyed calmness and resolve when finding the truth. Whether witnesses and suspects wanted to profess it or not.

Now, the chief inspector had an entire homicide team assigned to her. Carl gave himself four years before he would be an inspector himself. Although, some would say, that was an overly optimistic thought.

'What's up, Gov?' he said, as he entered her room, and sat down in a chair opposite her.

'We have a murder at Cricklewood Hall in Kent. I need you to ready the incident room, and I want a list of everyone who works and lives at the Hall. Make sure forensics collect DNA and fingerprints from everyone ASAP. Then I want a list of all visitors to the Hall within the last two weeks, and I want their DNA and fingerprints taken. As its Sunday, I won't bring the team in yet. Let them enjoy their day off. We won't have any forensic evidence to dissect until tomorrow, so just let the team know I want them in by eight to kick start the investigation. You and I will head to Kent now and start the preliminaries and notify the family of the deceased once the body has been identified.'

'Yes, Gov. I'm on it.'

'I want to leave in fifteen minutes. I'll meet you at the car.'

'Right you are, Gov.' Carl left without any further instructions; he knew the drill.

It had been a career-making opportunity to work with the inspector. He was delighted when the DCI asked him to join her new team. It hadn't taken him long to appreciate her razor-sharp mind, which didn't come without the usual eccentricities found in most talented investigators.

Carl called each member of their team and quickly briefed them on their new assignment. Every one of them offered to come in on their day off, but Carl said Monday morning was fine. He knew they were all eager to impress the Chief Inspector and secretly pleased they didn't have to come in.

Sofia knew forensics wouldn't be finished for many hours, and, considering the murder took place on a large estate, they had a lot of ground to cover. She decided to turn on her computer and googled Cricklewood Hall to get a layout and size of the place. The site she found showed an array of beautiful award-winning gardens, which wrapped around the three hundred year old Hall. Sofia fell instantly in love with it. She knew a beautiful garden could make or break any house. She was openly proud of her own little garden in Teddington. But if paled in comparison to the grounds at Cricklewood Hall.

Sofia clicked on another link which announced the death of Bartholomew Goode, who had died of cancer less than a month ago. It was a Facebook account of a Verity Goode—the daughter. Sofia wondered who their victim was.

Sofia placed her laptop, notebook, pens and notepaper in her briefcase. She picked up her favourite travel cup and headed to the kitchen to re-fill her cup with fresh coffee, then downstairs to her car.

At forty-one, Sofia had been married and divorced. It started well but ended badly. Her husband's temper left her with no choice but to separate and eventually divorce. Initially, she had tolerated his bouts of anger, which never appeared to really be his fault. She finally drew the line when he struck her. The only good thing to come out of their marriage was her inquisitive daughter, Francesca, lovingly named after her nonna. Sofia's mother often told her the Yin and Yang of her personality were down to her level-headed English father and her feisty and passionate Italian mother.

Sofia held a degree in psychology from Oxford. But it was always the criminal mind that had fascinated her. Detectives needed to understand the victim to understand their killer. When piecing together a murder, Sofia would dissect the victim's past and present life, including the suspects that surrounded them, to understand why and how they died. Most murders were crimes of greed or passion, which often made them *personal*. Her unorthodox manner had gotten her knuckles rapped more times than she cared to remember, but her conviction rate was one of the highest at Scotland Yard. Her last conviction was a high-profile case, which came with a codicil: solve this and you'll be promoted.

Sofia's promotion finally came through a month ago, and, to celebrate, Sofia treated herself and Francesca to two weeks in Tuscany, where she added another three Italian cookbooks to her collection and one more pound to her hips. Unfortunately, Sofia was one of these women who loved to say, 'I'll start my diet on Monday'. But that Monday always came and went without any calories lost.

For now, however, she had a murder to solve.

Carl was downstairs in the carpark waiting for her. They headed out of London and onto the A2 towards Kent. While Sofia drove, Carl updated her on the particulars of where and when the body was found. Sofia recounted the obituary she found and said the first item on the agenda was to identify the body in the library. Then, she wanted to know who had inherited the Hall from Bartholomew Goode.

Cricklewood Hall

12.45 pm

Sofia presented her warrant card to the police officer posted at the gates of Cricklewood Hall. She drove up to the entrance and was met by a local PC. From what Sofia could glimpse from her car, the Hall and grounds were even more beautiful in person.

But now wasn't the time for sightseeing.

The local police force had closed the Hall to all visitors. The three family members who discovered the body had been escorted to the cottage of Ariadne Goode.

Sofia and Carl were escorted to the library, where they found an ashen-faced man waiting in the corridor. Sofia was informed he was the estate manager, George Fox. Sofia and Carl put on their shoe coverings before entering the library. They walked up to the body of a man slumped in an armchair. Sofia thought he looked a lot like the Facebook image of the man who had died over a week ago.

The forensics team was still busy dusting for fingerprints. They were completely covered in white overalls and white shoe coverings and wearing white face masks. They were putting items into plastic bags and labelling them as evidence. The pathologist had placed plastic bags over the dead man's hands to protect any evidence that might be found under his fingernails. He stood up to greet them when Sofia and Carl arrived by his side.

'Argh, Chief Inspector Faraday and Sergeant Brooks, always a pleasure,' Dr Harry Budd said, giving them a salute instead of a contaminated handshake.

'Hi, Harry. What can you tell me so far? And please don't say, "he appears to have been stabbed in the chest".'

Harry smiled at the Chief Inspector, who had beaten him to his own punchline.

'Well, he died between 10.00 pm last night and 4.00 am this morning. But I can't be more specific until I get him back to the lab.'

Sofia noticed a book inside an evidence bag. He had been reading Oscar Wilde. There was blood splattered over the book cover.

'We have retrieved quite a few fingerprints. The housekeeper said she polished and dusted in here on Thursday, so we can assume any prints found have been left since that time.'

'That's if she polished and dusted as well as she said she did,' Sofia added.

'True. There is only one stab wound, so it wasn't a frenzied attack. He was killed where he's sitting. If he was awake when he was attacked, the assailant would have had to come around here to face him. The angle of the wound suggests a front-on attack. I'd say he would have known his assailant. However, there are no defensive wounds, so the attack took him by surprise.'

Carl was jotting down everything Dr Budd said in his notebook.

'But he could just as easily have been asleep when he was attacked,' Carl remarked.

'Correct. In which case, it's anybody's guess. However, there is bruising on the side of his face. Unsure yet whether he was hit at the time of his death or before. The fire was lit in the room, so it was quite warm in here. Once I've done more tests, I'll be able to narrow down the time of death. But I don't want to jump the gun, there's some discolouration around his mouth, and his expression appears to be very strained, both of which are a little unusual. I'm not sure about that yet, but you'll know soon after I do.'

'Anything else?' Sofia asked.

'Yes. Congratulations on your promotion, Chief Inspector,' Harry said, winking at her.

'Thanks, Doc.' Sofia began to blush.

'Do we have a name for him yet? Is he related to Bartholomew Goode?' Sofia continued. Before Harry

Budd could give an answer, a voice from outside the room replied.

'He *was* Bartholomew Goode!'

George showed Sofia and Carl into the sitting room. He offered them tea or coffee, but they both declined the offer. They were too intrigued.

'Could you please explain how a man came to die twice, Mr Fox,' Sofia asked.

'He was diagnosed with cancer last year. At first, Bart thought there was no treatment, but it turned out his second diagnosis wasn't as dire as the first. I was told he was heading to Jamaica to enjoy what time he had left, then he would return to the Hall for his final days. But we were informed of his death several days ago by his lawyers. He was supposedly cremated, and his ashes were returned to the Hall.'

'So why did he pretend to be dead? It must have distressed his family!' Sofia asked, thinking the pretence was a thoughtless act on the victim's part.

'Bart was a decidedly twisted man. He loved the Hall, his work, and his family, in that order. Before he left, he invited his family over for the weekend to tell them about his illness. The only one remotely upset was Ariadne, his sister. You see, Bart didn't know who to leave his fortune to. He didn't believe any of them deserved it, not even his children. Which is why he created a game, to test them. I knew he was up to something, Hugo Billingsworth and Sam Potts told me about the game, but I didn't know what it entailed or that Bart was still alive. You would have to talk to them about that, they were his friends and lawyers. But I swear I didn't know he was alive until last night. I should have *known* he'd beat the cancer.'

'What did you think of his game?'

'I thought it was in poor taste.'

'How long has he been back in the country?' Carl asked.

'Bart said he arrived home about ten days ago.'

'I'm surprised his lawyers went along with it,' continued Sofia.

'Hugo and Sam are old school friends. The three of them have always been as thick as thieves.'

'Is that so?'

'His family believed whoever solved all three clues in his game first would win the prize, that being Bart's estate. However, it turns out the prize was, in fact, Bart.'

'Someone obviously didn't think it was very funny,' replied Carl.

George looked at the Sergeant. He didn't like what he was implying.

'You can't suspect one of his own family killed him…'

'Did anyone else know he was alive and living back at the Hall?'

'Only his lawyers.'

'So, no one else knew he was here?' Carl asked, with his pen ready.

'No.'

'Who discovered the body?' he asked.

'Ariadne and Eleanor, Bart's sisters, and Bartie, his son. They're currently at Ariadne's cottage.'

'Where can we find this cottage?'

'I'll take you,' George said, standing up to leave.

'That won't be necessary, Mr Fox,' Sofia said, standing up. 'Just point the way, we're good at finding things.'

Carl and Sofia walked to the door, but before leaving Sofia turned to George and asked him one final question.

'When was the last time you spoke with Bartholomew Goode?'

'I saw him at around 7.30 pm, when he walked into my office, alive. That was the last time I saw or spoke to him. I left the Hall around 8.00 pm.'

'Where were you between 8.00 pm and 6.00 am this morning?' Carl added.

'Maidstone, The Brenchley, it's a pub. I was there all evening. Got home around 1.00 am.'

'How did you get home?'

'A cab. I was too drunk to drive. I woke up when I heard someone screaming.'

George walked them outside and pointed them in the direction of Ariadne's cottage.

Carl headed for the passenger door of their car, but Sofia had other ideas. She opened the boot and retrieved her wellingtons.

'Come on Carl, the walk will do you good. Besides, I want to check out these gardens.'

'What if it rains? It always rains in the countryside,' he said, looking up at the cloudy sky. He grumbled something under his breath before he zipped up his jacket.

'You know, this is like something out of Cluedo. Colonel Mustard, in the library, with a dagger. Does Bartholomew Goode have a butler?' he asked.

'Very funny. If only murder were that simple,' Sofia replied, who would never admit to Cluedo being her favourite board game.

Their walk took a little longer than necessary, as Sofia took her time strolling through the beautiful estate. 'Will you look at these gardens Carl, *bellissima*!'

Carl had to admit the gardens were stunning, but he cursed himself for not bringing his own wellies. His expensive leather boots were taking a battering. They were a recent gift from him to himself to mark his promotion.

'I want to know everything about this game Mr Fox spoke of. I want the details of each clue and who participated in it. Until proven otherwise, each player is a suspect.'

'Right you are, Gov.'

'We're going to have to speak with Bartholomew Goode's lawyers first thing tomorrow morning and see what they have to say for themselves. Have one of the team look into them, will you?'

'Yes, Gov.' Carl made a mental note as he trudged across the gardens.

Sofia had to admire the architecture of the gardens. Walking through them, they emitted a tranquillity and left you feeling calm. It was hard to believe a murder had taken place here. As she walked across the estate, her thoughts drifted towards her retirement. What she would give for a place like this! Not the house, but the gardens. She hadn't given much thought as to where she was going to retire to, all she knew for sure was that she must have a larger garden.

She only wished it wasn't a murder that had brought her here.

Rose Cottage

2.30 pm

On their arrival at Rose Cottage, a constable was standing outside to make sure no one left or entered without permission. He stood aside once Sofia and Carl showed their warrant cards. They found all three witnesses in a quaint little sitting room. One woman had a small glass of something in her hand, obviously to calm her nerves. A second woman, with long straggly hair, was sitting beside her with her arm around her. Lastly, a young man, obviously the dead man's son, was sitting in an armchair; he appeared to be in total disbelief. His hands had clearly been gripped tightly around the armrests for some time, his knuckles were stubbornly white.

'Good afternoon, my name is Chief Inspector Faraday, and this is my colleague Sergeant Brooks. I'm very sorry for your loss, again.'

The scruffy-looking woman spoke, 'I'm Ariadne Goode, this is Eleanor Sharp, my sister, and Bartie is my nephew.'

'This whole affair is quite unusual, Ms Goode. Can anyone explain how your brother came to be dead in his library when you buried him a week ago?'

'He was cremated actually,' Ariadne said offhandedly, 'or so we thought.'

Ariadne decided in that moment to take the lead. Eleanor was in no state to talk, and Bartie, well…

She took the police officers through the will reading on the previous Monday.

'Do you know why your brother created this game?' she asked.

'If you want to know how or why he created it, you will need to speak with his two vile friends, Hugo Billingsworth and Samuel Potts,' Eleanor interrupted, speaking for the first time. 'They're Bart's lawyers and old friends. They held all the clues, and no doubt knew Bart was still alive. You will find them in the city, down near Canary Wharf.'

'Thank you. Did any of you know Bartholomew Goode was still alive?'

'*What?* What kind of question is that?' interrupted Bartie.

'A straightforward one, sir,' replied Carl.

'No, I didn't,' he replied, lowering his head again. Ariadne and Eleanor both nodded the negative. Sofia continued her questioning.

'How many people participated in his game?'

'Seven family members participated, plus Felicity, Bart's ex-wife who was assisting her daughters, Charity and Verity.'

Carl couldn't help the derisive snort that escaped him, but quickly recovered and began writing their names down in his notebook after a sharp look from Sofia.

'Could you please tell me where you were between 10.00 pm last night and 6.00 am this morning?'

They all looked mortified by the Inspector's question.

'I was here with Ariadne, all afternoon and night,' Eleanor said, rather too quickly.

'I was at home yesterday afternoon with my fiancée Chloe and our son. We were solving the final clue if you need an alibi. I left home around 08.00 am this morning and arrived at my aunt's cottage around 9.00 am.'

'Thank you,' Sofia said, 'we'll need to speak with you all again separately to take your statements. Your fingerprints and DNA have already been taken by forensics at the Hall, so you can go to your respective homes now. But please stay away from the Hall.'

They all nodded the affirmative. Bartie stood up and kissed both his aunt's cheeks before heading out the room.

'Oh, before you leave. Do any of you know who inherits your father's estate now that he is actually dead?' Sofia was trying to be as tactful as she could.

'I don't know,' Bartie replied, 'I assume my sisters and I will inherit. Considering the game was a hoax. But, with my father, who knows?' Bartie stopped at the door and turned to his aunts.

'I'll let my mother and sisters know.'

'Thanks, Bartie, I'll tell Augustus and Zachary,' replied Ariadne, who could see Eleanor was still in no state to speak to anyone. She usually had nerves of steel. Ariadne had never seen her sister so lacking composure.

Ariadne gave Sofia the clues to Bartholomew's game and explained how she solved them.

Sofia and Carl left Rose Cottage and walked back to the Hall. They met with Harry Budd once more before leaving the estate. They agreed to meet at the forensic institute tomorrow at 10.30 am for the autopsy.

Sofia and Carl stopped for a bite to eat in Maidstone before heading back to London. While in The Brenchley, they confirmed George Fox's alibi with the barman. On their journey home, they reviewed what they knew so far and coordinated their team's assignments for the next few days.

Sofia allowed Carl to drive so she could study the clues Bartholomew Goode created for his ludicrous game.

'Well, he had a sense of humour, I'll give him that,' she said.

'Yeah, but someone in his family obviously doesn't.'

Bartie was too distraught to drive, he sat in his car as the image of his dead father kept playing in front of him. He wanted to scream, but he was too deflated to find the energy. In that fleeting moment, when he glimpsed his father in the chair, he thought, just for a second, that they had a chance of repairing their relationship. He was momentarily excited, until he saw the knife sticking out of his father's chest. He lost his father all over again, only this time he felt defeated. There was definitely no coming back from this now. He'd lost his chance.

Bartie cried, a dry convulsive sob; he would never know him now.

'Augustus! It's Ariadne.'

'What do you want?'

Ariadne always found it hard to talk to her oldest brother. His resentment hung over the family like a waterlogged tarpaulin.

'I have some bad news. We found Bart dead this morning.' There was a pause on the other end of the line.

'What? Do you mean Bartie?'

'No. Not your nephew. Your brother, Bart. We found him dead this morning, at the Hall.'

'What the fuck are you talking about? Have you been smoking some of your herbs again?'

'No, of course not. Eleanor, Bartie and I solved the final clue last night. We went to the Hall this morning to collect the prize and found Bart dead in the library. He had been murdered, someone stabbed him.'

There was another long silence on the other end of the line. Ariadne thought the line must be dead.

'Are you there?'

'*That fucker!*'

Then, the line did in fact go dead. Ariadne called Zachary, who showed only a little more dignity in his response. Neither brother was pleased by her news, but Ariadne wasn't entirely sure if they were angry that their brother was actually dead or that he had played them for fools.

Eleanor had been quiet since the detectives left. The only person she spoke to was Timothy. The previous night, she had slept intermittently, tossing and turning till the early morning. During her agitation, she heard Ariadne moving around the cottage, then she heard her leave around midnight, not returning until 12.45 am. Now, she was too afraid to ask her where she went.

It had been a long day, Sofia told Carl to go home as they had an early start in the morning. They would begin the family interviews tomorrow. Sofia took the three clues home with her so she could try to solve them herself. She wanted to understand the type of man Bartholomew Goode was.

Once home, Sofia kicked off her shoes and changed into a pair of jeans and a polo shirt. She then prepared a chicken and mushroom risotto in the slow cooker. While it was slowly cooking, she mulled over her future while helping Francesca with her homework.

While in Tuscany, Sofia had considered her life after the police force. One of her goals, after retiring, was to write English/Italian cookbooks. Her father, being a traditional Englishman, even though he loved her mother's Italian cooking, also loved his traditional English dinners. Her mother couldn't quite ween him off his traditional dinners of steak and kidney pie, egg and chips, fish and chips, and steak and chips. She often reiterated to her husband that not everything had to be served with chips.

Sofia hoped she could write books that would bridge this cultural divide. Her goal was to write an Italian cookbook for the everyday Englishman. Sofia had learned everything she knew about herbs and spices from her nonna. She wanted to make English cooking as exciting as Italian, by educating her readers on the art of herbs and spices. She was going to need a large garden to grow her many herbs and vegetables, which would be the heroes of her cookbooks.

After tucking her daughter into bed, Sofia settled down with a glass of red and worked her way through the three clues. Ariadne had already written down the answers, but Sofia wanted to understand how the cipher worked. When she built up the cubes, Sofia recognised the entrance to the walled garden, with its brick wall and the red door she had seen earlier that day. She made a note to request a copy of the video played at the will reading from the victim's lawyers.

Making extensive notes about each of the three games, Sofia finally went to bed dreaming of winning the lottery. The image of her dream home consisted of four acres of articulated designer gardens with a pond, maze, walled garden, and a fountain, until an image of Bartholomew Goode's dead body crept into her tranquil thoughts.

Sofia roused herself from her delirium and turned over. The only thing she was sure about was that Bartholomew Goode's murder was personal. He was murdered by someone he knew.

31

Offices of Potts & Billingsworth

Monday, 09.00 am

'Sir, Chief Inspector Faraday and Detective Sergeant Brooks are here to see you,' Alyson announced.

'What do they want?' Hugo asked, looking up from his paperwork.

'I don't know. Do you want me to interrogate them?'

'Show them in,' he said. *What now?* he thought. *It can't be about the break-in, they wouldn't send a chief inspector!* It was never good when the police came snooping around. *Could it have something to do with…*

Before he could finish that thought, Alyson showed the detectives into his office. Without even pausing for Alyson to offer them anything, Sofia walked up to Hugo's desk and stretched out her hand.

They shook hands cordially, as Sofia introduced herself and her colleague. Then she showed Hugo her warrant card. She asked if a Mr Potts was available. Hugo pressed the intercom button on his telephone and asked Sam to come into his office.

Interviewing lawyers was a different kettle of fish from interviewing the general public. Sofia would have to handle the situation deftly. They would be naturally cagey and standoffish. Not to mention, fiercely protective of their friend and client. Lawyers were always good at answering a question with a question and never divulge information about their clients unless the police handed them a subpoena.

Sam entered Hugo's office, and, after the same formalities, Sofia asked her first question. Both men were still standing.

'Can you please tell me the last time you both saw or spoke with Bartholomew Goode?'

'Argh, excuse me,' Hugo replied, taken aback by the question.

'It's a simple enough question, Mr Billingsworth,' she replied. Carl's pen was at the ready. Obviously, no one in Bart's family had informed them of his latest untimely death. Or if they had been informed, the lawyers chose to hide that fact.

'What is this about, Inspector?' Hugo asked. *First question*, Sofia marked.

'That's *Chief* Inspector,' corrected Carl.

'Bartholomew Goode is dead.' Sofia threw the information out and watched them closely, gauging their reaction. There was a calculated pause before Sam Potts answered.

'Yes, we know. He died of cancer a few weeks ago.'

'Oh, well that's a lie right there, Mr Potts. Bartholomew Goode was found dead at Cricklewood Hall this morning. He had been murdered.'

Neither lawyer spoke. Both genuinely looked shocked. Hugo sat back down behind his desk, while Sam allowed himself to fall gently back onto the sofa. Neither man spoke.

They looked at each other for clarification. Sofia could see both men had been caught off-guard. She allowed them a moment to recover, but only a moment.

'Are you sure it's Bart?' Sam asked.

'Quite sure, his sisters and son found him.'

Both men looked genuinely distraught.

'Argh, shit,' was all Sam could muster.

'I'll ask you again, when and where was the last time you spoke with Bartholomew Goode?'

'I spoke to him on Saturday around 6.30 pm, and I saw him two days prior.'

'And you, Mr Billingsworth?'

'I met Bart along with Sam for dinner last week. I spoke to him yesterday. I did leave him a message this morning, but he didn't return my call.'

'Have either of you been to Cricklewood Hall in the last seven days?' Carl asked.

'Yes,' they both replied.

'It was last Monday for the will reading, but not since,' Hugo said.

'Where was Bartholomew staying, if not at the Hall?'

'When he first arrived back in England, he stayed at The Willows, it's a holiday cottage I own on the Essex coast. Then, he moved into a vacant cottage on his estate. I believe he was going back to the Hall permanently on Saturday evening after everyone left for the day.'

'Do you know who was at the Hall on Saturday?'

'His entire family, I think,' replied Sam. 'His children and siblings. George Fox, of course, and the housekeeper, I think her name is Tina. Felicity was there with her entourage.'

'Last time we saw Bart he was happy,' Hugo said, still in shock. 'He had recovered from his cancer and was finally back in England. He was looking forward to seeing his children and returning to the Hall.'

'Whose idea was it to play a game on his family?'

'Bart's, of course,' Sam said. 'I advised against it. But he had a new spring in his step and wanted to have a little fun. He thought it would be a laugh seeing his siblings' reactions when they discovered he was still alive.'

'I bet it would've been,' Carl said offhandedly while he kept scribbling.

'How was he killed?' Sam asked.

'Stabbed through the heart,' Sofia replied. She saw no reason to keep it a secret, considering how many people found the body.

'Oh my god,' Hugo said, who sat forward in his chair. Both men were clearly appalled. If not, they were good actors. Sofia still wasn't convinced.

'How many people knew Bartholomew Goode was still alive?'

'Sam and myself. My assistant Alyson knew, nothing gets past her, and unless Bart told someone else, no one. Although… I think his ex-wife Felicity knew.'

'Why on earth would Mr Goode play such a game?'

Both lawyers eyed each other, silently conferring. *How much should we tell the police?*

'We'll find out in the end. We always do. Please don't waste my time,' Sofia said in answer to their silent questions.

'Bart wasn't just our friend but a client also, we have to consider client confidentiality,' Sam said.

'A warrant will sort that out. Or we could come back with sirens blaring. But I really doubt you'd want the police doing that.'

'Think of the publicity that would follow,' Carl added, finally looking at Hugo.

Hugo eyed Carl with a 'don't come at us with that' look on his face. But he decided to answer their question.

'Bart had a large fortune,' Hugo said. 'His net worth is around £70 million. He sold his business while convalescing in Jamaica. His family didn't know this until the will reading. They have always expected a great deal from Bart. He had been generous in the past, but he didn't trust his siblings. Nor did he believe they deserved his fortune. His cancer made him take stock of his life. He was testing them all. Watching how they behaved during the game. The winner, of course, would receive nothing, only Bart's respect for winning.'

'It was foolish, I know,' Sam said. 'Bart said he had an epiphany during his recovery. His reprieve from death made him frivolous. He wanted to live life to the fullest and not waste any more time dwelling on the past.' He held up his hands as if to deflect blame. 'His words inspector, not mine. More importantly, he wanted to get to know his children again. That was his greatest regret. They may have hated him for a while after the game, but he was planning on making it right with them.'

'He was just having a little fun, that's all,' Hugo added. 'He also wanted to vex his ex-wife Felicity, who has always clawed at his fortune.'

'Was their divorce amicable?' Sofia asked.

Both men smirked at the question.

Neither wanted to tell them the truth that she took him to the cleaners.

Instead, Hugo said. 'He gave Felicity a generous settlement when they divorced. However, Bart had made most of his fortune since then. Felicity feels she's still entitled to it.'

'I want a copy of the video from the will reading.'

'I'll organise that now for you,' Hugo said, before pressing the intercom and asking Alyson to fetch a copy of it.

'Who actually inherits Bartholomew Goode's estate?' Sofia asked.

Both men looked at each other again, before Sam replied, 'Well, that's the thing. Bart was supposed to come in today to sign his new will. He was changing his will. Leaving it in favour of his three children. He was going to leave small annuities to his siblings to keep the peace. George Fox was to receive a small sum, while Hugo and I would receive a small annuity for our expenses and legal fees.

'As he didn't sign it, the original will, which he wrote up after his divorce, is still his legal and only will,' Sam continued.

'Okay, so who inherits in his legitimate will?' Sofia asked.

'Ariadne Goode.'

'One last question, gentlemen. What type of family are the Goodes?' asked Sofia.

Sam looked at Hugo before speaking. 'Sir Augustus I made his fortune through unscrupulous business endeavours. Although, he preferred to call them *smart business ventures*.' The sarcasm was evident in Sam's voice. 'He married well above his station. Abigail Downs came with a rundown estate. *He* wanted prestige and a pedigree bloodline, while *she* wanted his money. But, as they say, you get what you pay for.'

Hugo picked up where Sam left off. 'You'll meet Bart's siblings during your investigation, no doubt, Inspector. I'd say they're all dysfunctional in one way or another. If you're asking us who we think killed him... Well, I'd hate to speculate.

'Augustus has always been jealous of Bart. Eleanor envied him, Ariadne depends on him, and Zach, well, I wouldn't trust him as far as I can throw him.'

'What about his children?' Carl added. Sam looked at Hugo, who nodded. There was no point staying silent. The chief inspector would find out eventually.

Sam continued, 'Bart wasn't close to his children. His son is his own man. But his daughters are spoilt. Charity had always allowed others to dictate her decisions. She's overshadowed by her sister, and her mother's forcefulness. I believe she has a drug problem. Verity, on the other hand, is a clever manipulator. Just like her mother. Whether she does it to seek attention, or simply for the pleasure of it, Bart wasn't sure. Verity has no appreciation for the value of money, which is how she's ended up with a gambling problem. Win or lose, she always had a steady income to replace the one she lost. Bart had learned recently she tapped Ariadne for a loan, which all three knew would never be repaid.'

A heavy silence was left after Sam finished speaking. No one seemed to know what to say.

'Thank you,' Sofia said, before walking out of Hugo's office. The lawyers had given her a lot to think about.

Sofia and Carl had a post mortem to attend. They arrived to find Harry had already started. He welcomed them, then continued on with his dictation. Sofia and Carl watched from behind a large glass wall as he performed the autopsy.

Once the examination was over, they met Harry in one of the conference rooms where he brought up the pictures he had taken during the procedure.

'All the DNA and fingerprint samples will be back later today or tomorrow at the latest, along with toxicology. I'm concerned about the condition of his kidneys and his respiratory system, so I've taken samples. But, unless something unusual appears in his blood work, my report will say Bartholomew Goode died between midnight and 2.00 am on Sunday morning, due to a stab wound through the heart with a letter opener. I'll leave it up to you to figure out who put it there.'

'Thanks,' Sofia replied. 'Could the condition of his kidneys have anything to do with his chemo treatment?'

'No. This is something else. They're badly damaged and only recently. I'll know more later.'

'Anything under his fingernails?'

'I took samples, but he had some scratch marks on his neck. I think he did it to himself. You'll have the full report tomorrow once the lab results are back. There's one other thing, your victim was punched in the face shortly before he died. But not at the time of his death. I'd say a few hours before.'

'Thanks Harry,' she replied, 'we have a lot to get on with. We'll need those DNA and fingerprint results as soon as possible to clarify who was at the Hall in the last few days, especially in the library.'

From her many years of experience, Sofia had learnt that suspects had a tendency to lie or leave out or embellish the truth. Witnesses interpret the same event from varying perspectives. It was forensic medicine that was the only reliable witness that enabled the truth to be told. It was unemotional.

Interviewing suspects and witnesses had to be handled with scepticism, as people's reactions vary when questioned. They could be spontaneous, irritable, cagey, aggressive or unpredictable. Some witnesses would say barely anything while others wouldn't stop talking—which was usually down to nerves.

Sofia's team would paint a picture of the events leading up to Bartholomew Goode's death. Every family member was a suspect until eliminated. One thing detectives knew from experience was murder was mostly personal, which meant their suspect list was surprisingly short.

Their victim was in an altercation with someone shortly before his death. The only person known to be at the Hall late Saturday night was George Fox. He was their likely suspect. If not him, then someone else had known Bartholomew Goode was alive and back at the Hall.

32

Scotland Yard

Monday, 11.00 am

Sofia's homicide team was made up of four detectives of various ranks, DS Carl Brooks, DC Devish Das, DC Ronnie O'Farrell and DS Shirley Smith. All were highly experienced and excited to be working under the newly appointed DCI Faraday.

While Sofia and Carl were at the lab, her team prepped the incident room at the Yard. Their incident room was a large rectangular room with six desks. A row of windows ran along one wall which looked out over London. At the end of the room was Carl's desk, which was nestled against Sofia's office.

All relevant information was stored and displayed on an electronic database and whiteboard. However, Sofia still preferred to do things the old-fashioned way, with a non-electronic whiteboard that had a picture of Bartholomew Goode at its centre and pictures of his family surrounding him.

On their arrival back at the Yard, Sofia took her team through Bartholomew's game and who had played it. Then they all watched Bart's video from the will reading.

'I know it'll take time for all of you to settle into our new digs. But I've assembled the best homicide team in the country, and you're right here in this room.'

'Hear, hear's went up around the room.

'This is our first case together, so let's show the Yard how it's done.'

This was followed by 'hear ', hear's' and palms being slapped on tables.

'To learn why our victim died, we need to discover how he lived. Not many people knew he was still alive. Was our victim's deceit enough to justify his murder? Or was he killed for another reason? Most answers are found in the past, so that's where we need to dig. Once we find our motive, we'll find our murderer. So, everyone is a suspect until proven otherwise. I want to know everything Bartholomew Goode did leading up to his murder. That includes before he left England to seek treatment for his cancer. I want background checks, including financial records, on every member of his family. I want all evidence scrutinised as soon as it arrives. We have a basketful of suspects and a timeline for his murder. Midnight to 2.00 am Sunday morning.'

Sofia handed her team their respective assignments to get on with. They knew the drill.

'Carl and I will interview the family members today. We'll update you as we go along so you can get on with verifying their alibis. I want to see that board,' Sofia pointed to the whiteboard, 'awash with evidence, names and motives by the time we return this afternoon. We'll re-group then. One last thing. Bartholomew was stabbed with a letter opener. The housekeeper will confirm if it was the victim's. If so, then the murder was not premeditated. It was impulsive.'

Sofia and Carl decided to interview Eleanor Sharp first, followed by Felicity Goode and her children, then Zachary Goode to round out the London-based suspects. Then they would head back into Kent and interview Ariadne and Augustus Goode, concluding with George Fox.

Unless their victim was murdered in a random act of violence, which Sofia doubted was the case, then it was personal. Which meant their suspects were limited to his acquaintances. Even the most respectable families had dark secrets. Some families just buried them deeper than others. Sofia would dig as deep as necessary to find her murderer.

Residence of Eleanor and Timothy Sharp

12.00 pm

Eleanor appeared more composed than yesterday when she showed Sofia and Carl into her living room. She offered them a seat and a drink before they began their questions. Timothy arrived shortly after, carrying a tray of coffees, which rattled as he walked into the room. He appeared more anxious than Eleanor. But, after a warm handshake, he took a seat opposite Sofia. He sat forward in his chair, twitching his thumbs together while his hands rested on his lap.

'Did you know your brother was still alive, Mrs Sharp? Or may I call you Eleanor?'

'No, certainly not! Sorry, I mean, yes, you can call me Eleanor, and no, I thought he was dead.'

'What about you, Mr Sharp?'

'No, I didn't.'

'What did you think of the game your brother set for you?'

Eleanor took a moment to think about her answer.

'At first, I was angry at what he did. He insulted everyone at the will reading. Then mocked us with his stupid game. But I thought, right, I'm going to play, and I'm going to win. Stick it to him, you know.'

'Did you get on well with your brother?'

Eleanor needed another moment to consider her answer. If she lied and said it was great, it would only take one family member to contradict her. Then she would look guilty. So she decided to simply tell the truth; she had nothing to hide.

'My relationship with my brother had always been strained.'

'Why?'

'My father was an old-fashioned man. He left Ashburton Manor and the family business to my oldest brother Augustus, who ran it into the ground. There's no point hiding that fact, I'm sure you'll find that out for yourselves. He just doesn't have a head for business. My father should have left everything to Bart or myself. But he flatly refused. I hated being brushed over simply because I was a woman. He always favoured his sons. Ariadne and I were always designated as second-class citizens in his eyes, and my mother wasn't much better. I took it out on my brothers.'

'Would you say Augustus Goode is in financial trouble then?'

'Yes. He was relying on Bart to bail him out.'

'Had he done that in the past?'

'Yes. Bart purchased large portions of Ashburton Manor whenever Augustus put acres up for sale.'

'What about you? Did you need Bartholomew's money?'

'No... I played only to beat my brothers, and I didn't want Felicity to get her hands on Bart's estate.'

'You don't get on with your brother's ex-wife?'

'No. I never knew what Bart saw in her. She looked down on him and our family from the moment she met him. But if Bart's game was all just a hoax, then I'm sure his children will inherit, and she'll get her grubby hands on it eventually.'

'Well, that's the thing, his children don't inherit their father's estate.'

Sofia could see Eleanor was genuinely shocked by her revelation. Clearly, she knew nothing about the contents of her brother's previous or current will. Her expression then changed from shock to a mischievous grin, and she started to chuckle.

'Who inherits?'

'I'm not at liberty to disclose that at present, but I'm sure you'll know before the end of the day.'

Timothy had remained quiet throughout the interview, but Sofia had the feeling he was quiet for another reason. He seemed agitated. She had found that sometimes people thought it best to say nothing for fear of letting something slip. Sofia made a mental note to follow up. His fingers were still twitching. Sofia wondered if he knew more about his brother-in-law's death than he was letting on.

'Where were you both between midnight on Saturday and 2.00 am Sunday morning?' They both looked at one another before answering.

'I was at Ariadne's on Saturday night, as I said before. We didn't leave her cottage for the Hall until Bartie arrived at around 9.00 am on Sunday.'

Eleanor didn't know why she felt the need to lie again, simply that she had to protect Ariadne. She was sure Ariadne had a genuine reason for going out late on Saturday night.

'What about you Mr Sharp?'

'I was here by myself all night. I went for a walk at 9.30 am on Sunday morning to get some milk.'

'So you don't have an alibi for Saturday night.'

Timothy became defensive.

'No, I don't. I had no reason to kill Bart. I barely knew him.'

'Really? He was your brother-in-law.'

'Eleanor and Bart weren't close, we met at family events but didn't socialise together. So no, I didn't really know him.'

'Would you mind if we took your fingerprints and DNA?' Carl asked, already retrieving the plastic bag with the test kit inside.

Timothy was indignant but agreed. His fingerprints were scanned on Carl's phone and a swab was taken.

'Well, thank you both,' Sofia said, as she stood up to leave. But before she left the room, Sofia turned back to them and said, 'We'll be in touch should anything else arise.'

Out on the street, Sofia looked back towards the Sharp's house. It was worth a couple of million pounds, easily.

'Start digging into Timothy's business affairs and bank records.'

'Right you are, Gov,' Carl said, making a note. 'Did you get the impression Timothy was a little standoffish in there?'

'Yes, I did. We'll speak with Bartholomew's lawyers again. They're a wily pair. If anything was amiss with

Timothy's business affairs or anyone else's for that matter, those two would know about it. Let's have a chat to Felicity Goode next. I think it will prove very interesting.'

Residence of Felicity Goode

Pimlico, 12.45 pm

Felicity's butler answered the door. He requested their warrant cards and, after taking a little longer than needed with them, stood aside to allow Sofia and Carl to enter. Sofia could see straight away that Felicity had done well in the divorce.

They were shown into the sitting room and waited a full five minutes before Felicity joined them.

Sofia took in the decadence of the room; it was jaw-dropping. The room definitely had a regal elegance to it. The drapes were a golden-mustard colour that draped down to the floor beside six wall length windows. The furniture, high wingback chairs and a sofa, was covered in a golden linen and had multi-coloured decorative cushions. The rug matched the furniture perfectly, with its deep reds and browns. The fireplace had an expensive ornate grill in front of it. Small photos sat atop a piano in the corner of the room, while large paintings hung from two of the walls. Sofia couldn't stifle a soft gasp when she looked up at the chandelier.

Immaculately dressed, Felicity finally made an appearance. She welcomed her guests and offered them a seat but no refreshments.

Sofia chose an expensive armchair and made herself comfortable. Carl followed suit then pulled out his notebook and pen ready to take notes.

'I would prefer my lawyer to be present on any matters involving my ex-husband or the police.'

'That's fine Mrs Goode, we can continue this down at Scotland Yard if you prefer our interview to be official. Or you can just answer my questions. It won't take very long,' countered Sofia.

Felicity eyed Sofia with contempt, but, weighing up her choices, she decided to play along.

She ran a critical gaze over Sofia's attire before deigning to speak.

'What is it you want to know? We've been divorced for many years. I don't know how I can help you.'

'You were at the Hall last week, on numerous occasions.'

'I was there on behalf of my daughters.'

'Where were you between midnight on Saturday and 2.00 am Sunday?'

'Am I a suspect?'

'Everyone involved in your ex-husband's life is a suspect until eliminated from our enquiries.'

Felicity looked down at Sofia's shoes then rolled her eyes disparagingly.

'On special, forty pounds at Marks and Spencers, if you're interested.'

Sofia wondered why Felicity felt the need to play a power game against her and try to shift the status quo by belittling her. Still, she allowed Felicity a little leeway as long as it kept her talking. Sofia had no intention of letting Felicity take control of the interview.

'Now, where were you between the hours in question?'

'I had a dinner engagement here in London on Saturday night and was home by 11.00 pm. My butler let me in, and I was up early on Sunday as I had an early appointment in the city.'

'Who with?'

'Hugo Billingsworth.'

'What was the reason for your visit?'

'That's private.'

'Would it have something to do with your ex-husband's game?'

Felicity took a moment to respond.

'You know about that then… well then, you know the type of man my husband was.'

'Yes, I'm starting to build a picture of him. However, why were you there? You weren't a participant in the game.'

'I was helping my daughters.'

'Oh yes, Charity and Verity,' Sofia quickly looked at Carl with a 'don't you laugh' look on her face. 'I'll need to speak with them also. Do they live here with you?'

'No, they have a flat in Notting Hill. But they are presently upstairs. They were staying with me until the game was over.'

'Well, that will save us some time then. We can interview them while we're here. If you would be so kind.'

Felicity rang for her butler, and, on her instructions, he went upstairs and summoned Charity and Verity to come down.

'Did you know your ex-husband was still alive?' Sofia asked.

'I had my suspicions but no proof. He was devious enough to create this stupid game. I should have known he wouldn't want to miss the ending.'

'When did you suspect?'

'Saturday, while at the Hall. My husband's game was crude. Seeing his family there, all squabbling amongst themselves for his money… it was something he wouldn't be able to miss. When I climbed into my car to leave, I thought… I felt like there was someone watching me. That's when I had my suspicions. I confronted Hugo at home on Sunday morning. He wouldn't bite. But he didn't deny it either.'

'Did you speak to anyone regarding your suspicions?'

'No.'

The twins arrived dishevelled and in a state of undress. They had obviously had a late night. They were identical in appearance and appeared as indifferent as their mother about the news of their father's murder. Although that could have been down to sleep deprivation. Sofia couldn't tell if their indifference was an act, or if they truly had no feelings for their father.

Both daughters confirmed they were out on Saturday night. Verity had been at a London casino all night and didn't arrive home until 2.30 am. Charity was on a date and returned home around 3.00 am. Carl noted down their alibis, including people, times and places to be followed up. Sofia asked Charity and Verity when they last saw their father.

'A few days before he left for Jamaica. Although, that was a lie. He went to Switzerland for treatment, it appears,' Verity replied indignantly.

'Why weren't you close to your father?'

The girls looked to their mother before answering. Felicity spoke for the both of them, 'He wasn't father material. He cared more about his business than his family. My daughters were away at school most of the time anyway.'

Verity appeared defiant and refused to show emotion over her father's death. But Charity was now struggling to hold back her tears. She was agitated and fidgeted.

Sofia began to notice that they weren't entirely identical.

Sofia wondered if Felicity was capable of killing her ex-husband. Stabbing him in a moment of anger might be plausible. Hiring someone to do it for her might be a stretch. If she knew he was alive, and having fun at her expense, there was a motive. Or she could be covering up for one of her children. The woman was clearly vindictive but also a protective lioness.

'Did either of you know your father was still alive?'

Both twins replied in the negative.

'What about your brother. He was at the Hall yesterday with your aunts?'

'My son chose not to play my husband's game with us, for strategic reasons,' interrupted Felicity.

'The game was obviously a hoax, but do you know who inherits your father's estate now?' Sofia threw the question out casually.

'My children, of course,' Felicity said.

'Actually, they don't,' Sofia replied.

Felicity's stare turned icy.

'Who then?' she asked. Her tone was moderate and without emotion.

'That would be Ariadne Goode.'

'*What?*' Felicity pounced out of her chair but quickly composed herself and walked over to the window, keeping her back to Sofia, all the while staring out the window onto the street below with her hands on her hips. After a minute, she turned around slowly to face her guests.

Her face was thunderous. She had turned red. Sofia thought she saw steam coming out of Felicity's ears. The twins' expressions were a mixture of bewilderment and shock about their father's will and their mother's uncharacteristically uncouth behaviour.

'That can't be right,' Verity said, she was becoming annoyed.

'How do you know?' Charity asked.

'Your father's lawyers confirmed it this morning. Your husband had written a new will leaving the bulk of his estate to his three children. Unfortunately, he hadn't signed it before his death. So, the original will, made shortly after his divorce many years ago, is his only legitimate will.'

Felicity looked like she wanted to kill someone. With forced dignity, she asked Sofia, 'Is there anything else? I have an appointment in the city.'

Sofia knew exactly who she intended on seeing.

Once Sofia and Carl were back on the street and safely seated in Sofia's car, Carl forwarded the particulars of the three Goodes' alibis onto their team to begin verification.

'You know, Carl,' Sofia said, looking up at Felicity's house, 'she was really pissed.'

'I thought she was about to attack you in there. I was getting ready to tackle her for you. I was kinda looking forward to it.'

Sofia chuckled, then said, 'Check her phone and computer records and see who she's been talking to. It wouldn't have been difficult for her to check with the hospital or clinic in Switzerland. In fact, check with the clinic and see if anyone had made enquiries about Mr Goode during or after his visit.'

'Will do, Gov'. But she obviously didn't know about the new will not being signed. Otherwise, why kill him if her children receive nothing?'

'Good point,' Sofia said, starting the car. 'Unless she had reason to believe he *had* signed it.'

Residence of Zachary Goode

Chelsea, 1.30 pm

Zachary welcomed Sofia and Carl warmly, albeit a little too politely, into his home. He introduced them to Beatrice, who didn't look too happy. This, however, didn't seem to have anything to do with the police.

Sofia couldn't decide if Zachary was shocked his brother had been alive all this time or shocked to hear he had been murdered. One thing Sofia noticed: he wasn't distraught.

Throughout the interview, Zachary used wit and charm to brush off Sofia's questions. The tactic didn't work on them, but Sofia and Carl enjoyed the charade.

Zachary made it known that he was shocked to the core by the news of his brother's death, although his behaviour didn't convey that emotion.

'It's like *déjà vu*. Don't you think, Bea?'

'No. Not really,' she replied, bluntly. Zachary simply smiled at her rebuke.

Sofia sensed discord in their marriage, but she gave Zachary credit for trying to hide it. She decided to play along for the time being.

Carl asked for their alibis on Saturday night until early Sunday morning. Both confirmed they were tucked up in bed with each other all night.

'Did anyone see your brother's body before it was cremated?' Carl asked.

'Ahh... No, I don't believe anyone did. We were told he went downhill fast. He was cremated overseas. His lawyers were following Bart's wishes.'

Zachary couldn't say a bad word against his brother. They were as close as brothers could be. Sofia decided not to mention that they had watched the video of the will reading.

'I was told you hadn't finished the second clue in your brother's game?' she asked.

'I was fed up with it.'

Sofia caught Beatrice's expression as her eyes rolled to the side, as if to say '*for fuck's sake*'. 'Do you know who inherits your brother's estate, considering the game was a hoax?'

'No. I assumed it would be his children. Why, do you know something different?' Zachary sat upright and became more alert.

'I'm afraid I can't say anything at present, but you'll know soon enough,' Sofia replied. For the first time during their interview, Zachary showed genuine surprise.

After taking their fingerprints and DNA, Sofia thanked them and said they would be in touch.

Sofia decided to interview Ariadne before she spoke with Bartholomew Junior. Word would undeniably spread faster than a bush fire about who inherited Bartholomew Goode's fortune. She was sure Felicity would have called her son by now. Sofia wanted to gauge Ariadne's reaction.

As for Zachary, Sofia thought him a fool, but was he a killer? She didn't think so.

'Thank you for that,' Zachary said, as he closed the front door on the police officers.

'Where the hell were you on Saturday night? And don't lie to me, or I'll call them back in,' Beatrice snapped.

'I went to Cricklewood Hall.'

'*What?*' Beatrice was livid. Initially, she'd thought he was out with his latest girlfriend. She had no intention of covering up a murder.

'I didn't go there to kill him. I wanted to solve that bloody clue. I headed back to the walled garden, but I saw someone cross the grounds, so I didn't go in there.'

'Who? Who did you see, you fool?'

'I don't know. It was too dark. All I saw was a dark figure carrying a torch. They were wearing a tracksuit, you know, the kind with a hoodie. I didn't want to be seen, so I stayed hidden, then I legged it back to the car.'

'You idiot.'

'Well, what would you prefer, I go to jail for murder or embezzlement?'

'Either would suit me just fine.' Beatrice walked away from her husband.

Residence of Ariadne Goode

Rose Cottage, Allington, Kent, 3.20 pm

Stopping on their way for a quick late lunch, Sofia and Carl arrived at Ariadne's cottage around 3.30 pm. Carl drove this time so Sofia could take in the beauty of the Kent countryside. George Fox answered the door and invited them in. They weren't alone.

Ariadne had a visitor, a friend she introduced as Angeline Toussaint, who was not only a good friend, but also a highly gifted cartomancer. Angeline could see this was a family matter and gave her *adieus*, as she had errands to run. She kissed Ariadne on both cheeks and left the cottage without any further explanation.

'If you don't mind, Mr Fox, I would prefer to speak with Ms Goode in private. But I will need to speak with you shortly. Where shall we find you?'

'I'll be in the pub, in Maidstone, The Brenchley. You have my number.'

'The Hall is still off limits. Where are you staying for the time being?' Carl asked.

'I'm staying in a cottage on the estate.'

'Is it the same one Bartholomew Goode was using?'

'No. I'm staying in "Little Hollows'. It's not far, it's still being renovated.'

Carl made a note as George said goodbye to Ariadne. They whispered something at the door, which neither detective could hear clearly.

George wasn't looking forward to being interrogated about Bart's murder. He was in need of a pint to steady his nerves before being questioned again.

'Condolences again for your loss, Ms Goode,' Sofia began.

'It's Ariadne, please.'

'You have a beautiful name.'

'Thank you. It means "most holy" in Greek.'

'Mine means "wisdom".'

'I don't know what mine means,' interjected Carl. 'I should Google it.' They both looked pointedly at Carl before taking a seat across from each other. He decided to stay quiet and removed his notebook and pen from his jacket pocket.

'Were you aware that your brother was still alive?' Sofia said, 'I only ask again as your brother had had an altercation shortly before he died.'

'No. I wasn't.'

'How did you feel about the game he created for you and the rest of your family?'

'It was typical him. Having fun at everyone's expense. I should have known he would have wanted to see everyone's reactions when he turned up alive.'

'Do you know of anyone who would want to kill your brother?'

'No. No, I don't.' Ariadne fidgeted with her hands where they rested in her lap.

'Did he ever speak to you about anyone he had trouble with, through business dealings or in his personal life?'

'No, I knew nothing about his business. If he had any enemies, he never shared that with me. Besides, he sold his business while he was away. If that's still to be believed.'

'What about his ex-wife, Felicity? Do you think she's capable?'

Ariadne snickered before answering. 'She certainly hated him enough. But murder? That would be beneath her. Financial revenge would be more her style.'

'Yes, I spoke with her this morning. She wasn't very pleased by the time we left.' Ariadne chuckled again on hearing that.

'I thought she would be ecstatic, considering she'll probably get her hands on Bart's fortune now.'

'Well, that's the thing. Bartholomew hadn't signed his new will. His old will still stands. The one he signed shortly after his divorce.'

'You don't say.' A smile spread slowly across Ariadne's face.

'I take it you know he left everything to you.'

'Yes, I do.' Ariadne let out a soft laugh, but it was replaced quickly by a sting of regret. Sofia watched her closely, she could tell by her puffy eyes that Ariadne had been crying.

Ms Goode had trouble making eye contact with her; it seemed she felt uneasy in her presence, so she redirected the focus back to Felicity.

'Felicity Goode wasn't happy after I broke the news about Bartholomew's will.'

'I would have loved to have seen Felicity's face when you told her it was me.'

'I thought she was going to attack me at one point,' Sofia said, lightly.

Ariadne chuckled, then went solemn again.

'Poor Bart,' she said, 'after their divorce, he didn't want her to have any control over his assets or future income. His children were too young and needed a custodian. So, he asked me to stand in, until they came of age.'

'So, am I to presume you will look after his children now?'

'Of course I will.'

'Did he love his children?'

'*Yes*. Of course, he did. What a strange question to ask.'

'Not really. We watched the video he made for the will reading. Nobody came away unscathed. Not even you.'

'Yes, that was in poor taste, I grant you. Bart's relationship with his children was complicated. Felicity can be devious when she wants to be.'

'What was your relationship with your brother like?'

'He was hard to love at times. But I did love him. You had to know his other side.'

'Can you explain his other side to me? I need to build a picture of your brother.'

Ariadne studied Sofia; she knew the police would keep digging until they found something. She wondered if they believed Bart was killed by a family member. After all, *she* certainly did.

'He was a clever and resourceful businessman. But he had a kind and protective side to him. He could still be ruthless at times. Put it down to bad parentage. None of us came out of our childhood unscathed. But Bart made his fortune on his own. Hugo and Sam could probably tell you more about that side of his life than I can.'

'What will you do with his estate?'

'I don't know. Bart's children will inherit the majority of his fortune. I'll also give Augustus, Eleanor, Zachary and George an annuity. I'm sure Bart would have wanted that.'

'Bart wasn't very empathetic towards his siblings from what we've discovered so far. Are you sure he would want that?'

'I don't know, to be honest. But he trusted me back then, so he'll have to trust me now. I think his game was a test. To see how we behaved towards each other, not just how we solved the clues. In part, it worked. I have my sister back. Maybe that wasn't his intention, but that was the outcome. Our family needs to heal itself.'

Sofia thought that was an odd word to use. *Heal.*

'Where were you between midnight on Saturday until 2.00 am Sunday morning?'

'I was here all night, with Eleanor.'

'You didn't go out at all during that time?'

'No.'

Sofia and Carl drove into Maidstone. Before entering The Brenchley, Sofia asked Carl to have the team check out all the cameras installed at the Hall, plus the footage captured on Bart's laptop from within the walled garden. Hopefully, Bart recorded the day's events and didn't just view them.

'I want to know everyone's movements at the Hall on Saturday.'

'Will do, Gov,' Carl said, climbing out of the car.

Carl made a quick phone call to DS Smith. She confirmed they had Bart's computer and the tapes from the security room at the Hall; she was watching them now.

When Sofia and Carl entered the pub, they found George Fox sitting by himself, he was already three sheets to the wind. Sofia ordered a glass of lemonade and a cola for Carl, both of them wishing it were something stronger. They joined George at his table. Sofia hoped he would open up a little, considering the amount he had already drank. Bart's family might close ranks, but George Fox was an employee. Hopefully, he would speak more openly about Bart's life. Sofia decided to start off gently with some easy questions to get him talking.

'How long had you known Bartholomew Goode?'

'Over thirty years. My father worked as the overseer at Ashburton Manor. Bart offered me a job at the Hall when he bought it.'

'What was he like to work for?'

'Decent and fair. We were friends.'

'It must have been tragic, when you heard he died?'

'Yes. He's always been a strong and confident man. I thought he would beat the cancer. I should have *known* he would.'

'How did you react when you found out he was still alive?'

George took a moment to reply. 'I was shocked, at first. Then relieved he was still alive. Then angry. He shouldn't have done that to Ariadne and the rest of his family. Bartie was distraught.'

'Did you see anyone at the Hall on Saturday night?'

'No. Like I said before, I went out and didn't get back until after 1.00 am. I drank too much and caught a cab home. It wasn't until I heard Eleanor scream that I got up and ran into the library.'

'How did you know the scream came from the library?' Sofia asked.

'What...? I, I ran through the house but didn't see anything. I heard one of the dogs bark and ended up in the library.'

'Do you know of anyone who had a grudge against Bartholomew Goode? Personal or work related?'

'No. He made a lot of money during his life, but he made it honestly. He was a sharp businessman. He didn't tolerate fools and always rewarded loyalty.'

'There was no love lost between Bartholomew and his ex-wife. Who else did he have such a hostile relationship with?'

George looked at the Inspector, she clearly had done her homework.

'The only person who hated him more than his ex was his brother, Augustus. But I expect you already know that.'

Sofia didn't but asked why.

'Bart was better than him. Plain and simple. And Augustus knew it.'

'Then why would he sell to his brother?'

Sofia's last question put George on edge.

'I... I don't know. You'll have to ask him.'

'What about Bartholomew's children?'

'What about them?'

'Did they get on with their father?'

'No... Not really. They came to the Hall infrequently. Felicity saw to that.'

'Why was that?'

George quickly regretted his last remark and cursed himself for the slip.

'You'd have to ask her.'

'I'm asking you, George.'

George refrained from saying anymore. He was realising that going to the pub wasn't such a good idea after all.

Sofia could see she hit a nerve. She wasn't going to stop now.

'I'll ask you again, why didn't Bart play a more important role in his children's lives after his divorce? Was he abusive or violent in some way, was he a drinker?'

'*No.* No, of course not.' The suggestion was offensive. George wanted the inquisition to end.

'Then *why* wasn't he a part of their lives? *Why* did his children dislike him?'

George didn't want to betray his old friend, but he reasoned they would find out eventually. Someone had murdered Bart. That was undeniable.

'Felicity told lies about him, that's all. She used her children like pawns to get what she wanted.'

'What lies?'

'I don't know. You should ask her.'

'Do you really think we'll get a straight answer from her?' Sofia asked.

'She turned her children against Bart, accused him of cheating on her. That he didn't love them enough to stick around. That sort of rubbish.'

'He could simply have denied it,' Carl supposed.

'There would have to be more to it than that,' Sofia added.

'Did you believe the lies?' Carl asked.

'Of course not. But, if they were true, who could blame him. She's a nasty piece of work. Now, are we finished? I have things to be getting on with.' George downed the last of this beer and stood up to leave. He had to steady himself, but, once he was upright, he found more self-control.

'Thank you, Mr Fox. That will be enough for now. Do you need my sergeant to drive you home?' Sofia asked.

'No. I'll catch a cab.' George left without any further ado.

Sofia and Carl stayed to finish their drinks and review what they had learned so far.

'We need to re-interview Felicity and find out what she had on Bartholomew. I'm sure Ariadne knows something too. Check Felicity's bank records going back before their divorce and see what Bartholomew has given her since then. I want her daughters re-interviewed alone. I want to know what she said to them about their father. If he hadn't done anything wrong, why didn't he defend himself?'

'Understood,' Carl said. 'I'll have DC O'Farrell and DC Das re-interview the sisters. My guess, Felicity had dirt on Bart and used it against him. Although, it would mean Felicity has kept his secret, since before their divorce. So… what changed now?

'I don't know. But if he was paying her to keep quiet about something, killing him would bring an end to the payments. Unless she believed her children would inherit.'

'Yeah… But he hadn't signed his will,' Carl said, finishing off his cola, wishing it were a pint.

'Let's talk to the son.'

Home of Bartholomew Goode Junior

London, 5.15 pm

Sofia evaluated Bartholomew Junior's appearance. He was dishevelled and appeared to be still in shock. He had been the one to inform his mother and sisters of his father's death. That would have been difficult for anyone. Seeing his father for a fleeting moment, possibly alive, then realising he was dead must have been a shock. Unless he knew in advance that he wasn't alive. Sofia felt for him, but she had to tread carefully, as he was still a potential suspect.

'Can you explain your relationship with your father?'

'I barely had one, thanks to my mother.'

His directness caught Sofia off guard. She hadn't expected that.

'Can you explain why?' she asked.

Bartie decided to explain what he had learned on Saturday from his Aunt Ariadne. He was beyond angry.

Sofia could see he felt cheated out of a relationship with his father.

'My mother blackmailed my father for something that happened a long time ago. My mother saw to it that we didn't see much of our father growing up. She told us stories about him, which made me despise him for years, and I've just learnt they were all lies.'

Bartie didn't care whether he aired his family's dirty secrets in public. *To hell with them all*, he thought. He was angry with his mother for causing his disassociation with his father. He also didn't care what his father had done all those years ago. Someone had killed him.

Bartie confessed that he didn't know what the secret was. 'Aunt Ariadne was going to tell me once the game was over. She believed I deserved to know. Can you believe that? It's typical of this family. Whatever it was, it was bad enough for my father to keep paying my mother all those years.'

'What exactly did your mother tell you about your father?'

'That he cheated on her and broke her heart. That he didn't really want to be a father. That it inhibited his life and work, and he found it an inconvenience. And, because we didn't see very much of him, I believed everything she said.'

Chloe confirmed her fiancé's alibi for Saturday night, up until he left for Kent early Sunday morning.

Sofia felt for the young man, to have spent most of his life believing his father didn't love him when it was all a lie. He and his sisters had been used like pawns on a chess board, sacrificed and discarded by their parents. Bart's secret must have been significant for Felicity to hold that amount of power over him. Sofia wondered if the wrong person had been murdered. It wasn't the first time that had happened during her career.

Sofia and Carl headed back to the Yard. They had a lot of information to review with the team before heading home for the night. One thing Sofia new for sure, both Ariadne and Felicity knew Bart's secret. She would have to re-interview both women again tomorrow. Only this time, she would press harder.

She still hadn't questioned Augustus Goode; time had gotten away from them. But, if he was as spiteful as Sofia believed him to be, he could stew for another day.

Scotland Yard

London, 6.00 pm

By 6.00 pm, Sofia's team were gathered for their evening briefing.

They had spent the day checking up on the alibis Carl provided and watching security footage. They had requested bank records and were conducting background checks on everyone associated with Bartholomew Goode. Sofia's team had made great progress throughout the day.

DS Shirley Smith was up first and informed the team that forensics had finished their fingerprint analysis in the library. Four sets of fingerprints had been found.

'Tina, the housekeeper, George Fox, the estate manager, Bartholomew Goode, the deceased, and Eleanor Sharp, his sister. Coincidently, Eleanor's prints were also found on the book that was sprayed with the victim's blood. It was found on the floor next to the victim's chair.'

'Well, well, well… Thanks, Shirley,' Sofia said, who was resting against one of the desks in the room. 'I want confirmation no one touched anything when they entered the library on Sunday. Check that will you, Shirley?'

'Yes, Gov.'

'The whole family was at the Hall throughout Saturday trying to solve the second clue in Bartholomew Goode's game,' Shirley continued, 'but only Eleanor's prints were found in the library. There were no fingerprints found on the letter opener, and Tina, the housekeeper, confirmed it was the victim's letter opener. It was resting on a side table, she remembered it when she cleaned the room. So, the murder wasn't pre-meditated.'

DC Devish Das was up next.

'The CCTV cameras picked up two intruders at the Hall on Saturday night. We don't have much to go on, as we can't see their faces, one wore black trousers and a black jacket with a black cap, the other a dark tracksuit with a hood. Unfortunately, the cameras were switched off at 12.45 am.'

'Could one of them be Bartholomew Goode?' Carl asked.

'No,' replied Devish, 'one has a small build and is walking towards the Hall, carrying a torch. The other was seen walking towards the walled garden, carrying a torch and what looks like a shovel.'

'However,' he continued, 'there is a motion sensor camera at the entrance to the Hall at the front gate. A car drove past there at approximately 1.15 am. Couldn't read the rego unfortunately, but it was a Vauxhall. Plus, another car drove past at around 1.30 am.'

'Well, that narrows it down then,' Carl said, sarcastically.

'George Fox said he returned to the Hall very early Sunday morning around 1.00 am but slept in his room until around 9.00 am,' said DC Das. 'This is confirmed by the camera at the front gate. However, there are no cameras inside the Hall. He knows the security codes. He could easily have killed our victim.'

'Good work Devish. Find out when the motion sensor cameras were put in,' Sofia said. 'I also want all rego details of each family member.' DS Das scribbled the request in his notebook.

'Have you checked the video footage on Bart's computer yet?'

'I've started, Gov,' Shirley said. 'I'll have it finished by morning.'

'I spoke with Charity and Verity Goode this afternoon,' interjected DC Ronnie O'Farrell. 'They both confirmed they were estranged from her father. They only reconnected with him in the last four to five years but weren't close. It seems their mother had told them petty things about her father over the years. You know… that he was greedy, only cared about making money, his business came first, that sort of thing. As he wasn't around much, they believed what they were told and spent most of their childhoods resenting him.'

'That fits with what we've been told about our victim,' Sofia said.

'They were sent to boarding school when they were eight, so neither of them saw much of either parent,' Ronnie said. 'I'm still checking their alibis. But the casino remembers Verity quite well. She's run up considerable debt. They're reluctant to hand over surveillance footage but said they will provide footage of her arrival and departure on the night in question. Charity's date confirmed her alibi. Although, they were both pretty drunk and stoned by the end of the night by all accounts. She could have slipped out, if he was unconscious during the night.'

'It's clear Felicity Goode turned her children against their father. But, speaking to Bartie today, he said his mother was blackmailing our victim. I want to know everything we can about that,' Sofia said. 'I want Bartholomew's siblings re-interviewed to see if they know anything about it. Carl and I are heading back into Kent tomorrow to speak with Augustus Goode. We'll see what he has to say on the matter. Bartholomew was buying up his brother's estate. I want to know why. But before we go, we need to reinterview his ex-wife and see what she has to say for herself.'

Sofia's team had their new assignments. They were making notes and would follow up on their enquiries tomorrow.

'All right, let's call it a day and pick up where we left off tomorrow.'

'Fresh day, fresh mind' was Sofia's motto. That did not apply to her of course, as she planned to take more work home with her. She had all the evidence and interviews her team had compiled throughout the day to read through before their morning briefing. Once they had examined Felicity and Bartholomew's bank records, they'd be able to confirm if there was indeed blackmail involved.

Sofia headed home to Francesca and a carbonara.

33

Scotland Yard

Tuesday, 9.00 am

DS Shirley Smith handed Sofia Bart and Felicity's bank statements going back several years. She had marked off all matching transactions. It was clear Bart had been very generous to Felicity over the years, more generous than was necessary. Especially towards someone he supposedly hated.

However, before Sofia and Carl left the station to speak with Felicity, PC Hubbard entered the incident room. She had heard through the Yard grape vine that the chief inspector had visited the Potts & Billingsworth law firm in relation to a murder investigation and told them of the break-in last week.

'Nothing was taken, but they haven't forwarded the CCTV footage yet or informed us which I.D. card was used to access their offices during the night,' PC Hubbard stated proudly.

'Why are they dragging their feet?' Carl asked.

'Not sure, but they didn't seem too worried about it. Mr Billingsworth confirmed nothing was taken. I assumed he didn't want to take the matter any further.'

'Is that so?' replied Sofia, who hated coincidences, especially during a murder investigation. 'Chase up the video footage, and I want to know how the intruder got in. Go back yourself and wait there until you have it, PC Hubbard, and good work.'

PC Hubbard left the room feeling pleased with herself. She wanted to work in homicide but had been turned down on her last request. If she impressed the chief inspector, she hoped the chief inspector would put in a good word for her.

'When the footage arrives, have it compared with the footage from the Hall on Saturday night,' Sofia said to Carl on their way out. 'I want to see if this intruder has a similar build to our two suspects at the Hall on Saturday night.'

They were off to reinterview Felicity Goode. Sofia was looking forward to the encounter. Especially when she confronted Felicity about the blackmail allegations. She was hoping Felicity's claws would come out. It was the only way to provoke her into revealing something she normally wouldn't. Self-preservation can make people more assertive with their answers. Sofia believed Felicity was one of those people.

Residence of Felicity Goode

Pimlico, 9.40 am

Felicity's butler answered the door, and, after showing their warrant cards for a second time in as many days, Sofia and Carl were escorted into the sitting room, while the butler went upstairs to fetch his mistress. They had to wait a full fifteen minutes before Felicity made an entrance.

Just as impeccably groomed the second time around, she walked casually into the room and took a seat. Felicity was clearly setting the boundaries of who was leading who in their second interview.

'What can I help you with this time, Inspector?'

'That's Chief Inspector, Mrs Goode, or may I call you Felicity?'

'No, you may not!'

Sofia conceded to her sparring partner and allowed Felicity to believe she had the upper hand for the time being. Sofia took the seat directly opposite Felicity, so she could gauge Felicity's reactions. She waited until Carl had his notebook and pen ready before she began her first question.

'What was your relationship like with your ex-husband after your divorce?'

'None of your business,' Felicity snapped.

'You came away handsomely in the divorce. Plus a monthly allowance for your children. So, can you explain why Bartholomew Goode kept paying you, *just you*, large sums of money after your divorce?'

The DCI had done her homework. Felicity had known the police would dig into Bart's finances, and now obviously hers. Her steely eyes bore into Sofia. *What the hell does she know?*

'Do I need to repeat the question?'

'He gave me the extra funds for our children. Not that that's relevant.'

'I don't believe you. He would have put the money into a trust for his children, not given it to you directly. Judging by the extravagance of your home, you clearly spent it on yourself.'

'Go to hell. This interview is over,' Felicity said, rising from her chair.

'Sit down, Mrs Goode. It's over when I say it is. Unless you'd prefer to do this down at the station with your lawyer present.'

Felicity and Sofia squared off.

Felicity knew when to retreat, and so she slowly cupped her hands behind her skirt and neatly straightened it as she sat back down.

'What was the money for?'

'He was a poor father. The money was his way of making amends.'

'Your daughters live in an apartment paid for by their father. That doesn't sound too uncaring to me.'

Felicity ignored Sofia's sarcasm.

'Why have you lied to your children about their father since your divorce? So much so that they didn't want anything to do with him?'

'I don't know what you're talking about,' Felicity replied, wondering who had spoken to the police.

'That's your second lie. One more, and we *will* make this an official interview down at the Yard.'

'I *beg* your pardon.'

'By all accounts, Bartholomew Goode loved his children. It was you who prevented him from having joint custody. You who damaged his relationship with them because it suited your needs. A loving father would have fought for them, so the only reason I can think of why he couldn't is that he was being blackmailed.'

'You're talking rubbish.'

'I'll find out the truth. I have your bank statements.'

Felicity took a moment to regroup. She was losing the upper hand. She knew when to put up a fight, but now was the time to withdraw.

'Who have you been speaking to? Bart's family have never liked me. I wouldn't trust anything that comes out of their mouths.'

'It was your son, Bartie.'

Felicity was momentarily taken aback. She hadn't expected her son to betray her and divulge family secrets. *Does Bartie actually know anything about my arrangement with Bart? Who could have told him?*

Felicity was thinking quickly. She had to choose her words carefully, especially in front of this policewoman. She wasn't sure how much the police already knew.

Sofia's mobile rang. Annoyed by the interruption, she quickly pulled it out of her handbag and turned it off. Now was not the time for distractions. DS Smith would have to wait.

'As I see it, you've been receiving large sums of money for years. However, the funds stopped last year when your husband left for his treatment. Obviously, you thought he was going to die, and no longer had any hold over him. That's a motive in itself right there. Maybe you knew about the new will but didn't know he hadn't signed it?'

'Don't be ridiculous!' exclaimed Felicity.

'Then enlighten me as to why he kept paying you. It wasn't because he cared about you or that he was a generous man. Blackmail is a serious crime, Mrs Goode.'

'It wasn't blackmail,' Felicity finally blurted out. 'I simply heard something a long time ago. I had no idea if it was true or false. I just reminded him of it from time to time. That's all.'

'What did you hear, a long time ago?'

Carl's mobile rang, he quickly pulled it out of this jacket pocket and turned it off. DS Smith would have to wait. This interview was just getting interesting.

'Mrs Goode!' prompted Sofia.

Felicity was clearly thinking about her next move.

'I'll find out eventually. But if we uncover embezzlement or blackmail, we will have to take it seriously and make it official.'

Felicity had no intention of being taken down to Scotland Yard and relished even less having her arrangement with Bart exposed publicly to friends and family.

'My agreement with Bart had nothing to do with his death!' exclaimed Felicity, who was growing more agitated by the minute.

'Everything in a murder investigation is relevant to our inquiries, Mrs Goode. Until I say otherwise. The longer it takes, the more we'll turn your life upside down to find out the truth.' Sofia allowed a moment to pass before adding, 'The longer it plays out, the more likely the press will get wind of it, and your life will become fodder for the tabloids. I'm sure you wouldn't want that.'

Felicity wanted to scratch Sofia's eyes out. She was playing her, in her own home. But the inspector was right, she had no intention of being a laughingstock in society or in the tabloids. Besides, she hadn't committed any crime, only benefitted from it from time to time.

'It's only hearsay. I doubt it's even true.'

'Who told you?'

'Augustus. Bart's brother.'

'Why would he tell you something incriminating about his brother?'

'Because he was drunk at the time. Besides, he's always hated Bart.'

'What did he tell you?'

'He said… He said Bart had killed someone and covered it up. That is all I'm going to tell you. Except, I did *not* kill my husband. The act of murder is contemptable.'

Strangely enough, Sofia agreed. The act itself would be beneath her. But that didn't mean she hadn't hired someone to do it. Or wasn't possibly acting to protect one of her children.

Sofia had finally found her smoking gun. Bart's death may have something to do with a past crime. If, in fact, there were one.

'Withholding evidence about a crime is also a crime in itself.'

'I'll simply deny it. Look… what happened back then was before I ever met Bart. It has nothing to do with me or my children. Look to his family.

'Augustus hated Bart more than anyone else. Including me. Besides, anything I was told in that drunken moment is hearsay. Now, if you don't mind, I have an appointment I cannot miss. Any further questions *will* be conducted in the presence of my lawyer.' Felicity stood up, signalling the interview had come to an end.

Sofia knew she wouldn't get anything else out of Felicity today. She held the upper hand and allowed Felicity to keep a morsel of dignity. Sofia and Carl thanked her for her time. Sofia had to give Felicity credit, she had completely shifted the blame away from her own family and in the direction of Augustus Goode.

Felicity watched from her living room window as the police officers walked to their car. She hated the idea of laundering family secrets in public; nevertheless, she wasn't going to be accused of something she didn't do. Felicity doubted Bart's death had anything to do with his past. But she knew it had everything to do with his detestable siblings. She fed them Augustus out of self-preservation. Besides, if he were present at the time of this alleged crime, that made him an accomplice, not her. Felicity knew Augustus hated his brother enough to kill him. Zachary, if the stories floating around town were true, was sufficiently desperate. Eleanor, too, could be resentful enough.

The only sibling Felicity gave no thought to killing Bart was Ariadne.

'Well, well, well, I guess our next stop is Augustus Goode, Carl.'

'Do you really think our motive lies in the past, it would be nearly thirty years ago?' Carl asked, climbing into the car. 'It's a stretch after all this time.'

'Maybe something happened recently that made it resurface. Can you check with PC Hubbard, I want that video footage of the intruder at Potts & Billingsworth. It may not be relevant, but I don't like coincidences.'

'Right you are, Gov.' When Carl pulled out his mobile, he saw there were four messages waiting his response. He rang Shirley back, who told him Dr Harry Budd at the lab needed to see them urgently. Sofia decided to visit the lab before heading back into Kent.

On the way, Carl called PC Hubbard for an update.

Sofia's spirits lifted when she entered the lab to find Harry Budd talking to an intern. He had a pleasing manner, a calm disposition and a wicked sense of humour that Sofia relished. He wasn't bad looking either.

'You said it was urgent, Dr Budd,' she said, as she approached him.

'Harry, please.'

'Ok, Harry, what have you got for us?'

'The murder of Bartholomew Goode has just taken an unusual turn. Good or bad will be for you to decide.'

'How so?'

'He was stabbed, which goes without saying. The letter opener pierced his heart. But he was also poisoned, possibly hours earlier.'

'*What!*' exclaimed both Sofia and Carl simultaneously.

'Technically, he was killed twice. The poison would have killed him, to be sure, if allowed to run its course, but someone stabbed him before he died of the poisoning.'

'*Maledetto inferno,*' Sofia whispered.

'Bloody hell,' Carl said.

'My thoughts exactly,' Harry replied.

'So, we're now looking for two murderers. Or are we?' Carl asked.

'I'll leave that one up to you,' Harry said.

'Why would you stab someone if you'd already poisoned them?' Sofia said, more to herself than anyone present in the room. 'Unless you believed the victim hadn't taken the poison, and time was of the essence...'

'Would Bartholomew Goode have been showing symptoms of the poisoning by the time he was stabbed?' Carl asked.

'Yes, it would have started to take effect.'

'Who do we actually charge with murder then? The poisoner or the stabber, assuming they are two separate people?' Carl asked, looking at Sofia for clarification.

'Both. I think.' Sofia wasn't entirely sure. This sharp turn of events had taken her by surprise. 'Our time of death has now expanded until we can determine when our victim was poisoned and how. So, everyone is once again a suspect.

'What type of poison was used?' Sofia asked. 'Do you have a time frame for when it was administered?'

'Strychnine. Not a very nice way to go, I'm afraid. It's an odourless powder that can be taken orally, inhaled, mixed with a solution or given intravenously. I'll take another look at the victim's body to see if I can find any needle marks. But I doubt I will. He wouldn't allow anyone to inject him willingly, unless he was asleep at the time. There are no signs of a struggle, but there was discolouration around his mouth. I would suggest, unless you rule out suicide, it was given orally. Probably in his drink or food, up to one to two hours before he would have died. It all depends on how much he ingested and on the strength of his immune system.'

'He had just beaten cancer,' interrupted Carl. 'So, his immune system would've been weakened, isn't that correct?'

'Yes. You're right. He may have started to feel symptoms leading up to the stabbing. Agitation, painful muscle spasms, fever, rigidity in his arms and legs. Maybe that was why he couldn't fight off the person who stabbed him. There was an empty glass on the coffee table beside his armchair and a half-smoked cigar in an ashtray. I'm waiting on the test results to confirm what he ate and drank to determine if the poison was ingested. I'll also test all the cigars in the cigar box.'

'Cheers,' Sofia said. 'My window of opportunity has just been extended by an unknown timeframe. Someone could have spiked his food, drink or cigars days ago.

'Sorry about that.'

'That would mean our killer definitely knew Bart was alive before returning to the Hall,' Sofia said.

'Do we assume the killer brought the poison with them or found it in the Hall somewhere? That's going to be a big job, searching the Hall. The strychnine may no longer be there, or the killer could've brought it with them,' Carl said.

'We'll wait for the lab's results before starting an extensive and expensive search,' Sofia said. 'I'd say the killer brought the poison with them. That's what I would have done. Leave no trace evidence.'

'Your call. I have to wait for toxicology to confirm my findings on how the strychnine was induced. That will give us an idea of when he was poisoned. It wouldn't have been in the air, or in vapour form, if his dogs were with him in the library that evening. They would also have died from the fumes,' Harry replied.

'Thanks, Harry,' Sofia said.

'What I know right now is that the poisoning came first. He would have died from that within hours of ingestion, regardless of being stabbed.'

'I would like to keep the poisoning under wraps for the time being. Someone out there thinks he or she just got away with murder,' Sofia said. 'Let them believe he was stabbed.'

THE DEVIL

The sixteenth card of the major arcana

The Devil will enslave you to your ideals and relationships.
He represents greed, materialism and temptation.
Try walking away from these negative forces before
it's too late.
Do not succumb to temptation.
Only in reverse can The Devil appear more hopeful. It
may suggest you have moved away from this temptation,
enslavement and other addictive habits.

34

Ashburton Manor
Home of Augustus and
Henrietta Goode

Maidstone Kent, Tuesday, 1.00 pm

The trip into Kent was as beautiful as the previous day's journey, so Sofia took the opportunity to relax while Carl drove. The idea of retiring to the countryside was becoming more and more tempting. Sofia could see why Kent was known as the Garden of England.

'Do you believe we're looking for two murderers?' Carl asked, interrupting Sofia's thoughts. 'Maybe someone planted the poison but decided to speed it up. A time factor might be involved, especially if they didn't want the new will signed.'

'It's a possibility. But remember, he was found dead beside an empty glass and half-smoked cigar. If it was the same killer that poisoned Bartholomew, they would have realised he was on the doorstep of death. There would have been no need to stab him.

'Either way, the poisoner knew Bartholomew's habits. Enjoying a nightcap and a cigar in your favourite armchair with a good book wouldn't be hard to set up. But what we need to know is how many people actually knew Bartholomew Goode was still alive and residing back at the Hall. If there were two people, it would mean both killers knew that.'

'Yeah, but the killer was still taking a risk. I mean, which glass would he have chosen, or which beverage. What cigar would he have taken out of the box and smoked. What if the poison was planted before he left for his treatment months ago?' Carl said.

'I don't think so. Our poisoner could have removed it long ago.' Sofia went through which suspects knew Bartholomew Goode was still alive: George Fox had only recently found out, Hugo Billingsworth and Sam Potts had known all along. Sofia doubted Tina, the housekeeper, was a killer. Her background check had come back clean, and they hadn't found a motive for her wanting her employer dead. Excluding the contract gardeners who worked at the Hall, George Fox was their most likely suspect. But Sofia's instincts told her George was not a killer. She hadn't ruled out Felicity or Ariadne knowing Bart was still alive.

'Well, someone knew he was still alive,' said Carl. 'He had a fight with someone. I think it was George Fox.'

'I agree.'

On their arrival at Ashburton Manor, Sofia and Carl drove down the long country driveway. Instantly, Sofia could see the dissimilarity to Cricklewood Hall. Sofia wondered what Bartholomew's motive was in buying up his brother's estate when the Hall was far more breathtaking.

The deterioration of the gardens was immediately clear. The Manor looked bleak and in desperate need of repair.

She couldn't shake off the feeling that the Manor was cold and unloved and wondered if the same could be said for its occupants.

The police officers were shown into the drawing room, where Augustus II and Augustus III, accompanied by their respective wives, greeted them. Maude excused herself as she went off to organise some tea.

Henrietta confirmed that James, their youngest son, was at work in the city. He wouldn't be home as he was visiting his cousin Bartie after work, in case they wanted to talk to him.

Sofia decided that this interview would focus on the stabbing and everyone's whereabouts at that time. Henrietta gave Augustus and herself an alibi by confirming they were in all night. Augustus III also confirmed he was tucked up in bed with Maude after putting their son to bed.

Their attitudes during the interview appeared fake and well-rehearsed. They corroborated what each person said rather too efficiently and were, altogether, too cordial. So much so, that Augustus showed no emotion regarding his brother's recent death. He appeared cold and disassociated from everyone.

Sofia decided to rub some salt on the wound of his malcontent. She needed to unnerve him to get him to talk.

'You weren't faring very well in your brother's game?'

'It was a stupid game, typical of my brother.'

'You were angry, by all accounts.'

'Wouldn't you be?'

'Did you know your brother was still alive?'

'No, of course not.'

Augustus still showed little irritation. Sofia put her earlier concern about the Manor being cold and unloved down to him.

'Our records show your brother Bartholomew owned more of this estate than you do. Per acreage, that is.'

Augustus took a moment to respond. His expression shifted slightly from irritation to annoyance, which he tried to suppress.

'That was between my brother and I, madam.'

'That's chief inspector, Mr Goode.' Carl corrected him. Augustus eyed Carl coldly.

'I believe your brother finally refused to bail you out. That must have made you very angry.' Sofia continued.

'On the contrary, he was happy to buy the land. We preferred to keep it in the family.'

'Why would he do that, he has a much larger estate in Allington?'

'That's what brothers do for one another.'

'Yes, but you didn't like him, and vice versa by all accounts.'

'Who told you that?'

'You wouldn't be blackmailing him would you, regarding an incident that happened many years ago?'

Augustus's expression shifted to icy. But Sofia finally saw some alarm on his face. She had rattled his cage.

Augustus hadn't expected that line of questioning. He was momentarily taken aback. Someone had been talking. *Fucking Felicity*, he thought.

Augustus's son looked at him for clarification. He apparently didn't know anything about the blackmail.

'Felicity Goode spoke to us in confidence this morning. She mentioned a serious incident which took place over thirty years ago.'

Sofia had called Augustus's bluff. One thing she knew for certainty, Felicity hadn't called Augustus to warn him about their conversation. There was obviously no love lost between them.

'Maybe we can discuss this new line of questioning in private, Mr Goode.' Sofia sounded sympathetic and understanding. 'Shall we take a walk outside? Unless you're happy for your family to know everything, if they don't already.'

He nodded his agreement, and they exited the room, leaving Carl to smile politely at the remaining family members, who were perplexed by this new line of questioning.

Carl sat quietly and drank his cold coffee.

Henrietta started to fidget. She kept smoothing the creases in her pleated skirt. The interview had taken a sharp turn. She wasn't prepared for the inspector's blunt questions. Henrietta held an uneasy feeling that her husband had killed his brother. Although, at the time of the stabbing, he had been asleep beside her.

Walking across the lawn, Sofia allowed a few minutes to pass before she prompted Augustus to start talking. This gave him time to weigh up his options. She had a lead, which would lead somewhere or nowhere. She wondered who else knew about this crime.

'You were drunk at the time, otherwise I'm sure you wouldn't have betrayed your brother in that manner,' Sofia said, creating an opening for Augustus to step into.

'Look... I'm not proud of myself but it happened a long time ago.'

Sofia said nothing but allowed Augustus to continue at his own pace. She kept him walking across the grounds.

'About thirty years ago, a man attacked Ariadne. George confronted him and killed him, and Bart helped cover it up.'

Sofia kept her cool. *No past deeds go unpunished*, she thought.

'Did you witness this incident?'

'No. I arrived on the scene much later.'

'Did you know the attacker?'

'No. I didn't recognise him. I assumed it was a vagrant or trespasser.'

Sofia led Augustus further away from the Manor.

'All I remember from that night was finding Bart digging a grave. There was a dead body lying on the ground next to him covered in plastic. This was very early in the morning. My parents held a lavish party each year during mid-summer. Bart and I came home from Oxford for it. He brought a few friends with him. I remember we all had too much to drink, it was a very warm night. When I confronted him about it, he said the man attacked Ariadne, and George killed him. It was an accident. Plain and simple. But Bart covered it up to protect our family.

'I know I should have said something, but he was my brother. Years later, I had a verbal confrontation with Felicity. She has a habit of bringing out the worst in people. I was drunk, and to my regret, it just came out. The vicious bitch used it against Bart during their divorce. Because of my indiscretion, my relationship with my brother has been on shaky ground ever since. I may have exaggerated the story a little, when telling Felicity, by stating it was Bart who killed him, but it wasn't. It was George Fox.'

'And were you blackmailing your brother over it. To buy up acreage after acreage when you needed money?'

'No. I didn't need to. Bart didn't want the Manor falling into someone else's hands. The new owners might start digging up the past, literally. He bought the land out of self-preservation.'

'Please show me now where you saw your brother digging the grave?'

'It was a long time ago, Inspector.'

'I doubt your memory from that night has diminished over the years. You walk these grounds every day.'

Augustus sighed and looked deflated. He nodded and took Sofia into a small wood, which looked as though it had been untouched for centuries. He led her to an old oak tree. It stood over twenty metres tall. Augustus pointed to a spot on the ground near it.

'Look… I had no part in the murder. My brother didn't either. Bart didn't want our family dragged through the press, not to mention poor Ariadne. So, he dealt with the body. Maybe Bart was going to say something. Maybe he had grown a conscience since his illness and wanted to set things right. Maybe he told George what he was going to do, and that's what got him killed.'

Sofia had to hand it to Augustus, he just shifted the blame away from his family and straight towards George Fox. But now that Bart was dead, there was no one to corroborate either side of the story.

'It was just an accident,' he said, looking squarely at Sofia.

'Is that why George has worked for Bart all these years?'

'I guess so, George felt indebted to Bart. I believe George has a drinking problem and had trouble finding a job. So, Bart helped him out. He's been working at the Hall for many years. He also likes to keep an eye on Ariadne. She's always been an overly sensitive and feeble woman.'

'Being attacked has a tendency to do that,' remarked Sofia, shocked by his lack of empathy.

'Yes, of course. What I meant to say was, Ariadne has procrastinated throughout her life. She's weak-willed and has allowed that one night to dictate her whole life.'

'She would have won your brother's game.'

Augustus allowed the slight to go unanswered.

'Ariadne has always depended on Bart and his charity.'

'So have you, by all accounts.'

'She was desperate to win, because she was afraid of losing her cottage. Maybe George is still protecting her.'

'If you had won, would you have let Ariadne keep her cottage?'

'Of course.'

It wasn't lost on Sofia that Augustus had now managed to provide two suspects for Bart's murder, while simultaneously exonerating himself. Bart wasn't alive to defend himself, which only left George and Ariadne. Sofia wondered if Ariadne had been in any state to know what really happened all those years ago. But, if she did, she'd kept quiet about it ever since.

Everyone was pointing the finger at someone else. *But that would be down to self-interest*, thought Sofia. She told Augustus he would need to give an official statement, and that a member of her team would come by later to take it.

Sofia thanked Augustus and they walked back to the Manor.

'One last thing,' she asked, 'who were Bart's friends at the party that night?'

'Sam Potts and Hugo Billingsworth.'

'Thank you.'

Carl called the forensics team to Ashburton Manor and cordoned off the area around the oak tree.

When Harry Budd arrived, he and his team were escorted to the burial site, where they erected a white tent over the immediate area before they started digging.

Sofia ordered George Fox and Ariadne Goode be picked up and taken to the Yard for questioning. She wanted them to stew for a while before she interviewed them.

By 5.00 pm, Dr Harry Budd confirmed the presence of a body. It had been covered with a large plastic bag. All he could say at the present time was that it was likely male. Once the body was carefully removed, it was bagged and taken back to the lab, where the autopsy would be carried out in the morning.

On the drive back to London, Carl asked Sofia what she thought of this new development. 'Whaddaya reckon, Gov?' A little *too* convenient?'

'I agree. Augustus could have said Bart killed this man, then had George and Ariadne confirm it. Case closed, unless forensics said otherwise.'

'True. If he knew Ariadne inherited Bart's fortune... By laying the blame at Bart's feet for the murder, Ariadne and George would be off the hook, allowing her to be generous with Bart's inheritance. But he didn't, he pushed the blame onto them. I guess his sister can't spend or inherit Bart's fortune if she's charged with his murder and that of this unknown victim. Clever.'

'I agree. Let's wait and see what the forensics have to say.' Sofia had far too many suspects for each murder.

Scotland Yard

London, 5.25 pm

Sofia and Carl had to wait for Ariadne's lawyer to arrive before interviewing her, so they decided to interview George Fox first.

Any allegation of rape was taken very seriously, no matter how long ago the act. Regrettably, there could be no justice now, as the alleged perpetrator was dead.

Was this old crime a motive for murder? Was Bart really going to confess his part in it to the police? Sofia doubted that. Sofia knew it would be easy for George and Ariadne to make up whatever story they liked now. They would be able to shift the blame to Bart. Augustus hadn't seen who killed the man, he said he'd arrived to find Bart digging a grave.

Sofia freshened herself up and drank a short black before she entered the interview room.

'I apologise for keeping you waiting, Mr Fox,' Sofia said, as she and Carl entered the room and sat down across from him.

Carl turned on the recorder.

'This conversation will be recorded. As you have already been read your rights and have declined legal counsel, we shall begin.'

'I've already told you, I had nothing to do with Bart's death.'

'You're not hear in regard to Bartholomew Goode's death.'

'What then?' he asked, sensing something was amiss.

'The murder of a yet unidentified man, who has been buried for nearly thirty years at Ashburton Manor. And the alleged rape of Ariadne Goode.'

If George weren't already sitting, he probably would have collapsed to the ground. He was shaken to the core. It looked like the blood had drained from his face. Sofia could see he was unnerved, shaken. He hadn't denied it though.

She allowed him a few moments to compose himself. He was breathing heavily; he dropped his head down. His elbows were on the table. He spread his hands through his hair and squeezed them tightly. He was physically shaking now.

Sofia had seen over the years how secrets and lies kept hidden could eat away at a person's soul, robbing them of a fulfilling life. George's drinking obviously hadn't been able to bury his memories deep enough.

George took a deep breath, then looked up at the police. His voice was soft and subdued but remarkably calm.

'It was an accident, I swear… one stupid punch. Ariadne had nothing to do with it. None of it is her fault. Do you understand me?' he said sternly.

'OK,' Sofia said, 'if she is truly a victim here, then I will treat her with all due respect. But if you lie to me, I'll throw the book at both of you. That man has been buried in a shallow grave for over thirty years. His family deserve to know what happened to him. You've denied them closure.'

George's will was gone, he simply nodded his cooperation. In a way, he was glad the truth was finally out.

'Is Ariadne here?'

'Yes, we're waiting on her lawyer before we interview her.'

'Can I talk to her?'

'No. Not until we have interviewed you both.'

George shifted in his chair and sat upright. He was ready to talk.

'It was the night of the Goodes' annual mid-summer party. Some of us had drunk too much, smoked a little pot. We were happy that we were all together again, Ariadne and myself. Bart, Augustus and Bart's friends were back from Oxford. It was getting late, and Ariadne had gone for a walk. She was hot and had drunk too much. I don't know his name, but he looked vaguely familiar. Bart never wanted to talk about it. He appeared to move on from it. The man may have worked at the Manor over the summer. If he did, it won't be too hard to find out his name from the estate's employee records.'

'Go on,' Sofia said. Carl was still taking notes even though the recorder was doing his work for him.

'We were all together most of the night, us young ones. Eleanor and Zachary had already gone to bed. But we eventually drifted apart. I went looking for Ariadne, someone said they saw her walking towards the woods. I followed after her, but when I entered the wood I heard a scream, then some muffled sounds. I found Ariadne with a man on top of her. He was pulling at her clothes, one hand was under her dress, and the other was trying to cover her mouth.'

'I raced up to them and pulled him off her. We wrestled on the ground. I managed to get on top of him, and I hit him hard across the face. He fell back unconscious, so I thought. I carried Ariadne back to the house and came across Bart on the way. I told him what happened, and he raced into the woods. I thought he was going to detain him. I stayed with Ariadne until she calmed down. She didn't want anyone to know about the incident. Later, I ran back into the woods and found Bart digging a grave. The body was beside him, wrapped in a plastic bag. He said I killed him.' George paused for a moment.

Sofia sensed remorse in his voice. One punch is all it can ever take.

'What happened next? Why didn't you simply call the police? If it was truly an accident,' Carl said, 'and under the circumstances.'

'I wanted to, but Bart said it was too late for that. We were all drunk and a little stoned. We weren't thinking clearly. Ariadne was in a terrible state, she didn't want the police involved. Neither did Bart. Knowing the Goode family, like I did, Bart's father would have buried the whole incident, just as Bart did. Bart said it was done and dealt with. He told me to go home. We never spoke of it again, and he returned to Oxford shortly after. We hadn't spoken in years. But when he bought Cricklewood Hall, he offered me a job. I was drinking a lot more back them, and I couldn't hold anything down. The memory of that night has always haunted me, as it has Ariadne. Bart has been a good friend to me. His job offer saved my life.'

'Did you punch Bart the night of his death?'

'Yes. When he entered my office on Saturday afternoon, I was shocked, but briefly happy he was alive. I knew he could beat the cancer. But then I grew angry. How could he do that? To Ariadne and his family. I started yelling at him. He didn't expect that kind of reaction. He turned on me. We were both shouting, and then I hit him. I also quit before storming out.'

'Thank you, Mr Fox.'

Sofia asked one final question.

'Did Bart's friends know what happened in the woods that night?'

'I don't think so. Not unless Bart told them. But why would he?' George took a long deep breath, then exhaled slowly. As he did a heavy weight was finally released, as did all his pent-up guilt and fear. He was ready to accept his punishment now.

Sofia finished the interview and asked a PC to fetch Mr Fox a cup of tea and something to eat. But before leaving the room, Sofia offered him some advice.

'I think you should get a lawyer, George.'

It was nearing 6.00 pm by the time PC Hubbard informed Sofia that Ariadne's lawyer had arrived.

'I want you to all go home,' she said to her team back in the incident room. 'We have a big day tomorrow. I want our new victim's body identified. We know exactly when he went missing, so start on missing person records from then, and I want one of you to go to Ashburton Manor tomorrow and obtain all the employee records for that year. Get a search warrant if you run into any flack there. Hopefully forensics will have dental records and DNA for us tomorrow. That's our main priority now, finding out who this man was, and how he fits into Bartholomew Goodes death.'

Sofia's team said their goodnights and left the Yard. Carl remained behind to interview Ariadne with Sofia.

Before she started her next interview, Sofia took a minute to call Francesca and see how she was doing. Sofia's mother had picked Francesca up from school, as she did each day, and stayed with her until Sofia arrived home from work. As it was going to be a late shift, Sofia asked her mother to give Francesca her dinner.

Sofia entered the second interview room, where Ariadne was waiting. She was surprised to see Hugo Billingsworth sitting beside her. But, then again, who else would Ariadne call.

'I would like to start by saying my client knows nothing about the murder of her brother,' Hugo said. 'And the insinuation is offensive.'

'I'll make a note of that, Mr Billingsworth. I'll be wanting to talk to you about that a little later, but for now Ms Goode, you're here to answer questions about an attack that took place at Ashburton Manor over thirty years ago and the murder of a young man during a mid-summer party. You would have been around sixteen at the time. You may also remember it Mr Billingsworth, as you were present too.'

Ariadne's face went white. So did Hugo's. Sofia realised Augustus hadn't warned his sister about their interview earlier in the day. Sofia was starting to paint a picture of what the Goode family was actually like.

Ariadne started to become anxious. Her chest constricted and her breathing came heavily. She was clearly taken off guard. She looked at Hugo for help; he appeared as shocked as she was.

'I... I... don't know what you're talking about?' she whispered.

'We were under the impression you wanted to talk to my client about her brother's death.'

'I do, but I believe one may be connected to the other.'

'No!' cried Ariadne.

Ariadne closed her eyes. She didn't know what to say, she was afraid for George. She *knew* he couldn't have had anything to do with her brother's death.

'What has George said?' she asked Sofia.

'I'm afraid I can't tell you that.'

Hugo, who was also caught off guard, said, 'I need a few minutes alone with my client.'

'I appreciate that,' Sofia said. 'We can certainly give you time to consult with your client. Or you can just tell us what happened all those years ago, Ariadne, and put an end to it now.'

Ariadne looked again at Hugo, who was shaking his head, signalling her not to say anything. Then she looked at Sofia. She felt trapped; she didn't know what to do. She wanted to protect George. *Who told the police? Was it George... or Augustus?* Her thoughts drifted to Felicity. *How much does she know?* Ariadne was afraid where this would all lead. Right to George's feet. She looked pleadingly at Sofia for help.

Sofia remained inscrutable. 'George Fox has just given us a statement under caution. I only need you to corroborate what he said.'

Ariadne asked for some time with her lawyer. Sofia agreed but said she would return in fifteen minutes.

She and Hugo didn't really speak, she just needed time to compose her thoughts. Each was absorbing the shock of what they'd heard. It didn't matter, Finally, Ariadne had made her decision.

Now that it was all out in the open, Ariadne began to surrender to the idea of being free from her past. She finally understood what Angeline meant. She had to let go of her past if she ever wanted to move forward. She needed to unburden herself.

When Sofia and Carl re-entered the room, Ariadne took a deep breath and recounted her story. Her account appeared to marry up with what George had said. But only so far as being carried back to the Hall by George and running into Bart.

'George was just trying to protect me. Most of it is a blur, but I remember how afraid I was, the fear still hits me at times, and I get panic attacks, especially when I feel claustrophobic.'

'Can you describe him?' Sofia asked.

'He had dark hair, and I remember, when he tried to kiss me, his breath smelt of alcohol, and he'd been smoking.'

'You should have told the authorities. It could have been all over with many years ago. You could have received counselling for the trauma.'

'My parents would never have allowed that,' Ariadne smirked wryly. 'Bart made it all disappear. I was grateful to him for that at the time.'

'Do you think your parents knew what happened?'

'No. No, I doubt Bart told them. He never really got on well with our father. They were opposites in every way. As for my mother, she would have just hushed it up and pretended it never happened.'

'Did you know the man? Did he work on the estate?'

'I'm not sure, sometimes I get a sense of recognition. When I try to remember, I get a feeling that I had seen him prior to that night, around the Manor. I remember him saying something to me, during the attack, but I couldn't understand what he said. I was so scared, it sounded like he was drunk. But sometimes, when I'm watching TV, I hear the same words, pronounced the same way and it brings it all back.'

'What do you mean?' Sofia asked.

'I think he had a Geordie accent. When I hear that accent, certain words said, I get a chill down my spine.'

Sofia said that was enough for today. Ariadne was free to go. Sofia wasn't sure yet what to charge her with. Concealing a crime, possibly. But if she was in shock and was taken away from the scene, then she had no part in the aftermath of the attack. She had only helped cover it up all these years.

Sofia couldn't see a jury convicting her of any crime. Even if they did, she would probably get a suspended sentence. But Sofia couldn't rule out Ariadne or George having something to do with Bart's death. As for George Fox, Sofia decided to wait until the autopsy on the decades-old corpse was completed before deciding what to charge him with.

Ariadne and George were released and driven home. Sofia told them she would speak with them again after the autopsy was carried out.

Back in Sofia's office, she and Carl debriefed quickly about the interviews.

'If he wasn't a local, we'll have to extend our search nationwide. That's going to take a while,' Carl said.

'Agreed.'

'They could have killed Bart to keep him quiet, if they thought he was going to blab.'

'I know. Let's find out who this guy was first. We should find what we need at the Manor tomorrow. But right now, I'm going home to my daughter. Goodnight, Carl.'

'Good night, Gov.'

Residence of Sofia Faraday

Teddington, 12 miles from London, 7.50 pm

Sofia walked through her front door, kicked off her shoes, tossed her keys into a bowl on the sideboard, and walked into her living room and threw herself on the couch. She was too exhausted to get herself a drink. She unhooked her bra and pulled it off, sighing with relief. Her mother walked into the room with a glass of red wine and told her that her lasagne was in the oven when she was ready to eat.

'*Sei la migliore, Mamma,*' Sofia said, as she took the glass of red wine and had a long slow drink.

'*Lavori duramente, tesoro,*' said her mother, concerned by how tired her daughter looked.

'*Io so,*' she replied. Sofia knew how much her mother worried about her and loved her for it.

Sofia had inherited her mother's good looks, along with her dark hair and soft brown eyes. The only significant difference was their height. Sofia took after her father, while her mother only came up to her shoulder. Although, she was as feisty as an Amazon.

'Why is my granddaughter learning Spanish at school instead of Italian? I couldn't help her with her homework.'

'She wants to be multi-lingual, Mamma,' Sofia smiled. 'She wants to work at the Foreign Office.'

'*Mamma mia,*' her mother cussed, rolling her eyes to heaven, '*cosa succedera dopo?*'

She kissed her daughter goodnight and went home, which was only a two-minute walk down the street.

After dinner, Sofia opened her laptop and started Googling house prices in Kent. She was curious to know if the thought of retiring there was out of her reach. Writing her cookbook at home in the Kent countryside was getting more enticing by the day. Although, she was a long way off from retirement, she liked to dream.

Later than night, while dozing on the sofa, her thoughts drifted to a certain doctor of forensic medicine. She blushed inwardly, then put Dr Harry Budd out of her mind. Although, a small trace of a smile remained by the time she finally fell asleep.

35

Scotland Yard

Wednesday, 9.00 am

Sofia's team re-capped the previous day's findings at their morning briefing. DC Devish Das was up first and confirmed Bartholomew Goode had made a phone call from the Hall earlier in the evening to Sam Potts. It lasted two and a half minutes.

'Potts forgot to mention *that*,' interrupted Carl.

Devish said they couldn't rule out Bartholomew turning off the surveillance cameras himself, then leaving the Hall after making his phone call. Although the DC couldn't imagine why, given the risk of being seen and recognised. He ruled out Bartholomew being either of the two suspects captured on video Saturday night. His physique didn't match either suspect. Devish also noted that Hugo Billingsworth left the victim a message on his phone on Sunday morning, but it had not been opened.

Up next was DS Shirley Smith.

'The Hall was busy with comings and goings all Saturday. I reviewed all camera footage on Saturday, but there were no cameras inside the Hall, only motion sensors scattered around the grounds and on the front and back doors. The cameras caught images of someone entering the Hall via the back door. But there is no evidence of them leaving. The camera was turned off approximately fifteen minutes after the intruder arrived. So there is no record of them leaving and nothing recorded afterwards. We only have footage of the two unknowns walking across the grounds, one carrying a shovel.'

'PC Hubbard obtained the CCTV footage of the intruder at Potts & Billingsworth, and we have identified the owner of the stolen security card,' Devish jumped in. 'We've ruled out the cleaner having any involvement in the break-in and accepted her story that her card was stolen. I've asked PC Hubbard to re-interview the cleaner and find out exactly when she realised her card was missing.'

Before heading to the lab to talk with Harry, Sofia and Carl decided to visit Bart's lawyers once again. Ronnie and Devish were tasked with searching through missing persons files to identify their thirty year old corpse. While Shirley was off to the Manor in search of old employee records.

Sofia doubted Hugo Billingsworth or Sam Potts would admit to knowing anything about Ariadne's attack or the thirty year old murder. But she believed they knew more than they were saying about Bartholomew Goode's divorce.

Offices of Potts & Billingsworth

Canary Wharf, London, 9.45 pm

'The Old Bill are here to see you and Sam again,' Alyson announced.

Hugo sighed. He had been expecting them.

'Invite them in, will you, Alyson.'

Alyson headed back to reception to fetch the chief inspector and her sergeant, while Hugo asked Sam to join him in his office. On their arrival, Alyson asked if anyone would like tea, coffee or doughnuts.

Hugo raised his right eyebrow dubiously at her, before she turned and left his office.

'How can we help you today, Chief Inspector?' he asked.

'Did Bartholomew ever discuss his divorce or his brother's blackmail with you, formally or informally as a friend?'

'That would be under client privilege for the first and none of your business for the second, Chief Inspector,' Sam said. Sofia didn't have the luxury of time to play *tête-à-tête* with them.

'This is a double murder investigation now, Mr Potts. Everything is relevant, especially if it goes to motive. Our investigation can be long and drawn out, or it can be over quickly and painlessly.'

'We don't know anything about either murder, Chief Inspector,' he replied, appreciating her candour.

'I believe you do. I'll keep digging up your lives until I find what I'm looking for. It may take some time. So I would re-think your last remark, as search warrants may uncover more than we bargained for,' Sofia replied.

The partners looked at one another. They valued their privacy more than a dead friend's past.

'Bart had mentioned from time to time how Felicity was sucking him dry. To use Bart's words,' Hugo said. 'But he never said how she was able to do it.'

'Everyone has a past, Chief Inspector,' Sam said. 'Even you, I'm sure. We simply thought Bart had done something foolish and his ex-wife knew about it.'

'Foolish enough for Felicity to turn his children against him?'

'You don't know Felicity, Inspector,' Sam said.

'I'm beginning to.'

'We never asked him directly, because we didn't want to know. We took care of Bart's business affairs. We're not criminal lawyers,' Hugo said.

'What makes you think Bart committed a criminal act?'

'Bart changed when we returned to Oxford after the party at Ashburton Manor,' Hugo continued. 'He was cagey and anxious for some time, which was out of character for him. His family was complicated, we assumed he had a falling out. We never asked, because we didn't want to know.'

'Ignorance is bliss, Chief Inspector,' Sam added.

'Why did you help Ariadne last night?'

'She was in a state and didn't know who else to call. Of course I helped her. We've known her for many years. She didn't kill Bart. She couldn't kill anyone.'

'Did you know about Ariadne's attack?'

'No,' came back two replies.

'Even though you were both at the party that night?'

'Yes, we were there,' Hugo said, not bothering to hide the fact, 'and at a few others over the years. But we crashed before Ariadne's attack took place.'

'But it makes sense now. It explains her demeanour,' Sam said.

'Look. It's obvious Bart only thought to protect his sister and family. He could have hung George Fox out to dry, but he didn't,' Sam said.

'If that's how it actually happened,' Sofia replied.

'What do you mean?' asked Sam.

'I'm just saying, we can't corroborate what actually happened now that Bartholomew is dead. We only have

George's and Ariadne's testimonies to corroborate the events that night. And the hearsay of Augustus after the fact.'

'Are you suggesting Ariadne made up the attack? Hugo said.

'No, I'm not. I believe her about that,' Sofia replied. 'Were you drunk that night, had you smoked anything?'

'You know, Inspector, I simply can't remember,' Hugo answered, in true lawyer style. Sofia eyed both men with a 'give me a break' look on her face.

'All right, but it was a party Chief Inspector. Everyone was having fun. We may have drunk and smoked a little weed, but that's all.'

'Did either of you notice anyone hanging around Ariadne at the party that night? Did anything happen earlier that night that stands out in your minds?' Sofia asked.

Both men thought for a moment but shook their heads.

'Sorry, Inspector, it was a long time ago. It was just a party. But if we had seen someone harassing Ariadne, we would have done something about it,' Sam said.

Sofia held no doubt they would have.

'Did you oversee the payments to Felicity or write up the legal documents relating to the purchase of land at Ashburton Manor for Bart?'

'No, to the first. Bart would have taken care of that himself. Yes, to the second, which was legitimate land purchase,' Sam said.

'Why did you think Bartholomew wanted to buy up his family's estate?'

Hugo and Sam looked again at each other. They didn't want to betray a friend, but it didn't really matter anymore now that Bart was actually dead, so Hugo answered for both of them.

'We thought Bart wanted to stick it to his father. Show him that he should have chosen Bart over Augustus to run the family business. Bart had a vengeful side. He liked getting what he wanted. But Bart's father died over fifteen years ago, and I doubt it would have mattered to him how clever Bart was. Augustus was his heir and the future owner of Ashburton Manor.'

Hugo clearly had contempt for Bart's father and his legacy. Sofia wondered if it was enough to cover up a crime of murder for a friend.

Sofia showed Hugo and Sam two pictures on her iPad of the intruders at the Hall on Saturday night. Along with the image of the intruder at their office early Thursday morning. Neither man recognised anyone in the photos. Although, they did agree that the person who broke into their office looked like a woman, due to their physique and size. They had their suspicions but no proof. Hugo told Sofia that Eleanor hadn't solved the first clue at the time of the break-in.

'What do you know about Zachary Goode's company?'

Both men shifted a little, not too sure how much they should reveal.

'You know we'll find out eventually. Our forensic auditors will uncover any wrongdoing. Please don't drag this out.' Sofia was becoming impatient.

'Put it this way, Timothy Sharp is a shrewd financier, he just got into bed with the wrong Goode. Zachary on the other hand, I wouldn't trust him with my grandchildren's pocket money,' Hugo said.

'One last thing, Mr Potts. What did Bartholomew want to talk to you about on the night of his death?' Sofia asked matter-of-factly.

'Nothing...' Sam said, with a hint of hesitation.

'He left you a message which lasted,' Carl flicked through his notebook, before answering, 'two and a half minutes.' He gave Sam a pointed look. They had applied for a warrant to access Bart's phone records, but he was hoping Sam would co-operate.

Sam looked at Hugo, who nodded his confirmation.

'Um … He said, "the game will be over my morning. Felicity saw to that." He also said, he'd misjudged everyone's reactions to the game. And that George quit after laying into him and storming out.'

'Was that all? That wouldn't have taken two and a half minutes,' Carl said.

Sam hesitated before he continued.

'He also said, "I need to buy the Manor. Now."'

'Did he say why?' Sofia asked.

'No. He wanted me to call him back. I didn't get the message until Sunday morning. But I swear, if his death had to do with a crime thirty years ago, we had no part in it.'

'What about you, Mr Billingsworth?' Carl asked.

'I turned my phone off late Saturday night. I had plans on Saturday evening. I warned him on Sunday after Felicity came to see me. I had just given her the final clue. She said she had her suspicions that Bart was still alive. She also said Bart was going to pay this time. She wasn't pleased.'

'Did you mention this to anyone else?'

'No.'

'Thank you for your time, gentlemen.'

Sofia and Carl left the building. She wasn't entirely sure if she believed them, but she couldn't prove it one way or another. Not until they had evidence to the contrary. The three men had been friends most of their lives, and friends kept secrets.

Once back on the street, Carl spoke, 'If they were all drinking and smoking pot that night, I doubt they could remember if Ariadne's attacker was a guest at the party or not. I'll get Shirley to check at the Manor to see if there were any photos taken that night.'

'That's a good idea,' Sofia replied.

'Maybe Ariadne knew him in passing, as a handyman or gardener at the Manor. If he was drunk too, his actions may have been out of character for him.'

'People are ultimately responsible for their actions, Carl.'

'Point taken,' Carl said. 'But then so were Bart, George and Ariadne in covering it up.'

'We can check our database for any other assaults on women around the same time in Kent and see if we get any hits. Get someone onto that will you,' Sofia asked Carl.

She continued, 'We can't rule out Eleanor or even Zachary witnessing something that night and not realising its relevance.'

'Well, someone clearly knows. If not Ariadne, then who?' Carl said.

'I'm not sure yet. Have we heard anything from the clinic Bart attended in Switzerland? I want to know if anyone made enquiries about his visit.'

'I'm on it, Gov.'

Forensic Lab

London, 11.00 am

'Argh, Chief Inspector, I'm glad you've arrived. Your case gets more intriguing by the minute,' announced Harry Budd.

'I'm glad we're entertaining you, Doctor, and please it's Sofia.'

'Only if you call me Harry. But I do like the sound of chief inspector. It's more commanding.'

'Thank you, Harry,' Sofia blushed.

Carl felt like a third wheel in the room and wondered where the bathroom was.

'So what have you got? Please tell me you found his name on a clothes label?' she said, smiling for the first time that day. It had nothing at all to do with the case, and everything to do with Harry Budd's charismatic presence.

'No, but I can tell you he didn't die because of a punch to the face.'

'Really…' Sofia said, back on the case.

'Yes, he was hit on the side of the head with a rock. I'm not saying he wasn't knocked out by the punch, he probably was, but that was *not* what killed him.'

Sofia looked at him quizzically, as she took in what he just said.

'I've taken samples from the wound, and we'll know more once the results are in.'

'Are you absolutely sure?'

'Yes, his skull is fractured. Here, look.' Harry brought up a CT scan of the victim's skull on a monitor and used a red laser light to show them the fracture. 'The samples taken from the skull appear to contain small particles of rock.'

'George Fox never mentioned hitting him again with a rock,' Carl said. 'Convenient.'

'No, he didn't. He said he punched him once, then carried Ariadne back to the Manor. Bart was the one who went back to the victim,' Sofia said.

'Oh, but wait, there's more,' Harry said.

'All right, dazzle me,' Sofia asked, she could see Harry was about to let the cat amongst the pigeons.

'Whoever buried this guy preserved the evidence by wrapping him in plastic. It was very considerate of him. But they also put the murder weapon in the plastic bag along with our victim. I might be able to obtain fingerprints off it and possibly DNA if we're really lucky.'

'*What!*'

'Look here,' Harry said, bringing up another photo of the rock which showed dried blood on it.

'*Dio mio!*' Sofia said, in bewilderment.

'I'll complete the autopsy with what's left of the body. I'll check the hair follicles, but unless I find something else in the toxicology reports, my finding will probably be epidural haematoma. I've taken dental images and DNA to help you identify him. You'll have my full report by the end of the day, Sofia.'

'Thank you very much, Harry,' she said, smiling.

'Always glad to help.'

'What would I do without you?'

Oh brother, thought Carl, as he started looking for the nearest door to make a quick exit. He had worked with Sofia for over three years, and after her divorce she had put everything into her work. He was secretly pleased his boss liked Dr Budd. She deserved someone special in her life. He just didn't want a front-row seat during their courtship.

Dr Budd was about to say something else but hesitated. He said he would email the reports as soon as possible.

Back in the car, Carl updated their team on the new cause of death. They were now heading back into Kent to re-interview George and Ariadne.

'Do you believe Bart killed this guy? Hitting him with a rock and letting George believe he killed him?' Carl asked, dumbfounded.

'It does appear that way, doesn't it? But Bart isn't around anymore to corroborate that,' Sofia said. 'We'll need to wait for forensics to confirm.'

'George could have hit him a second time, and Ariadne doesn't remember.'

'Possibly. Or the man woke up, and Bart fought with him. But he wasn't the only one there that night...' Sofia mused. Her case was getting more and more complicated. She still had far too many suspects for each murder.

'If George had finally found out what Bart had done... Well, it would drive anyone to commit murder.'

'I agree, Carl.'

'But why wait so long. If Bart *did* kill our victim, why would he go to the police and incriminate himself?'

'I'm not sure. His lawyers said Bart wanted to buy the remainder of the Manor. Maybe he was afraid someone else would go to the police and wanted to remove the body once and for all.'

'Let's find out, shall we.' Sofia started the car and headed back to Allington. She'd learned years ago that the past always had a way of catching up with you. Nobody can hold a secret for ever.

THE TOWER

The seventeenth card of the major arcana

The Tower marks a sudden change, whether it be a change in your ideals, dreams or relationships. It is inevitable and beyond your control.
You cannot hide away in your ivory tower and must accept these changes, whether spiritually or in the physical world. Once you have, you can rebuild again.
But when reversed, the Tower's collapse is inevitable; although, once it has collapsed, you can surrender to it and reaffirm where you stand. Then, you can rebuild.

36

Allington, Kent

Wednesday, 1.30 pm

It was turning into another beautiful day in Kent. The rain had eased by the time they found a pub in Allington and enjoyed a quick lunch before heading to the Hall to speak with George Fox.

They drove up to George's cottage, but he wasn't there. Searching the grounds, they spotted him walking Bart's dogs. Sofia watched him play with them. She still found it hard to believe he was a killer, even if he believed he was. Her instincts were usually right. Thirty years was a long time to carry guilt. He deserved to know the truth, although, as Carl had pointed out, it could all be a lie. Sofia reminded herself that it was Augustus who saw Bart digging the grave. *What else did he see that night?*

Sofia had to trust her instincts on this one, and they told her George was not a killer.

George Fox watched the police officers approach. He felt his freedom slipping away with every step they took. He could run, but where would he run to. He was tired of living in the shadows.

'Can we have another word, Mr Fox?' Sofia asked, once they were within ear shot.

'Can we walk through the gardens?' George asked, worried he may never have another chance.

'Fine by me, lets walk to the folly. I've been wanting to see it for myself.'

The dogs ran on ahead and jumped into the lake.

On their arrival, Sofia stood by the lake and took in the grounds, they were indeed beautiful. She reluctantly turned away and joined George on the garden bench. Carl stood up with his arms in his pockets in front of them.

Sofia turned to George and asked her first question, 'I want you to go over everything that happened the night of the mid-summer party once more. I know you've already given us a statement but please bear with me. I want you to recount everything in minute detail and leave nothing out. Especially where everyone was during that night.'

Carl pulled out his notebook as George relived the events of that fateful night once more. He tried to remember as best he could where everyone was and what time they left.

'The party was well and truly over, and the novelty of getting drunk had worn off. I just wanted to make sure Ariadne was okay. She was so young... We shouldn't have let her drink all that champagne.'

'Did you see anyone hanging around Ariadne earlier that night or did anything happen that made you feel uncomfortable?'

'No. It was after midnight, and we were so warm we all stayed outside.'

'You stated earlier that Hugo and Sam had called it a night before you went in search of Ariadne, are you certain that's what happened?'

The question surprised George. He tried to remember.

'Yes, they did. I'm sure of it. There was only myself, Bart and Ariadne left.'

'What about Augustus?'

'He wasn't with us. He didn't like Bart's friends. He kept to himself most of the night.'

'Can you remember if anything happened at the Manor during the week leading up to the party? Anything at all. Privately amongst the Goode family or something work related?'

George had to think a moment.

'I do remember my father firing someone a few days before. A work hand who had done odd jobs around the estate. My father caught him stealing and had to sack him.'

'Do you remember who that was?'

'God no. He hadn't been there very long.'

'Can you describe him?'

'Not really. I vaguely remember him around the estate. He was medium height, dark hair. My dad felt bad for the guy, so he never called the police.'

'Was he local, could you remember if he had an accent?'

'Um… I think he was from the north. Not so far north as Scotland, though.'

'Did you know him personally?

'No. I knew some of the workers on the estate well enough, but the casuals? Not really.'

'Did the man you attacked say anything?'

'I don't recall. It happened so fast. Why?'

'No reason. We just need to corroborate a few points.'

George looked at both Sofia and Carl.

'Have you identified the body? Was it him?'

'We don't know yet. How many times did you say you hit him? And did you see Ariadne hit him or lash out at him at all?'

'Once and no. Ariadne was in no state to do anything. That's why I carried her back to the Manor. I swear I just punched him once. He fell back, unconscious, I thought. I didn't need to hit him again. When I realised he was out cold, I ran back to Ariadne.'

Sofia thought George deserved to know the truth about the attack. If he already knew the truth about that night, she would tell by his reaction.

'I'm not sure how to tell you this, George. But our pathologist has confirmed the man didn't die from a single punch. If he was drunk, as Ariadne said he was, you probably did knock him out. But he didn't die from that. He was hit on the side of the head with a rock,' Sofia watched George closely as the news sunk in.

George's expression changed from confusion, to shock, then back to confusion. He stood up and started pacing.

'No, no... I swear I didn't hit him with a rock. On my life. Neither did Ariadne.'

'Did you go back to the sight of the attack again that night?' Sofia asked.

'Yes, I told you I did. Once I calmed Ariadne down, I went back. I found Bart burying him.'

'Did you actually see the man wrapped in plastic?'

'No ...'

George kept pacing, back and forth.

'Are you telling me... I didn't kill him? That someone hit him *after* I did?'

'Yes.'

George stopped pacing, he crouched down and placed his hands over his head. He was breathing heavily. Then he let out a long, drawn-out sound, followed by a roar that had been bottled up for nearly thirty years.

Sofia and Carl gave him time to recover. She couldn't imagine what was running through his mind. But she knew it wasn't an act. Relief would set in, but then a new anger would start to grow. One of betrayal. One caused by an old friend.

'All these years, all those fucking years, he let me believe I killed that man! Why? He could have left him to sober up, and it would all have been over with that very night.'

'I can only guess that when the man came around, he and Bart had words. Maybe a fight started. Bart panicked and hit him. Blaming you was the best way to protect himself, in case you or Ariadne decided to go to the police. Blaming you secured your silence and loyalty.'

'He must have seen how it affected Ariadne and me all these years.'

George looked to Sofia suddenly with alarm, 'Have you talked to Ariadne about this?'

'No, I thought you deserved to know first,' she said.

George exhaled, 'I need to talk to her.'

'You can, but not until after we speak with her. I need to gauge her reaction too,' Sofia said, with kindness.

'You can't think Ariadne knew and never told me. She would never do that.'

Carl had to state the obvious, 'Can't you see that this revelation has given you a motive for Mr Goode's murder? If you had found out what he had done, or if Ariadne knew, that would drive anyone to commit murder.'

George couldn't believe what he was hearing, he had just been absolved of one murder but was now accused of another. He couldn't believe this was happening.

'Mr Fox, I would like you to accompany us to Ms Goode's cottage. I don't want you to call and warn her. You'll have to wait outside until we've finished speaking to her.'

George nodded, he was agitated and couldn't keep still. He called Laurel and Hardy over to join him. He looked up at the sky and allowed the sun to gently warm his skin.

Sofia saw tears run down his face, which he quickly wiped away.

They walked in silence to Ariadne's cottage.

George felt a light-headedness that he hadn't experienced in many years. A serene sense of relief as he accompanied the police to Rose Cottage. Something that had been denied him all these years. He walked like a man who had just been given a second chance in life. How could all this have happened because of a lie?

Goddamn, Bart!

Rose Cottage

3.00 pm

Ariadne was interrupted by a knock at the door. She leant her head against the window and saw the police had returned, accompanied by George. Something was wrong. She felt instantly afraid. She put her paintbrush down and reluctantly opened the front door and let them in.

George remained outside; she could see he had been crying. But when he smiled at her, it was the warmest and sincerest smile she had ever received from him.

Ariadne closed the door and followed the police officers into her sitting room. Sofia asked her the same question she asked George about the night of her attack.

'I need to know if anything happened before the attack, or if you remember seeing anyone else in the grounds that night. It's important, Ms Goode.'

'I… I don't know what else to tell you. We were together most of the night, then we snuck outside with some bottles of champagne. But I drank too much and went for a walk to clear my head.'

'Who was with you when you were drinking outside?'

'At first, there were around twelve of us. But half had left with their parents just after midnight. Then, someone handed around a joint. About an hour later, Hugo and Sam called it a night. There was only Bart, George and I left by the time I went for that stupid walk. The rest had gone to bed.'

'Where was Augustus?'

'I don't know. I assumed he went to bed. I went to the toilet first, then came back outside. George and Bart were still lying on the grass. I never saw Augustus.'

Sofia repeated what she told George regarding the victim's skull fracture. Ariadne sat down, slumping into the chair; she rested her head in her hands.

'Then that only leaves Bart,' Sofia said.

Ariadne straightened quickly. It was a lot to take in.

'Bart would never do that,' she replied. 'George and Bart were friends. Someone else must have hit him.'

'Your brother Augustus witnessed Bart bury the body. It's possible Augustus saw Bart hit this man. It would explain why Augustus was blackmailing Bart all those years. Augustus told Felicity in a drunken moment, and she also used it against Bart.'

Ariadne said nothing at first, then she started to giggle. Sofia couldn't tell if it was from relief or shock.

'Well, that's karma for you, serves him right,' she said, before running out of the room and straight into George's arms. Sofia watched them hold each other tightly as they cried in each other's arms. She turned away from the window and decided to give them some privacy. Once their embrace was over, they re-entered the cottage to confront the police.

'What was Augustus and Bart's relationship like back then?' Sofia continued once everyone was seated.

Ariadne looked towards George before answering. They held each other's hands firmly.

'There has always been animosity between them. Bart was the smart one, but our father put all his efforts into Augustus, as he was his heir apparent,' Ariadne said, sounding indignant. 'There wasn't much time for the rest of us. Bart resented it. Truthfully, we all did. But Augustus resented Bart, because Bart was better than him. He was popular at school. He was smarter and had more friends. If anything, their dislike had only grown, especially since Bart started buying the Manor.'

'Did either of you know about the blackmail?'

'*No*,' George replied emphatically, before Ariadne had time to protest. 'I knew about the land purchase. Bart was pleased with himself about that. But I didn't know what Augustus was blackmailing him about. I did know Bart enjoyed buying the estate bit by bit from Augustus. He said as much once. As for Felicity, I had my suspicions about her blackmail. I overheard Bart on the phone with her one day. But Bart never spoke of it directly to me.'

'What about you, Ms Goode?' Sofia asked.

'I did know that Felicity was blackmailing Bart, Chief Inspector. Bart said she knew about what happened all those years ago. I don't think she knew that it was Bart who killed that man. Only that he'd covered it up. Otherwise, she would have fleeced him for more money.

As for Augustus… Yes, he's capable of anything where Bart's concerned.'

'What happens now?' George asked.

Sofia thought for a moment about her next move. 'I would like both of you to keep what we've told you about the manner of this man's death a secret for now. We still haven't identified the victim, and our investigation is still ongoing for both murders.'

They both agreed to remain silent. Sofia had her own suspicions about the murders but was keeping her thoughts to herself for the time being.

Sofia and Carl left Ariadne and George at Rose Cottage and headed back to London. DS Shirley Smith had returned from the Manor earlier that day with boxes of old employment records. Some boxes still had thirty years of dust on them from where they were stored up in the attic. However, others had been opened and rummaged through. Recently.

Augustus had initially refused the DS access to their records until she'd handed him a search warrant.

Scotland Yard

5.30 pm

Sofia's team were out to impress their new DCI. Shirley had been busy sifting through the Manor's employee records looking for a match to their victim and anyone else who had worked at the Manor during that summer. Every employee from that time would need to be found and interviewed.

The lab had confirmed the poison had been injected into Bartholomew Goode's cigars. The entire top row of cigars was contaminated. The second row was untouched. There were no fingerprints on the box of cigars, except those of Bartholomew Goode. Since the police had had an officer stationed at the Hall since Bartholomew's death, the killer hadn't been able to return and collect the remaining cigars. Sofia hoped the poisoner still believed Bart was merely stabbed and that the police might not have even looked at the cigars. The police had also set up a motion sensor camera in the library. If anyone returned to collect the remaining tainted cigars, they would be captured on video.

Sofia asked Devish to check all suspects' bank records and credit cards for any purchases involving chemicals of any kind that contained strychnine. It was a long shot, but they may have purchased it months or even years ago. Ronnie had obtained a warrant for Bartholomew Goode's business records and handed them to the police forensic accountants to review along with his laptop and phone. Sofia didn't believe his death was work related, but she couldn't rule it out either.

The team gathered for their evening briefing to recount what they had so far. Carl updated them on the causes of death, for both Bartholomew Goode and their thirty year old victim.

'Bartholomew Goode was poisoned prior to being stabbed. The Gov and I believe we are looking for two separate killers. So, we need all footage from the Hall checked and re-checked, as we don't know when the poison was put into the cigars. But if everyone assumed Bartholomew Goode was terminally ill, they wouldn't have put the poison in the cigars until after the funeral, when they realised he was still alive.'

'But couldn't one of the killers have known he was alive prior to the funeral?' Devish asked.

'Yes. That's true,' Sofia admitted. 'But putting poison in cigars and leaving them for what could possibly be months is risky. Devish, please find out who went to the Hall during Bart's treatment and in the weeks leading up to his actual death.'

'Shirley, have PC Hubbard speak with Tina the housekeeper and find out when she last cleaned the glasses and emptied the library of cigar ash. It may give us a narrower time frame.'

'I'll get her on it,' she replied.

'Our unidentified victim was hit twice, first by George Fox, then by who we can only assume was Bartholomew Goode,' Sofia continued. 'We are currently waiting on forensics to see if they can obtain any fingerprints from the rock or our victim. We can't unequivocally rule out that our victim was hit twice by the same person, but my gut says George Fox did not kill our victim.'

'If the victim fought with Bart, it's possible he left trace evidence on the rock. Or someone else did,' Ronnie commented.

'Anything is possible at this moment. We leave no stone unturned,' Carl said, hoping a little humour would go a long way.

'Ha. Ha. Funny guy,' Devish replied drily.

'I want each family member reinterviewed and their finances scrutinised thoroughly. Bart's wealth might not be the sole reason for his death, but it could have had something to do with it. I also want Eleanor and Zachary re-interviewed, as they may have seen something thirty years ago at that party and won't know if it's relevant or not,' Sofia said.

Looking at her watch, she realised the time.

'OK, it's getting late, go home and cuddle your kids and your partners. It'll be another long day tomorrow. Ronnie, did you put our suspects on flight watch? I don't want anyone leaving the country until we've made an arrest.'

'I did, Gov,' he replied.

Sofia gathered up her laptop, mobile and handbag, along with about half a dozen folders to read before morning, then headed home to Francesca.

Ten minutes from home, Sofia's mobile rang. She was tempted to let it go to voicemail, but during a double murder investigation she knew that wasn't an option. She was relieved when she heard a friendly voice resonate inside her car.

'Hi, it's Harry Budd here.'

'Hi, Harry, what's up, Doc?' Sofia rolled her eyes. She couldn't believe she said it. She heard him chuckle on the other end. 'Sorry!'

'Don't worry, I get it all the time. You police officers aren't very original. I had better hopes for you, Chief Inspector.'

'I'll be more original next time. I promise. I've got your latest report in my briefcase, ready to read. Please don't tell me you've found another cause of death for Bartholomew Goode.'

'No, he was only killed twice. Look, I couldn't ask you earlier today, with your sergeant in the room. I didn't want to get shot down like a Spitfire in front of him. But I would dearly love to take you out to dinner.' Sofia nearly swerved onto the wrong side of the road, momentarily taken off-guard by the invitation. She hadn't been asked out to dinner in a very long time. The car remained silent while Harry waited anxiously for her answer. Always cautious, Sofia was trying to think of a reason why she shouldn't. Oddly she couldn't.

'I'd love to, Harry.'

'Great, well how about this Friday, if you're not busy?'

'Sounds good to me, text me when and where, and I'll be there.'

'Phew… that was easier than I thought. I've been building up the courage to call you all day.' Sofia laughed before saying goodbye and disconnecting the call. Her smile remained plastered across her face for the remainder of her nine-minute journey home.

'How was your day?' Francesca asked as she watched her mum prepare dinner.

'Shouldn't I be asking you that?' Sofia replied.

'Oh, the usual. Maths, English, Spanish, science. Oh, and sport.'

'How did you go?'

'I suck at sport. I don't know why they make girls do gymnastics. We all hate it, and no one can get over the horse without hurting themselves.'

Sofia laughed despite herself. She had never liked gymnastics either. Her legs were too long.

She felt guilty coming home late again. During murder investigations, it couldn't be helped. Francesca understood. But it didn't stop Sofia from feeling guilty about it.

'Look… How would you feel if I went out on a date?' she asked, trying to be casual, as she started to peel the potatoes.

'A *real* one?'

'Yes, a real one. Would you be okay with that?'

'It isn't Carl, is it?'

'*No.*' Sofia cringed. Carl was nearly half her age.

'Who?'

'Someone I know through work. I'll tell you about him after our first date.'

'Why? In case there isn't a second?'

'Yes. Now clear the table. Dinner will be ready soon.'

Once Francesca's homework was done, and Sofia had tidied up the kitchen, she grabbed a glass or red and sat down in the living room and opened up the first of many files, to be read before morning. The task was proving harder than she thought. Her mind kept drifting to a certain forensic pathologist.

It was a pleasant distraction.

37

Scotland Yard

Thursday, 8.30 am

Sofia arrived at the team's morning briefing with a spring in her step. She had spent the evening reading work files, although some she had to read twice.

Once their daily assignments were confirmed, Sofia went to her office, which was located next to the incident room. Shirley tapped on her door before entering and confirmed Tina the housekeeper had cleaned the library on Friday. There was no ash in any ashtrays in the library or anywhere else in the Hall. The last time she cleaned away any ash or glasses was prior to Bartholomew's departure months before. Nothing appeared out of the ordinary.

'Good work, Shirley,' said Sofia.

Sofia still hadn't narrowed down her list of suspects. Everyone's alibis were now in question until they could establish when the poison was injected into the cigars. If they couldn't narrow it down, none of the suspects could be ruled out.

Within the hour, Carl entered her office. 'You're not going to believe this. Zachary Goode has just been detained at Gatwick. Airport police are holding him until we collect him. How did you know?'

'I didn't,' Sofia smiled. 'But both Timothy Sharp and Zachary Goode were twitchy about something. I don't believe it had anything to do with Bartholomew Goode's murder. But I thought one or both would try to leave.'

Zachary was too young to be involved in the thirty year old murder, and if Bart was killed because of it, it ruled both him and Eleanor out. From what her team had learned during their investigations, Zachary Goode was a womaniser, a schemer and a crappy financier, but not a killer.

But she decided to bring Timothy Sharp and Zachary in for questioning and see what she could flush out in the wash.

On their arrival at the Yard, both men were placed in a cell. She wanted them to feel a cold dose of reality before she began their interviews. She decided to interview Timothy first.

Interview with Timothy Sharp

11.00 am

The police forensic team hadn't finished their investigation into Zachary and Timothy's business affairs, so Sofia would have to interview them without any evidence. But she might be able to rattle their cages.

When Sofia and Carl entered the interview room, she found Timothy alone. He hadn't requested a lawyer. He was sweating profusely.

He felt as if his chest were being crushed by a boot. All the while, he could feel the interview room getting smaller and smaller with each passing minute. His fingers kept twitching as his hands rested on the table. He knew everyone would know soon enough. His partnership with Zachary might cost him his career, but he didn't want it to cost him his marriage and freedom. He had decided to come clean with the police.

Sofia asked her first question, 'I would like to talk to you about your investment company, Mr Sharp. I've been hearing rumours during our investigation about its financial viability and Zachary's hand in it. Would you like to start by telling me about that?'

A dejected Timothy looked solemnly at Sofia. 'You'll know soon enough. Zachary has been stealing money from my clients' portfolios. You see, he lost a substantial amount of his own clients' investments. He kept gambling on high-risk ventures. Bart wouldn't help him out anymore, so he transferred funds from my clients' accounts to cover his losses. I only found out the full extent recently. I can't make up the shortfall. You should also know I helped Zachary throughout Bart's game. I fed him information, which I learned from Eleanor. I knew he couldn't win on his own, so I betrayed my wife to help him, because I was desperate to repay the money in my clients' accounts.'

Well. That was easier than Sofia thought it would be.

'These are serious accusations, Mr Sharp.'

'It's the truth. I can prove it. But I had nothing to do with Bart's murder. Neither did Eleanor.'

Sofia could see the man was humiliated. He was on the verge of losing everything because of Zachary. Was it motive enough to kill his brother-in-law when he realised Bart was alive, mocking everyone? Would that push either man over the edge? Sofia thought not. Besides, it was

Zachary who Timothy was angry at. Did he lash out and kill the wrong man?

'Do you know if Zachary went to the Hall at all during the game, excluding his Saturday visit, when his whole family was present?'

'He went back Saturday night, as he still hadn't solved the second clue. Eleanor was on to me and gave me false information. Which I passed on to Zachary. The idiot was digging up half the walled garden,' he said, chuckling nervously. 'I believe he went back again later that night to keep searching.'

'Thank you,' Sofia said. That explained their suspect carrying a shovel. At least they had now identified one of their Saturday night intruders.

'What will happen now? Will you inform the securities commission?'

'Probably, if the money isn't put back by the time our investigation is over,' Sofia said, giving him a get-out-of-jail-free card. 'I'm more concerned right now about two murders. I'm not the fraud squad.'

Timothy's relief was palpable, she was giving him a lifeline. But only a very short one.

Interview with Zachary Goode

11.30 am

'My client has nothing to say,' Zachary's lawyer announced.

'About what?' Sofia asked.

'No comment,' smirked Zachary, with all the blind confidence of a turkey on Christmas Eve.

'The longer you say, "no comment", Mr Goode, the longer you'll remain at this station,' she replied.

'It's not a crime to travel on business,' he replied, as he ran his hand through his hair.

'True, but it is a crime to embezzle funds from your partner's clients' portfolios.'

'That's a lie!' Zachary sat upright and forward in his chair.

'Timothy Sharp is prepared to hand over the evidence of your embezzlement.'

Zachary wasn't looking so confident now. He hadn't counted on Timothy stabbing him in the back. He chose to remain silent, as instructed by his lawyer. Sofia could see he was rethinking his next move.

'You were fleeing the country and would have left Timothy Sharp to deal with all the fall-out,' Carl said, shaking his head. 'Or were you leaving to escape a murder charge?'

'Don't be ridiculous. I didn't kill my brother. He was my meal ticket.' Zachary just regretted his last remark.

'You mean he was until he refused to give you any more money,' Carl said.

'My officers are re-interviewing your wife as we speak. You were seen on video at Cricklewood Hall on Saturday night around 12.45 am carrying a shovel,' Sofia said.

Zachary looked at his lawyer for guidance.

'We would like to see that footage, Chief Inspector,' replied his lawyer.

'Of course,' Sofia said.

Sofia had to think quickly, the video footage didn't show the intruders face.

'Once your wife understands the penalty for perjury, I'm sure she'll change her testimony. Sergeant, will you please bring in the video footage from Saturday night,' Sofia asked. 'And bring Mrs Goode to the station.'

'Yes, Gov.' Carl stood up and walked towards the door.

'*Stop*. All right, I was there. But I only headed into the walled garden. I stopped when I saw someone heading towards the Hall. I panicked and hid until they were out of sight. Then I left.'

'Describe the intruder?' Sofia asked.

'God, I don't know, they were wearing a dark tracksuit. It had a hoodie.'

'Did you go into the Hall at any time, other than on the Saturday with the rest of your family?'

'No, only the grounds on Saturday night.'

'What about when you solved the first clue?'

'I didn't. Timothy gave me the answer. I went straight to Potts & Billingsworth for the second clue. I returned again Sunday morning, but when I saw the police there, I left.'

'Weren't you curious as to why they were there?' Carl asked.

'I thought there had been a break-in or something. As far as I knew, my brother was already dead.'

Reluctantly, Sofia had to accept Zachary's story. He was a louse, a charlatan and an embezzler, but not a murderer. He didn't have it in him. Timothy was released without charge, but Zachary was cautioned before being released. And his passport was seized.

When Timothy arrived home, Eleanor was waiting for him. She could see he was deflated. He had spent years building a reputation in London, only to have it destroyed by Zachary.

Timothy filled Eleanor in on what took place at the police station. She took a long look around her living room. She loved her house. Then she called Beatrice. It was time to settle the debt.

'I think I've found him!' Shirley yelled out, who had been sifting through the boxes of old archive records from the Manor all day. 'He fits our description. His name was Luc Dubois, he worked at the Manor as a gardener for two months during the summer. But his payslips stopped the week after the mid-summer's eve party.'

'Good work, Shirley,' Sofia said.

'Check his name against the missing person's database and then check with Interpol,' Carl said. 'Having a French name doesn't necessarily mean he wasn't English.'

'Will do,' she said.

'Are there any other employees that fit our victim's description? Ariadne Goode said her attacker had a Geordie accent,' Sofia said.

Shirley said she still had one more box to go through. It had taken her a while, as they were a mess.

'I need to know every employee that worked at the manor during that summer. Our attacker must be an ex-workhand or gardener. George Fox said one man was sacked for stealing a week before the party. We don't know yet if that was Mr Dubois. Keep looking. I want them all identified and located,' insisted Sofia.

'Right you are, Gov,' Shirley said, diving back into the box.

DC Das typed Luc Dubois's name into the police database and waited anxiously for a return on his efforts.

There he was, reported missing in August of that same year. Devish printed what was available on the database and gave his colleagues a copy.

Sofia's team was finally able to put a face to their victim, Luc Dubois. If it were truly him. The photo had been provided by his mother, over thirty years ago.

Devish read the police report out loud. 'The police interviewed Augustus Goode Senior, during the course of their investigation. He confirmed the young man worked at the Manor as a gardener during the summer but didn't know him personally. A statement was also taken from his mother, Emmanuelle Dubois, who said her son called her from England every week while he was abroad. He loved his job at the Manor and, by all accounts, was looking forward to returning to France to continue his degree.'

Another statement was taken from Henry Fox, the caretaker at the Manor during that time. Sofia had to assume it was George Fox's father.

Devish read it aloud. 'Luc Dubois was a hard worker and excellent gardener. I was surprised that he left. I thought he enjoyed his time here.'

The report also stated the police couldn't rule out he had met with foul play during his travels or even on his return to France. His case file was still open. The reports were written in both English and French, as copies had been sent to Interpol and the French police.

'Good work everyone! Get on to the lab and let them know we may have a name for our victim.'

Sofia didn't want Luc Dubois's family put through any further distress, especially if the victim wasn't him. She asked Harry Budd to make the DNA verification a priority. By all accounts, their victim didn't sound like the thief that was fired prior to the party.

'Who here speaks French?' she asked.

'I speak high school French,' Shirley said, raising her hand.

'All right, get on to the French police and update them on what we have. They should already have Luc's DNA on file. If not, we will need them to obtain a sample from a family member. Once we have a positive ID, I'll head to France to interview his mother. This needs to be done in person.' Sofia felt she owed it to Luc's mother to speak with her face-to-face. She deserved the compassion a personal visit would offer.

By the afternoon, the French police had emailed a file containing Emmanuelle Dubois's DNA profile. It was forwarded to the lab who later confirmed their victim was indeed Luc Dubois.

Sofia organised an early flight in the morning to Burgundy. But before she could do anything else, her mobile rang. It was Harry Budd, ringing about their dinner date on Friday night.

'*Oh merda*,' Sofia replied. 'I completely forgot. I'm flying to France tomorrow.'

'Do you speak French as well as Italian?' Harry asked, jovially.

'No. I was going to ask the French police for an interpreter.'

'Well, why don't I come with you, I'll be your interpreter, save the French police having to spare someone? We can have dinner before heading home. No one has ever said I don't go all out on a first date.'

'You're on.'

THE STAR

The eighteenth card of the major arcana

The Star offers hope and inspiration through times of darkness. She will heal the past and the present.
But in reverse, she can lure you into a false sense of security. You may be tempted to give up too easily on someone or something and feel a great loss.

38

Heathrow Airport

Friday, 7.30 am

At the airport, Sofia enjoyed a macchiato to wake her up, while Harry stuck to his traditional flat white. They sat in the coffee lounge while they waited for their flight to be called.

Harry had picked Sofia up from Teddington, and they had talked all the way to the airport. They continued to talk while sipping their coffees and then talked some more during their flight to Paris.

Sofia hadn't enjoyed anyone's company so much in years. She felt relaxed in his presence. She listened to everything he had to say with enthusiasm, which was equally reciprocated. Sofia respected Harry's confidence and charming manner, and he in turn showed great respect for her work, which made Sofia feel every inch his equal. Something she had never experienced during her ill-fated marriage.

They collected their hire car at the airport and drove to Burgundy. Sofia updated Harry on what she could about the case but hoped Emmanuelle Dubois may hold more insight into her son's work and life before he disappeared. As Harry drove, Sofia enjoyed the beauty of the French countryside. Then, for the last hour of their journey, she had to catch up on some reports she should have read on the flight over.

Luc's father had died when he was young, but his mother and sister were still alive. At least Sofia could offer them closure, now that they had a body to bury. Sofia wasn't sure how Emmanuelle Dubois would take the news that her son was possibly a rapist and that he had died thirty years ago. Sofia would be destroying what little hope Emmanuelle had that her son may still be alive. She didn't envy any parent that had to live through that.

Harry located Emmanuelle Dubois's house. She lived ten minutes outside the town of Chalon-Sur-Saone on two luscious acres. They found her in her garden, pruning her roses. Sofia was impressed. She assumed Luc must have had a hand in it.'

'*Bonjour, Madame Dubois*,' Sofia said.

'*Bonjour, Inspecteur*,' Emmanuelle replied. She welcomed her guests.

'Your garden is very beautiful,' Sofia remarked, joining her in the middle of the garden, envious as her own garden was quite small in Teddington.

'*Ton jardin est très magnifique*,' translated Harry.

'*Mon fils a fait tout les aménagement paysagers que vous voyez dans mon jardin. Je l'ai juste gardé pur lui*,' Emmanuelle replied.

'She said her son did all the landscaping you see in her garden. She's just kept it up for him.'

Emmanuelle showed her guests into her home and offered them refreshments.

'Is your daughter here?' Sofia asked.

'*Est-ce que votre fille est ici?*' translated Harry, who continued to translate for both women.

'No. My daughter lives in Paris, but I believe she is abroad at the moment, she often travels for work.'

'Could you give me her contact details, please? I will need to speak with her.'

'Yes, of course.'

Emmanuelle picked up her mobile and read out her daughter's mobile number and home address.

'*Merci, Madame Dubois.* I was told by the French police that they had already informed you that the DNA from our victim has been confirmed as that of your son. I'm truly sorry for your loss.'

Speaking in slow but confident English, she replied, 'Yes. I've known he was dead for many years. He would have been in contact, if he were still alive. Thank you for finally confirming it. I want my son's body back.'

'We're arranging that for you now, Madame Dubois,' Sofia said.

'Can you tell me what kind of boy your son was?'

Emmanuelle took a moment. She smiled as she reminisced.

'He was quiet, shy. He loved being outside, the gardens and the woods were always his favourite places to be, no matter the weather. He was so excited when he was offered the job as undergardener over the summer break at Ashburton Manor.'

'Why did he choose England and not a Chateau or botanical garden here in France?'

'He had learnt about some of the grand gardens in England during his studies. Kent was known as the garden of England, he used to say. One of his tutors organised the job for him over the summer holidays. I believe some English students came to France as well, like an exchange program.'

Sofia asked Emmanuelle delicately if she knew whether her son had ever taken drugs or had a drink problem. Emmanuelle found the suggestion offensive. She said her son never took drugs, he rarely drank and wasn't even a smoker. He was a gentle soul, who always preferred the company of plants and wildlife to people.

Emmanuelle's description of Luc didn't sound like the actions of their rapist. Sofia had to wonder if this woman really knew her son. Did alcohol change his personality that night? It was all too common for someone to act out of character under the influence of narcotics. It could have made him unusually aggressive. But something didn't sit right with Sofia. Was he Ariadne's attacker at all? The accent kept niggling at her.

Emmanuelle spoke at length about her son's dreams and aspirations. Sofia hadn't yet mentioned the attack on Ariadne to Emmanuelle. She thought it would be too hard for her to take. Too offensive. It didn't sit right with Sofia either. She decided to say nothing. At least until she was absolutely sure.

'May I use your bathroom, please?' Sofia asked.

Emmanuelle showed Sofia the way and returned to speak with Harry about how her son died and when they would return his body. Harry wasn't allowed to tell her how he died, but he told her where they found him. Emmanuelle sobbed at the thought of her beautiful boy being buried in a shallow grave all those years. She wanted him home.

Harry promised her he would make sure her son's body was released as soon as possible, and he would personally accompany him back to France. Emmanuelle blessed Harry and kissed his cheek. Harry found the whole interview heart-wrenching. He marvelled how Sofia was able to handle the sadness of death when confronted by the victim's family. The victims' families came to the morgue to see their loved ones. But it was mostly for identification purposes. It was carried out with the upmost respect, but it was an official act that the morgue took seriously. Harry tried never to get personally involved.

When Sofia finished up in the bathroom, she still had trouble getting her head around Luc Dubois being a rapist. For one thing, he didn't have a Geordie accent but a French one. Could Ariadne have mistaken the accent during the attack? Sofia doubted that. Ariadne was very specific about that. Sofia would have to interview Ariadne again.

On her return to the sitting room, she noticed some family pictures on the walls and on the sideboard. They were of a young Luc and his sister. Sofia took her time as she looked into the Dubois's past. They portrayed a loving and happy family throughout the years. There was also a picture of a married couple, Sofia picked up the picture and asked Emmanuelle who they were. Emmanuelle replied, it was her daughter and son-in-law.

Sofia didn't know whether to laugh or cry. Her case finally made sense. Sofia thanked Emmanuelle for taking the time to speak to her. Before leaving, Sofia promised Emmanuelle she would find her son's killer and bring him to justice. Madame Dubois kissed Sofia on the check and blessed her before they took their leave.

Once they were back in their car, Harry finally spoke.

'That poor woman, not knowing about her son all those years. I don't know how you do it.'

'This is the hardest part of my job. The victim's families always suffer the most. The reward is finding the perpetrators and bringing them to justice. That's all I can do.'

But before she did, Sofia was afraid she would regrettably cause this woman even more heartache. Emmanuelle Dubois didn't deserve any more suffering.

Sofia's mind was swimming with suspicion during their short ride into Chalon-Sur-Saone. The historic, picturesque town was even more beautiful on this sunny day. It lifted her spirits. They found a café in the town square and ate a late lunch while lapping up the warm sunshine. Sofia should have been in her element, eating good food at a great café with a handsome man by her side, but her case had just taken a new direction. She didn't like where it led.

'Penny for your thoughts.'

'Sorry, Harry. I think I might know who killed Bartholomew Goode. At least one of his killers, anyway. But I'm hoping I'm wrong.'

'Really. Why?'

'I'm sorry, but I can't say right now. But I think I know what happened. I just need a few more facts before I can make any arrests. But I don't believe Luc Dubois is a rapist.'

'I'm glad to hear that. You found something interesting at Emmanuelle's home, didn't you?'

'Yes.'

'I'll get you back to England on the earliest flight.'

'No. No, I want to enjoy today. I'll have tomorrow to work through the finalities. Saturday is going to be a difficult day for everyone involved. Besides, you owe me dinner in Paris, remember?'

While Harry drove back to Paris, Sofia made a few phone calls. One to Carl to update him on what she discovered at Emmanuelle Dubois's home. Then another call to Shirley for an update on whether she had found any other employees who fit their description.

Shirley confirmed there was one other man who would be of interest. He also ceased working at the estate during the summer. His name was Freddie Stuart. She was pleased to confirm he was born in Newcastle. He had a police record for petty theft and did a stint in HMP Northumberland for assault. But that was over twenty-five years ago.

Shirley said, 'There were two other groundsmen who worked at the Manor that summer. No police record, but they were a lot older than our victim was. I have someone checking on them anyway.'

'Good work, Shirley. Send me everything you have on Freddie Stuart. I want him found and brought in for questioning.'

Sofia rang off and tried to enjoy the rest of the drive into Paris.

On their arrival in Paris, Harry found a traditional Parisian restaurant. They ate, drank and talked continually through their dinner until it was time to leave for their flight home. Sofia couldn't remember having such a wonderful time in a man's company. Not even her husband's. Sofia didn't want the evening to end, but she found herself back at Charles De Gaulle airport by 8.00 pm and back in Teddington by 11.00 pm. She picked Francesca up from her parents' home and, while tucking her into bed, told her about Chalon-Sur-Saone and Paris. Francesca kept giggling; she could see how happy her mother was.

Francesca decided she would Google Dr Harry Budd in the morning and find out for herself what his prospects were.

THE MOON

The nineteenth card of the major arcana

The Moon speaks of illusions, dreams and turmoil. This card is in duality, with the sun and moon both fighting for their place in your subconscious.
While the Moon shows hidden depth and fear in a situation, the Sun can show light at the end of the tunnel. This will be a time of deep conflict as something may be brewing under the surface.

39

Rose Cottage

Saturday Morning, 9.00 am

Ariadne stood aside to let Angeline into her cottage. Her unannounced visit was a welcome surprise.

'I wanted to tell you in person, I'm leaving for France today. I don't know when, or if, I'll be back. My mother needs me.'

Angeline's announcement came out of the blue. Ariadne was going to miss her friend.

'What will I do without you for guidance?'

'You'll be fine, *mon chéri*, you have George. Who I suspect has loved you all along. My last piece of advice. Tell him you love him before it's too late, don't waste any more time in the past. Look to the future.'

'You're right, I actually feel unafraid of my future for the first time in a long time. I have you to thank for that. I'm going to miss you.'

'You need to trust yourself. When you finally do, you will realise you are deserving, Ariadne.'

'I hope we'll meet again, you're always welcome here.'

'*Merci*, maybe, one day.' Angeline kissed Ariadne on each cheek and held her tightly. Outside the cottage, Angeline waved goodbye to Ariadne.

Angeline had come to love Ariadne like a sister. She hoped her friend would find peace, now that her work was done. She climbed into her car and headed home to pack for the last time.

Justice would soon be done.

A sudden chill ran down Ariadne's spine as she closed the door. Already, Angeline's absence was felt. It was like a momentary shift in the seasons. But it wasn't long before her loneliness was interrupted by a visit from Eleanor, who appeared agitated and immediately began pacing the floor.

'Just say what's on your mind, Eleanor, you're going to tread holes in my rug.'

'The police know about Zachary's embezzlements. He actually tried to leave the country. The idiot.'

'Have they arrested him?'

'No. But he was cautioned. The chief inspector said if the money is put back before their investigation is over, then Timothy might be able to salvage his reputation and the firm. I'm putting our house up for sale on Monday, but I was hoping you could lend me the money, on behalf of Timothy, until the sale goes through. Beatrice and Zachary have agreed to do the same. I'm hoping it will be enough to cover the losses.'

'Of course I will. I'm not sure when I'll have access to Bart's estate, but I'm sure Hugo and Sam will authorise an early advance or transfer.'

Eleanor's relief was palpable. She started to sob and fell into the chair. Ariadne put an arm around her, reassuring her that this is what family was for. After supplying Eleanor with yet another tissue, they shared a quiet moment.

Ariadne was more than happy to give Bart's money away. Considering all he put George and herself through all those years. Payback was a bitch.

Ariadne felt it was time to tell Eleanor the truth about the mid-summer's ball all those years ago. She had promised the chief inspector she wouldn't reveal anything about Bart's part in the murder. But she wanted Eleanor to know what happened to her—no more secrets.

Once Eleanor's shock subsided, she cried even more at being so blind to Ariadne's pain. She finally understood the complexity of her sister's anxiety. Looking back, she remembered that party well.

'Mother had bought me a new dress, and I was allowed to stay up late. But I had to go to bed at 11.00 pm.'

'Yes, that awful blue thing,' Ariadne remembered.

'It was my first long evening dress. It wasn't that bad.' They chuckled at the memory.

'I was sitting on the bedroom windowsill for over an hour, looking outside. Listening and watching the revellers on the terrace.'

Then a memory stirred in Eleanor, 'Oh, God! I remember now. George was carrying you back into the house. It was very late. I thought you had fallen asleep, or you had too much to drink. I remember thinking, "what mother would say if she saw you in that condition?". What a naïve fool I was.'

Eleanor apologised for her ignorance. But Ariadne insisted—no more tears.

'The past belongs in the past.' This time, Ariadne truly believed it.

There was a short silence, which was broken by Eleanor.

'I told the police we were here all night at the cottage. But I heard you go out. I'll understand completely if you went to confront Bart, if you knew he was still alive. I'll never tell anyone.'

'What are you talking about?' Ariadne was taken by surprise by her sister's allegation.

'You left the cottage.'

Ariadne laughed at Eleanor's concern.

'I went to see George. I needed to speak to him. I let myself in via the servant's entrance. It's closest to his room. I told Bartie about his mother's blackmail. But I wanted to give George the heads-up before talking anymore to Bartie about it. I'm sick and tired of all the lies and secrets we all tell. They've destroyed this family. I know Bart loved his children. Bartie deserved to know the truth about his parents' divorce. But I didn't get a chance to speak to George... he wasn't there.'

'Oh my god!' Eleanor's relief was physically overwhelming.

The sisters shared a laugh.

'What does George have to do with Bart and Felicity's divorce? They weren't having an affair were they?' Eleanor looked shocked but excited.

'No. Don't be ridiculous. They aren't gay. There's more to that night than I've told you, but you'll know soon enough. Something happened that involved Bart, George and me. I'll tell you about it later.'

'Okay. Whenever you're ready. Come on, I'm going to buy you breakfast,' Eleanor said standing and offering her hand to Ariadne. 'While I still can.'

'Sounds like a plan. I'm starving.'

Ariadne gathered her shawl, and they left the cottage. She *had* failed to tell the police she went to the Hall. Was that a mistake? The thought preyed on Ariadne's mind all the way to the café.

Scotland Yard

Saturday, 10.00 am

Morning tea arrived for Sofia's team at the Yard. She notified them yesterday that overtime was on offer if they chose to work Saturday. No one ever turned down overtime. Sofia took them through what she learned in France and requested background checks to be carried out urgently.

DC Ronnie O'Farrell finally received confirmation relating to a suspicious payment on one of their suspects' bank statements. He had requested the invoice from the supplier to identify what service was carried out.

The police had just found their means to commit murder.

Forensics emailed confirmation that the fingerprints on the rock buried with Luc Dubois were Bartholomew Goode's. Sofia had most of her chess pieces lined up. She knew who poisoned Bartholomew Goode. But she needed a confession to seal the arrest. The evidence was circumstantial at best. She also knew who killed Luc, but she needed to speak with Freddie Stuart before she made her final move.

DS Smith had located Freddie Stuart on Friday night. He was living in Chelmsford. She had contacted the local police and had him picked up at home and brought down to London as a matter of urgency. He was currently waiting in an interview room.

Carl and Sofia entered the interview room and started the tape recorder. She repeated her offer for him to have a solicitor present, but Mr Stuart declined.

Freddie, now in his sixties, was overweight and slightly balding. He had had no criminal charges against him for nearly twenty years. Either he had gone straight, or he was never caught.

For Freddie's part, he'd known this day would eventually come. But he appeared neither afraid nor intimidated. He pointed out, when they took their seats, that he was happily married with three grown children.

'Thank you for helping us with our enquiries, Mr Stuart,' Sofia began, once seated.

'I divn't have much choice, did I,' he replied.

'I would like to talk to you about your time at Ashburton Manor.'

Straight for twenty-five years, he had always dreaded this day. *No past deeds go unpunished*, he thought. When he heard about the murder of Bartholomew Goode at Cricklewood Hall, he knew the police would eventually come knocking. He should never have talked to that Frenchie.

Freddie wasn't going down for a murder he didn't commit. Not then and not now.

'I divn't a kill 'im.'

'Who, Mr Stuart?' Carl asked.

'Bartholomew Goode, alreet.'

'We never implied that you did,' Sofia said. 'I want to talk to you about an assault and murder that took place thirty years ago, at Ashburton Manor. When you worked there. Before being fired for stealing.'

Freddie's chubby cheeks started to turn a darker shade of crimson.

'Calm doon, I divn't knaa nothing aboot that,' he said pointing his fat finger at Sofia.

His Geordie accent was very pronounced, Sofia was confident Ariadne would recognise it if she heard it again. Considering it'd haunted her all those years.

'We will be charging you with the assault on Ariadne Goode, who was only sixteen at the time of the rape.'

'Na. Na. Wait a minute. I never raped that wee lass.' Freddie was waving his arms about more vigorously now. 'I was propa mortal that neet. But I didnae rape na lass.'

'While we're at it, we might as well charge you with the murder of Luc Dubois. We found the remains of his body in the woods near where the assault took place, earlier this week.'

Freddie Stuart was getting agitated. He had nothing to do with a second murder. But he did know who the detective was talking about.

He wasn't that drunk that night that he didn't remember what he saw. Toffs always stuck together, even though nothing stuck to them, he knew that much. If he admitted to being there, they would stitch him up for it. He now had too much to lose.

'I wanna deal. I knaa tha truth about that neet.'

Sofia needed Freddie's cooperation and would eventually have to compromise on a lesser charge. She hoped Ariadne would understand.

'I can't promise anything, but your cooperation will be taken into account.'

'Yee lot always fuckin' say that.'

'That's the best I can offer you, presently.'

'I was drunk, alreet. So was that lass. I did get rough with the lass. But I didn't rape her.'

Sofia and Carl listened to his story. He admitted to the theft and the drunken assault. He remembered someone tackling him, then everything went blank. When he came around, another man was pulling at him. He couldn't understand him but lashed out at him as he was trying to detain him. He knocked him down before legging it.

Sofia showed Freddie a picture of Luc Dubois.

'Wey aye man, that deeks like him.'

'Sorry?' Sofia asked.

'I think he means, "that looks like him",' Carl said, getting used to the dialect.

'Aye,' Freddie said.

'What did you hit him with?'

'Nowt. I belted him, just the once.'

'Did you see anyone else there?'

'Aye, the son.'

'Bartholomew Goode.'

'Na. Da other one.'

'Where?' Sofia asked.

'When I legged it.'

'What was he doing?'

'Hiding in thaa bushes.'

Over the next hour, Sofia and Carl went over that night twice more with Freddie Stuart. By the time they left the interview room, Sofia had all the pieces she needed to make her arrests.

Sofia asked PC Hubbard to pick up Angeline Toussaint.

Sofia relayed to her team what she believed happened that night. But she would need a confession to seal the deal. Freddie was right about one thing. Rich people could afford expensive lawyers, and she only had circumstantial evidence. They couldn't physically place the murderer at the scene. Sofia needed a confession.

When Angeline arrived, she was taken into an interview room where she declined counsel. PC Hubbard told Sofia that Angeline's car was packed. She was leaving the country. Her passport was found in her handbag.

Angeline was read her rights, but before Sofia could ask her first question, Angeline spoke.

'I didn't kill Bartholomew Goode. I was at the Hall on Saturday night, but someone got to him first.'

Sofia had just had a spanner thrown into her wheel. If Angeline was to be believed.

'What time did you arrive at the Hall?' she asked.

'Around 2.00 am. Killing him wouldn't have helped find my brother's body.'

'Maybe he did tell you, before you killed him.'

'He was already dead.'

'How did you know Bart was involved?'

Angeline remained silent.

Sofia relayed what she thought happened on the night of Luc's death to Angeline.

Sofia said, "We believe that, although Bartholomew hit Luc with a rock, he was tricked into believing Luc attacked Ariadne."

Angeline looked startled. She was quickly evaluating what she already knew.

'Please take us through what happened on Saturday night.'

Angeline studied Sofia. She sensed an air of honesty in her, as if the Sun worked through her, emitting a positive charge. She believed she could trust the detective. Angeline told her story.

'I saw a light on in the library. I knew he had returned to the Hall. I entered through the back door. It was unlocked.

I wanted to confront him. I knew he killed my brother. If not him, then he knew who did. I just needed him to tell me where Luc's body was buried. Killing him would not have achieved that. I wanted to threaten him into telling me, but he was already dead.'

Angeline lowered her head at the thought of her brother being buried in the middle of a deserted forest for all those years. Alone and forgotten.

'I entered the library with the intent of threatening to expose him. But he was dead. He had been stabbed. His dogs sat beside him. I simply left and closed the library door on my way out.'

'Bart killed your brother. He blamed George Fox for the murder. But George was innocent. There was someone else there that night.'

'I know. Will you arrest him?

'Yes. I'll do everything in my power to secure an arrest.'

'Thank you.'

'Would you have killed your brother's murderer?'

'No. Like I said, I only wanted to know where my brother's body was buried. I couldn't dig up the entire estate. Besides, I could never do that to my mother. She's already lost one child.'

'We arrested Freddie Stuart for Ariadne's assault this morning. Unfortunately, your brother was just in the wrong place at the wrong time.'

'When Ariadne told me about her assault, I knew it wasn't my brother. He was no rapist. But I knew he must have been involved somehow. So I began my own investigation.'

'Why didn't you come to us with your suspicions?'

'When I first found out what the Goode family had done to my brother, I wanted justice so bad I could taste it. But can you truthfully say Bart would have gone to prison? With all his wealth and connections. All he had to do was remain silent. My brother's body would never have been discovered.'

'But George would have remembered the location. Besides, we have Bart's fingerprints on the rock used to hit Luc. It was found with your brother's body.'

'I didn't know that.'

Sofia asked Angeline one final question, 'How did you know your brother was killed at the Manor?'

'An email arrived last August. I couldn't trace it. It was very specific. It said Luc's body was buried on the grounds of Ashburton Manor. It did not state where precisely. I had put my brother's details on a missing persons website. I hoped someday, someone would recognise him and respond. Someone did. So, I came to England to seek the truth. I began my search from when he supposedly left the Manor. When I learned of Ariadne's assault, I knew my brother's disappearance was connected somehow.'

'How did you know Bartholomew was still alive?'

'I thought he was dying like everyone else. And that the truth would die with him. But I received a second email via the website. It stated clearly Bartholomew was alive and well. I broke into Potts & Billingsworth to confirm what I was told. I found Bartholomew Goode's latest will in a desk draw. Unsigned. A note on a desk diary stated the time and date Bartholomew would be in to sign it. It was the following Monday.'

'Did you tell anyone else Bart was still alive?'

'*Oui.*'

'Did you confront that person about your brother's death?'

'*Oui.*'

Angeline told Sofia and Carl who she had confided in in the hope he would shed more light on the night her brother disappeared.

'Will you help me bring this person to justice?' Sofia asked Angeline.

'Whatever it takes.'

It was time to put this investigation to bed. Sofia needed the entire Goode family present when she exposed Bartholomew Goode's killer. There were bound to be questions.

She asked Carl to round up Bart's family and have them arrive at the Hall by 3.00 pm that afternoon. She also requested the presence of Hugo Billingsworth and Sam Potts.

Luc Dubois's death was a needless crime, one instigated by a sadistic killer for his own gratification. Sofia wanted everyone together to help replay the events of that fateful night. She doubted she would get a confession without provoking her suspect but hoped the evidence they had so far would prove enough for a conviction.

Sofia still had a few tricks left up her sleeve and was ready to use them when and if she needed to.

Sofia needed to believe rather than hope Angeline didn't kill Bart. Maybe she was told where her brother's body was buried and didn't need Bart's confession. Even if she did stab him, Bart was already dying from the poison. Was Angeline capable of murder?

It was time for Sofia to bring secrets into the light and put old vendettas to rest. Her only regret was Emmanuelle Dubois. *Why do the innocent always suffer the most?* She thought as she gathered her briefcase and walked out of the Yard. She needed to go home and spend some time with her daughter before heading to Kent for the last time in this investigation.

THE SUN

The twentieth card of the major arcana

The Sun is a card full of hope and happiness, in life, work, home and family.
The Sun represents success and good health. Unlike its preceding cards, it is more carefree and full of achievements and positive changes.
Even in reverse, this card holds little to worry about, there may be small hiccups along the way but nothing that can't be overcome.

40

Teddington

Saturday afternoon

'I quite like him. He has two degrees, *and* he loves dogs,' said Francesca, reminding her mother that she didn't have one, yet.

Sofia chastised Francesca for her inquisitiveness. Francesca could find anything on the internet. Sofia didn't want to discuss her dating life, or lack thereof, with her ten year old daughter.

'We're just friends, Franny. That's all.'

'Yeah right. I think he's handsome, so do nonna and grandad.'

Great, thought Sofia, *is nothing private anymore?* She quickly changed her clothes then sat outside on the patio with her parents, enjoying the afternoon sun before Carl arrived to drive her to Kent. He texted to confirm all the family would be at the Hall by 3.00 pm.

Instead of adrenaline flowing through her veins as it usually did when she was ready to make an arrest, Sofia felt giddy and lightheaded. She couldn't stop thinking about Harry and her day in France. She felt a little apprehensive. She couldn't bear another failed marriage. But she knew it was time to let go of her own inhibitions and allow fate to guide her.

Sofia wondered if it was possible to be lucky in love a second time. Considering how badly the last one ended, she thought she should be in credit. She couldn't complain about her life. Her job was a success, she had a loving family that she adored. She knew she was blessed. But she wanted passion back in her life.

As the sun moved behind a cloud, darkness spread across her small garden and sent a shiver down her spine. She said a silent prayer, *Please let him call me back.*

Carl picked Sofia up and drove them to Kent. Sofia had much on her mind, but she was brought back to Earth when her mobile rang.

Her heart skipped a beat when she saw who it was.

'Hi,' she whispered, as she turned her head to look out the passenger window.

'Hi, yourself. I wanted to say I really enjoyed our trip to France.'

'Me too.'

'I would love to take you out to dinner. I'm classing the first dinner as work related, so it doesn't count.'

Harry's last remark made Sofia giggle.

'I would love to. When and where?'

Carl continued driving and concentrated on the road ahead, trying not to overhear everything his boss was saying. When Sofia finally hung up, he turned to her and said,

'Well. Are you seeing him again or not?'

'You're the detective, you figure it out.'

For the rest of their ride into Kent, Sofia looked out the window as the countryside passed her by. A wide smile remained glued in place.

Everything looked beautiful in the world today.

JUDGEMENT

The twenty-first card of the major arcana

*Before judging others, we must first judge ourselves.
Great changes could be on the horizon, but you
must address past actions before moving forward.
Only then will you be enlightened, and wisdom
will flourish.
Judgement is the card of renewal, both physically and
spiritually. But when Judgement is reversed, you may
be stuck in the past and unable to break free from past
decisions or actions.*

41

Cricklewood Hall

Saturday, 3.05 pm

'I don't appreciate being summoned like a servant,' spat Augustus, as he and Henrietta were shown into the sitting room by DC Das, who had shown great restraint when collecting Augustus, Henrietta and their sons.

Ariadne, George, Eleanor and Bartie were already present and seated. DS Smith arrived with a disgruntled Felicity and her daughters. She acknowledged her son but didn't speak to him. Her steely gaze was reserved for Ariadne. DC O'Farrell had escorted Zachary, Beatrice and Timothy to the Hall.

Everyone had to wait an agonising ten more minutes until Hugo and Sam arrived.

The only team member absent was PC Hubbard who was still to arrive with Angeline.

'Thank you everyone for coming,' began Sofia, once everyone was seated.

'You didn't give us much of a choice,' Zachary replied.

'For once, shut up, Zachary,' Beatrice replied. 'Let's just get this over with.'

Sofia finished her coffee while they waited for PC Hubbard to arrive. It gave her an opportunity to study everyone around the room. They all knew why they had been summoned.

PC Hubbard eventually arrived, accompanied by Angeline Toussaint.

Ariadne was surprised by her friend's presence. She stood up to greet her.

'What are you doing here?' she asked.

'*Je suis desole mon ami*,' apologised Angeline, as she put both hands on Ariadne's cheeks. She said no more but was escorted to a seat and waited for Sofia to begin her summation. Angeline had her part to play. She wanted justice, but more than that, she wanted to know the truth about the night her brother died. She wanted it for her mother.

Sofia finished the last of her coffee and walked into the middle of the room.

'The murder of Bartholomew Goode began over thirty years ago at Ashburton Manor.' Sofia allowed everyone a moment to absorb what she had just said.

'Then why am I here with my children, Miss Marple?' interrupted Felicity.

'Because all of you had a financial stake in Bartholomew Goode's life and in his death. You all sought to profit from him alive and dead. Some of you have even enjoyed blackmailing Bart for years.'

'I'm not listening to this,' Felicity said, standing up and heading for the door. DC Brooks blocked her exit.

'Sit down, Mrs Goode,' Carl said. She held her ground before Charity told her to sit down and be quiet.

'I want to hear what the police have to say, Mother.'

Felicity turned reluctantly on her heels and returned to her seat.

Sofia began.

'Bartholomew's death was the result of his thoughtless actions on mid-summer's eve, thirty years ago. Bart, Ariadne, Augustus and George have had to live with the consequences ever since. They were young and carefree that night. They drunk and smoked a little too much pot. Isn't that right Mr Potts, Mr Billingsworth?'

Both men nodded silently.

'But may I remind you, we had already retired to bed before the murder took place,' reiterated Sam.

'You don't need to remind me, Mr Potts,' Sofia said.

'Later that night, once most of the guests had left, Ariadne went for a walk to clear her head. She ended up in the small woods on the eastern side of the estate. It was there that Ariadne was assaulted.'

Those who already knew the story sat quietly while the rest of Ariadne's family looked shocked by the allegation. Carl handed Sofia some folders containing forensic evidence before she continued. Sofia thought of them as props, as she already knew what they contained.

'George arrived on the scene, and a fight erupted between him and Ariadne's attacker. The man was knocked unconscious. George then carried Ariadne back to the Manor. On their way back they met Bart. George told Bart what had happened, which sent Bart running into the woods to confront the man. For thirty years, George was made to believe he killed this man in the fight. However, that was a lie. Bart hit the man over the head with a rock. He then went to the gardener's outhouse and retrieved a shovel to bury him. George returned to the woods to find Bart digging the grave. Bart did the only thing he could think of, and that was to blame George for the man's death. He did it to protect himself. Probably out of self-preservation, George. That ensured you and Ariadne remained silent.'

Sofia allowed what she had said to sink in before she continued.

'We know Bart hit him with a rock, because Bart put the rock inside the plastic bag he used to wrap the man in. And in doing so, he preserved the forensic evidence. However, what Bart, George and Ariadne did not know was that Augustus saw what happened that night.'

Sofia turned to Ariadne to address her. 'Whether he witnessed your attack or arrived shortly after I do not know. Only he does.'

'This is absurd,' Augustus snorted, rising from his seat.

'Sit down!' yelled Henrietta. Everyone was speechless. 'Please continue, Chief Inspector.' Everyone looked towards the usually diminutive Henrietta who sat defiantly across the room from her husband. She waved her hand to prompt the chief inspector to continue her story.

Ariadne looked at her brother, frightened by the Inspector's accusation. *Did he actually witness my attack and did nothing, say nothing all these years?*

'Ariadne's attacker has been charged today with her assault. His name is Freddie Stuart, and he was a handyman working at the Manor up until the week of the party. He was sacked by George's father for stealing. Whether he attacked you out of anger towards your family, or if it was simply opportunistic, I doubt even he knows. He was drunk when he came across you in the woods, Ariadne.'

Sofia turned to Ariadne and continued to address her. 'He was originally from Newcastle. He came south for work. He has a Geordie accent, just like the one you thought you heard that night, Ariadne.'

'What? So who is the man buried in the woods?' she asked.

'My brother,' Angeline replied, with an even tone. Tears had begun to flow silently down her face.

Sofia looked solely at Augustus when she continued her account.

'You, Augustus Goode, saw Freddie Stuart come round, about the same time an undergardener arrived on the scene and tried to restrain him. He probably heard Ariadne's cries for help and came to investigate. You watched as Freddie attacked Luc Dubois, knocking him down unconscious. Again, you did not intervene. You simply watched.

'After Freddie left, Bart arrived on the scene. I can only assume Bart thought Luc had attacked his sister. Bart either hit him with a rock to teach him a lesson, or they fought, and Bart subsequently hit him during the tussle. Is that what happened, Augustus?'

'I wouldn't know. I wasn't there.' Augustus's tone was even. He was cold and unemotional.

'Yes you were,' interrupted Felicity. 'You told me you saw Bart kill a man. Or are you still full of shit?'

Sofia picked up where Felicity left off. 'I know you witnessed the attack. At least the one on Luc Dubois, because Freddie Stuart gave us a statement today admitting to the attack. He confirmed that after his fight with George, he lashed out at Luc before running away. He also stated, when he ran off, he saw someone crouched down in the bushes. He identified you as that man. The moon was full that night, it wasn't so dark that he didn't recognise you.'

'He's lying.'

'He has no reason to lie. He is being charged with attempted rape. You saw your brother approach Luc, and instead of intervening, you watched your brother attack and kill an innocent man. I would like to believe you didn't think Bart would actually kill him. Or maybe that was what you were hoping for? Obviously in the hope of using it to your advantage one day.'

Augustus remained silent. His face revealed nothing, it was completely devoid of emotion.

'Your only mistake was boasting about the murder during a drunken moment. Felicity was able to use that information against Bart during their divorce.'

'That's a lie,' remonstrated Felicity, although there wasn't much force behind the remark.

'It's the truth, Mother,' Bartie said. 'You cost me my relationship with my father. As you did for Charity and Verity. I hope it was worth it.'

Felicity knew to remain silent; she was already on shaky ground with her son.

Before Sofia could continue her recital, Augustus stood up to leave.

'Your accusations will have to be said in the presence of my lawyers, madam.'

Bartie jumped up and pushed his uncle back down.

'Sit down! This is coming out one way or another. Today!' declared Bartie to the entire room. DC Das showed Bartie back to his seat and urged him to remain calm. Verity couldn't believe what she was hearing. It was all making sense now. She had no intention of leaving, not when it was getting interesting. Charity sat quietly; tears ran down her face. She was finally understanding her family.

Augustus's steel-cold eyes bored into Sofia's. He finally spoke. Which was exactly what Sofia was waiting for.

'This has nothing to do with me or my family. My only crime is not reporting what Bart did. Bart killed Luc

Dubois, and you have Bart's killer right here,' he said, shifting his glare to Angeline. 'I killed no one.'

He rested back on his chair with a self-satisfied grin on his face.

'Your estate has been failing for many years, Mr Goode,' Sofia said, opening another folder. 'You knew your brother would buy up the Manor to protect his secret. But on learning of his illness and imminent death, he refused to give you any more money. He had nothing to lose. Your hold over him was gone. But I have been informed by Bart's lawyers, that, whilst Bart was convalescing after his treatment, he planned on buying the entire estate once it fell into foreclosure. No doubt forcing you out.'

'This is all hearsay,' Augustus snapped.

'I have here an email from Bartholomew Goode to Mr Billingsworth asking him to make an offer on the Manor. Can you please confirm what your client requested during his absence, Mr Billingsworth?'

Hugo spoke, 'Yes. I can confirm Bart asked Sam and myself to buy the Manor as soon as the bank foreclosed on it. Bart thought this would happen during his convalescence, but the foreclosure and bankruptcy hadn't come through by the time he arrived back in England. It was only a matter of time, though.'

Ariadne stood up and walked over to Angeline and sat down beside her. She felt only pity for her friend. Ariadne's miserable family had destroyed hers. Everyone started to stir. Except for Henrietta who sat quietly in an armchair, eagerly watching the proceedings.

As accusations started to fly around the room, the clamour became almost unbearable. Sofia asked for everyone to settle down.

'Augustus, you needed a hold over your younger brother. If George had actually killed Freddie Stuart, I doubt you would have covered it up. But when Bart arrived on the scene, you saw an opportunity. Maybe you knew Bart better than anyone else and hoped he would react the way he did. Nevertheless, you've been blackmailing Bart ever since.'

Augustus looked like he wanted to kill Sofia, which is exactly what she was aiming for. She needed to bait him.

'My brother was innocent,' Angeline cried. 'You took my mother's son from her that night. I knew something had happened to him. He would have contacted us if he was planning on leaving the estate. We had no proof and had to accept what the police said. That he may have died sometime after he left.'

Sofia looked from Angeline to Augustus.

'It wasn't until Angeline received an email telling her that her brother had been killed at the Manor that she began her own investigation. Is that correct, Angeline?'

'*Oui*, we didn't know he was missing until weeks after when he failed to call or write. I visited Ashburton Manor about a month later and spoke to your father, Ariadne, who told me my brother was paid up and left. I also spoke to a groundsman who also said my brother had left. So, I had to accept he died elsewhere.'

'I'm ashamed to say that was my father you spoke to all those years ago.' George spoke up for the first time. 'Bart told me to remove everything from his room, so it would look like he left. I'm so sorry. My father didn't know anything. It simply looked as if Luc left. Please believe me, I have lived with your brother's death every day and night since he was killed. Please forgive me.'

'But you never gave up hope,' Ariadne said, holding Angeline's hand. 'Did you?'

'*Non*, I put my brother's picture on a missing persons website a few years ago, in the hope someone might recognise him. We even offered a reward. It was about seven months ago that I received the email telling me Bartholomew Goode had gotten away with murder. I didn't know who sent it, so I couldn't question them. I didn't know if the accusation was simply vindictiveness or the truth. I came to Kent and swore to myself I wouldn't stop until I found out what happened to Luc.'

'But then Bart was diagnosed with cancer, and you thought he had died,' prompted Sofia.

Angeline turned to Ariadne, '*Oui*. I befriended you when I arrived because you were there that night. I also spoke to Augustus, who said he knew nothing. I sensed you knew something, because I could see you were struggling with your own demons. I hoped if I helped you, you would open up about what happened that night. Once you did, I knew my brother was not the man who attacked you. I had to find out the truth, for my mother's sake.'

'Did you kill my father?' Bartie asked Angeline.

'*Non*. I did not stab him. He was already dead when I confronted him on Saturday night. My mother wants Luc home. I thought… I thought Bart would do the honourable thing and tell me where he was buried. But it was too late.'

'It was Angeline who broke into the Potts & Billingsworth offices last week in search of proof that Bart was still alive,' Sofia said. 'You see, someone had emailed her and told her he was.'

Angeline paused and looked at Ariadne again before continuing, 'The second email I received said Bart was still alive. I knew his lawyers would know the truth. They were also there the night my brother died. I broke into their office looking for information on Bart. I knew the game must be a hoax. I should have told you, Ariadne, but I decided to let it play out. I wasn't sure what to do. Once the game was over, Bart would return, then I could question him, demand he tell me the truth.'

'I didn't know for some time what happened later that night. George finally confided in me years later. He said he only hit him once to defend me. But he's lived with the guilt of his death all his life,' Ariadne said.

'But Angeline wasn't the only one to know Bart was still alive. Isn't that right, Henrietta?' Sofia said, turning to her.

Henrietta looked up at Sofia. She remained silent and simply nodded.

'What is she talking about, Hen?' Augustus demanded. Henrietta ignored her husband.

'You're right, Chief Inspector. I knew. A friend of mine was staying at the Swiss clinic Bart attended. She was having plastic surgery to remove years of boredom married to her useless husband. She was shocked when she heard of Bart's death last week, considering she saw him leave the clinic happy and healthy. I rang the clinic, and a nurse told me Bart had left and headed to the Bahamas to recuperate before heading home.'

'Did you tell anyone what you knew?' Sofia asked.

'*Shut up, Henrietta!*' interrupted Augustus.

'Why don't you go fuck yourself?' she replied calmly. 'I was the one who emailed Angeline about what happened that night. And again, once I found out Bart was still alive.'

'Did you tell your husband?' Sofia asked.

'No. I wanted to see the look on his face when he discovered Bart was still alive. I hoped Angeline would go to the police with what she knew. I only knew that your brother was killed and possibly buried somewhere on the estate. I knew Bart and George were involved. I hoped, when it all came out, Bart and Augustus would turn on each other to save themselves.'

'Angeline confirmed with us today that she confronted Augustus after hearing Bart was still alive. Didn't you?'

'*Oui.*'

'So what if I knew. I didn't kill him. She did,' Augustus snarled, pointing his finger at Angeline.

'Angeline have you ever been to Ashburton Manor?' Sofia asked.

'*Oui*! Last year, I broke in. I was looking for documents that would help me find out about my brother. I wanted to know who else worked there, so I could talk to them. I searched in the attic.'

'Your investigation led you to Freddie Stuart, didn't it?'

'Yes! He was cagey, difficult. He didn't want to talk to me at first, so I knew he was involved somehow, especially after Ariadne told me about that night. She never said her attacker was French. Only that he spoke with a strong accent. It could just as easily have been an English accent.'

'What did he eventually say to you?'

'He admitted to being there. That he was drunk. But he was adamant that he didn't kill anyone. I showed him a picture of Luc, he remembered him as a gardener but couldn't recall who he hit that night. He said he was too drunk to remember. But he was lying.'

'Can you describe what you saw when you entered the library to confront Bartholomew Goode?' Sofia asked.

'*Oui.* I entered the Hall through the back door which was unlocked. I found Bart sitting in a chair, he had been stabbed through the chest. His dogs were sitting beside him. I've met them before with Ariadne, so they didn't make a fuss when I walked into the room. I was too late. There was nothing I could do, so I left the way I came in.'

Everyone remained quiet in the room, until Felicity broke the silence.

'Well done Miss Marple, so who killed Bart?' her patience was running thin.

'Actually, I've always preferred Hercule Poirot,' Sofia mused before continuing.

'Bart's near-death experience made him take stock of his life. He had offended all of you at his will reading. Then made fools of you again with his game. Zachary, he refused to bail you out of your corrupt business affairs. Charity and Verity, he refused to increase your allowances because of your frivolous lifestyles. He stopped paying you blackmail money, Felicity, and he planned to buy Ashburton Manor out from under you, Augustus. You had just as much to lose if the police became involved. You're the most desperate and vindictive person in this room. I no doubt believe Bart would have removed Luc's body from the woods once he owned the estate. Then refurbished it before re-selling it at a profit, no doubt. You couldn't have that now, could you?'

'I didn't stab my brother, as you well know, Inspector,' Augustus said, gritting his teeth. 'I have an alibi.'

'True. Bart was stabbed on Saturday night. But prior to being stabbed, he was poisoned.'

Sofia allowed the allegation to sink in.

'Angeline didn't know you witnessed her brother's death, only that you were seen that night. She asked you for help in exposing Bart. You hoped she would go to the Hall and confront Bart, lash out, maybe threaten or kill him. When you heard your brother had been stabbed, you assumed she had killed him. All your problems were solved.'

Augustus was turning red with rage. But he said nothing, staring Sofia down, daring her to continue.

'I believe you poisoned Bart. After Angeline told you he was still alive, you saw an opportunity. On Saturday, when everyone was at the Hall trying to solve the second clue, you snuck into the library and injected the top row of Bart's cigars with strychnine. You knew his habits. You knew he enjoyed sitting by the fire, drinking a scotch and smoking a cigar while reading a book. It was only a matter of time before your brother returned to the Hall. You didn't want Bart to go to prison, you certainly wouldn't get any money if he did. But if he were dead, you might.' Sofia paused to let what she said sink in.

'You knew the game would be over soon, then Bart would announce his resurrection. So, you played along. But then you learned that he had been stabbed, and you were off the hook. However, you couldn't go back and retrieve the cigars because the police had been posted around the Hall. Unfortunately for you, he smoked the cigar before he had been stabbed.'

'This is all conjecture, madam,' Augustus said.

Sofia shifted her attention. 'Rats are filthy vermin aren't they, Henrietta? Especially when you can hear them scurrying around in the attic.'

'Yes, they are, Chief Inspector.'

'The rats your wife said she heard in the attic. Those were, in fact, Angeline searching for old employee records. I daresay she visited the Manor on more than one occasion until she found what she was looking for.' Sofia removed a piece of paper from one of the folders in her hand. 'I have an invoice in my hand from a company you employed to fumigate the Manor last year.'

Snidely, Augustus asked, 'What does that have to do with anything?'

'We contacted the fumigation company and learned what chemicals were used in the pesticide. The poison used to kill your brother was a match to the chemicals used by the exterminators. Each time your brother inhaled on his cigar, he inhaled strychnine. He would have experienced tightness in the jaw, rigidness in his arms and legs, muscle pain, and, finally, he would have had difficulty breathing, then a slow, frightening and painful death.'

'Proof, Inspector, you can't prove any of it,' Augustus said, standing up to leave. 'I won't stand here any longer and listen to your insults. If you wish to discuss this further, then do it in front of my lawyers.'

'Yes. You will,' Bartie said, standing in front of him, blocking his exit. 'Sit down.' Bartie squared off against his uncle.

'*What would be the point in killing Bart?*' Augustus yelled. '*Without him, I'd have lost the Manor anyway!*'

'I daresay you believed your nephew or Ariadne would have given you the money needed to bail you out. Or maybe you're just a sadistic bastard who wanted to teach your brother a lesson. Like you did thirty years ago.'

'My lawyers will rip your theory to shreds.'

'Shut up, Augustus,' Henrietta snapped, from across the room. She stared her husband down. What she had to say was a long time coming.

'I saw Augustus, Inspector, in the garden shed on Friday night. I followed him. There was mostly rubbish in the shed. No reason for Augustus to go in there, he never did before. Once he left, I entered. I wasn't sure what he was doing in there, but there was a black plastic bag on the floor under the counter. It covered a used drum that the fumigators brought with them to kill the rats which I thought were in the attic. Which is ironic, as the only rat in my home is my husband. If you send your forensic team into the shed, I'm sure you'll find my husband's DNA all over the drum.'

'Shut up, you stupid bitch!' Augustus yelled.

'I'll testify in court if necessary, Chief Inspector,' Henrietta said, defiantly.

Augustus lunged towards Henrietta. He slapped her hard across the face.

'Shut your fucking mouth.'

Before he could strike her again, James and Bartie pounced on him. Tackling him to the ground. Carl joined them and quickly handcuffed Augustus. He hoisted him up and both Carl and Ronnie held onto him.

Carl looked at Sofia, with raised eyebrows, as if to say 'that was close'. Sofia was alarmed by Augustus' outburst. She was on shaky ground, but she finally had her smoking gun, thanks to Henrietta.

Bravely, Henrietta stood up and, with the dignity of a saint, she walked over to her husband and slapped him hard across the face. Henrietta knew Augustus better than anyone in that room. She knew he was a killer.

'I didn't know my husband knew that Bart was alive by the time we received the second clue. He obviously decided to play along with the game like I did. If I had known, I would have warned Bart,' she said.

'Augustus Goode, we are charging you with the murder of Bartholomew Goode and as an accessory to the murder of Luc Dubois,' Sofia said.

'My lawyers will destroy you,' hissed Augustus.

'Read him his rights please, Ronnie,' Sofia said, 'and get him the hell out of here.'

Ronnie escorted Augustus from the room, forcefully.

No one spoke again until he was gone.

Angeline sighed heavily; it was finally over.

Sofia was pleased with the outcome. She asked Shirley to send a forensic team to Ashburton Manor.

Sofia had an idea of who stabbed Bartholomew Goode, but she couldn't prove it. Considering the security cameras were turned off, anyone could have entered and stabbed him. George or Augustus, if Henrietta had fallen asleep. Ariadne or even Eleanor if one of them had slipped out that night. Even Angeline was still a suspect, but her instincts told her Angeline was not Bart's killer.

'Will you be charging Angeline with anything?' Ariadne asked.

'She did break into the law offices. But that will be up to Hugo and Sam, if they decide to press charges,' Sofia said, looking pointedly at the two men.

Hugo nodded his agreement; it was best to let the incident drop.

Ariadne walked over to Angeline. PC Hubbard took a couple of steps backwards to give them a moment in private.

'All this time. Was our friendship a lie?' Ariadne asked her old friend.

'*Non*, I truly care about you, *mon amie*. I could see you were in pain, and I truly wanted to help you. But I needed to know the truth about my brother. My mother and I have been living with this pain for thirty years.' Angeline put her fist to her chest. 'I wish you could have known my brother, you would have liked him.'

'I daresay I would have. I do remember a young French man working in the gardens that summer. There were three gardeners if I remember rightly. He always smiled at me and said *bonjour*, but I never knew his name. After that night, I was so messed up, I never thought of him again, I'm sorry.'

'It's not your fault, Ariadne. But I had to have justice for my brother. If you knew how my mother has suffered all these years. You would understand.'

'I do understand, Angeline. You've helped me, now it's my turn to help you.'

'*Merci*. But you have your sister back now, you must confide in her.'

Angeline kissed Ariadne on both cheeks, before rising and leaving with PC Hubbard.

Felicity watched Angeline leave the room with one of the police officers. She saw her opportunity to confront Ariadne. She stole herself stealthily across the room.

'We need to talk about Bart's will. Is tomorrow too soon?' she said, not seeming the least bit perplexed by what had just happened.

'I'll talk about the will when I'm ready, Felicity, and when I do speak, it will be to Bartie, Charity and Verity. Now, if you don't mind, please leave my home.'

Felicity took a step back. Her eyes widened. She needed no more persuasion and left in a stupor. Charity and Verity followed behind her but not as swiftly as they once did. Both girls nodded at their aunt before leaving.

'That felt good,' Ariadne said.

Bartie gave his aunt a wink and said his goodbyes. He was followed by Eleanor, who hugged Ariadne and said she would speak with her soon. She was going back to London with Timothy. Ariadne reassured them the money would be replaced. She would help Timothy and Zachary. But Zachary's days in the firm were over. Zachary wasn't able to protest before Beatrice accepted and marched him out. Her home was saved, but their marriage wasn't.

Ariadne said goodbye to Hugo and Sam. 'I'll be in touch shortly regarding Bart's will.'

'Anything you need, Ariadne. It's time to look to the future,' Hugo said, before both men said their goodbyes and left. Glad that the Goode family scandal would not tarnish their establishment.

James and Augustus III spoke with their mother quietly before leaving. Their lives had just been demolished. James reassured his mother they would rebuild elsewhere.

The only people left at the Hall were George, Ariadne, Henrietta, Sofia and Carl. Sofia still needed to clarify a few details with Henrietta.

'Why did you send that email to Angeline, telling her about Luc?' Sofia asked.

Henrietta replied, 'My husband talks in his sleep. He spoke about the murder from time to time. His gibberish didn't make sense most of the time, until I realised he was talking about the wrong man being killed. He was there that night with Bart. That's how he was able to blackmail him all these years. I searched for news reports of missing persons around the same time and found Luc's details on a missing person's website. I knew it had to be him, buried somewhere in the woods. I thought his family deserved to know the truth and I wanted Augustus out of my life, so I emailed Angeline. I thought he was only involved in the cover up. I should have known better. Then, I thought it would all come to nothing when we thought Bart was dying of cancer. It wasn't until my friend called with condolences about Bart that I learned he'd recovered and was still alive. I emailed Angeline again. I didn't believe for a moment that she stabbed Bart. She wanted the truth not vengeance. But my husband was another matter, Inspector.'

'Every action has a reaction, Mrs Goode,' Sofia said. 'Why didn't you simply come to the police, with your suspicions?'

'I had no evidence except the ramblings of a man who talks in his sleep. Bart and Augustus would have closed ranks. I would have been the only one to suffer, Inspector. Now, if you'll excuse me, I need to go home and pack.'

Ariadne had overheard their conversation and stepped in.

'Henrietta.'

Henrietta turned to her sister-in-law.

'I'll take care of any debts the Manor has. You don't need to leave, it's your home. Leave it with me.'

Henrietta nodded and said thank you with as much dignity as she could muster, then walked out of the room.

Outside the Hall, Henrietta climbed into the back of the police car and was escorted home. She leaned her head back on the head rest and sighed. It was finally over. If Ariadne was genuine about her offer, she had just been given a lifeline. She now had to rethink her position. She no longer had to sell the Manor, which she had put so much blood and sweat into over the years.

Henrietta pulled out her mobile and called her brother. She informed him she would now be in a position to clear the Manor's debts. She was calling in his promise to invest in the Manor and help her turn it into a hotel with an award-winning restaurant as she had always wanted.

Henrietta's brother agreed, now that her husband was out of the way. Her only task now was to inform her sons of her decision. And that she would now be in charge of the Manor, and its future success.

Back inside the Hall, Sofia and Carl said their goodbyes. Sofia would need to organise the transfer of Luc's body back to France. She agreed to let Angeline update her mother about her son's death. The last thing she had wanted was to tell Emmanuelle that she has arrested her daughter for break-in and entry, or worse, murder. But Sofia was confident Angeline did not kill Bartholomew Goode.

Driving back to London, Sofia remained quiet. Carl knew she was thinking about the case.

'Penny for your thoughts,' he prompted her.

Sofia looked over at him, 'I think I know who stabbed Bartholomew Goode. Only I can't prove it. Not now, maybe never.'

'You think it was Ariadne, don't you?'

'Yes. She had means and motive. She knew the grounds and the security system. She could have slipped out while Eleanor slept. If she knew that Bart was still alive and what he had done all those years ago. But it's only ifs and maybes.'

'Well... At least you have one of his murderers. Two would have been a bonus,' smirked Carl.

'True. But a crime was still committed.'

'And what about the crime committed against her? If she acted on impulse, it wasn't premeditated like Augustus's crime.'

'I know.'

'Then justice has been served. What would arresting her do?'

Sofia wasn't sure if justice had completely been achieved. Bart was stabbed in a moment of rage. It was a crime. Ariadne wouldn't have known he was dying. If she did indeed stab him.

After everyone had left, Ariadne and George took a long walk through the gardens. Her gardens. They watched Laurel and Hardy run ahead of them towards the lake, looking forward to their favourite pastime.

'Is it too late to start over?' he said. 'Do you think we deserve happiness after everything that has happened?'

'Everyone deserves redemption,' Ariadne said.

'To think, it could all have been different if Bart hadn't hit Luc. Our lives could have taken other paths.'

'We have to let go of the past, George. Nothing good will come from it.'

'What will you do with the Hall?'

'I'm going to keep it. I'm giving Bartie, Charity and Verity the bulk of the money. A small annuity will go to you, Hugo and Sam. Plus I agreed to bail out Zachary, for Eleanor and Timothy's sake. I'm also going to help Henrietta. Bart's children don't really want the Hall, they love living in the city. They don't appreciate it as we do. It will be theirs one day, but for now I want to look after it.'

'It won't be cheap to run.'

'A yearly allowance will help with the upkeep. I thought we could open the gardens up to the public. What do you say? We could look after the Hall together? Unless you don't want to marry me.'

George stopped in his tracks. His grin was as big as the mischievous quarter moon. 'I thought you'd never ask.'

Ariadne walked arm in arm with the man she would have married many years ago, if not for her brother's cruelty.

It was time to look to the future. The past no longer mattered.

Back at the Yard, Sofia congratulated her team for a job well done. Once all their reports were written up and Augustus was booked in, she offered to cook her team dinner tonight.

Walking into her office, she found a bouquet of flowers on her desk.

Sofia knew who they were from before she opened the card.

> Thinking of you.
> Till we meet again.
> *Harry*

Sofia dialled his number, 'Thank you for the flowers. They're lovely. When and where?'

'What about dinner tonight?'

Sofia cringed. *I have the worst luck!* She couldn't change her plans now. 'Argh, unfortunately, I'm cooking dinner for my team tonight, we've solved both murders.'

'Well done, smarty pants.'

'Thank you, for everything.'

'I'm accompanying Luc's body back to France. I promised Emmanuelle Dubois I would. Why don't you come?'

'I'd love to. You're a good man, Harry.'

'I aim to be. Well… What about tomorrow night?'

Again Sofia prevaricated, 'Oh, I can't. Francesca is eating at her grandparents tonight while I cook for my team. I can't flog her off to my parents three nights in a row.'

'Why don't I cook for both of you then? I would like to meet her,' he said.

Sofia took a moment to decide. She had never brought a man home before. But she was more worried about Harry than Francesca. He would have to deal with her daughter's inquisition. But… Then again!

'Sounds great. I should warn you, my daughter Googled you the other day.'

Sofia heard Harry laugh on the other end of the line.

'Then I better wear my best tie.'

'Goodnight Harry. Till we meet again.'

'Night Sofia.'

Sofia picked up some groceries on her way home and prepared dinner. She walked Francesca over to her parents' place before her team arrived.

'We're having dinner with Harry tomorrow night. So be on your best behaviour.'

'Can I have a dog? *Please.*'

'Will you walk it, feed it, brush it and bath it?'

'Probably not.'

'I'll think about it.'

THE WORLD

The twenty-second card of the major arcana

*The World signals success and completion.
You have come full circle and can now rejoice in your
success and happiness. Your dedication will pay off
through work, relationships, finances and life. It is a time
for celebration.
However, if in reverse, you may feel you do not deserve
these rewards and don't know how to let go. You must
believe in yourself and that you are deserving of your
success. Then you will have come full circle.*

EPILOGUE

Mid-Summer's Eve

Summer solstice, 30 Years ago

'Ariadne!' George called again. He headed into a small wood which was nestled on the far side of the estate. The moon helped guide him as shards of light resonated through the trees. The air was still and warm as he walked on. A cry echoed around him. Is sounded like a red fox. He turned around, unsure of where it came from. Then he heard it again and raced towards the sound. He found Ariadne on the ground with a man on top of her. One of his hands was trying to cover her mouth, while the other was removing her underwear. She was struggling underneath him.

George's anger flared up instantly; he flew at the man, grabbing him from behind, pulling him off Ariadne. They tussled around on the grass and away from her. The man elbowed George in the ribs, but he recovered quickly, raised himself up and punched the man squarely in the face, the man fell back with force, unconscious. George could smell alcohol on his breath. The man didn't move, he lay lifeless. He wasn't a guest at the party, but there was a familiarity about him. He was shabbily dressed and unshaved.

George rushed to Ariadne, he picked her up in his arms and carried her back to the Manor. He could feel her body shaking in his arms as she whimpered. He wanted to hold her for eternity and make everything all right. When they approached the clearing, Bartholomew was there. He ran towards them.

'What the hell happened to my sister?'

'She was attacked. I'm taking her back to the Manor,' George said.

'Shit! Take her up to her room and use the servant's entrance.'

'I'll call the police,'

'Noooo!' cried Ariadne.

'Just take her to her room. Did he run off?'

'No. I left him in the woods.' George nodded his head to indicate where he left the unconscious man. George was dimly aware of Bart running towards the woods while he carried Ariadne back to the Manor.

On George's instructions, Bart found a semi-unconscious man, who was beginning to stir. He grabbed at his hair as he tried to stand up. Bart didn't recognise him as a guest from the party. Neither as an estate worker. But he'd been away most of the year at Oxford, so it could have been anyone.

The man mumbled something unintelligible. Bart was reeling, but he had no intention of calling the police and dragging his family name through the mud. He decided to teach the deviant a lesson. He threatened him and shook him. The young man tried to find his feet. He yelled something in French as he tried to fight Bart off. As they tussled and grabbed at each other, they fell to the ground. The young man elbowed Bart in the face. Bart grabbed a rock nearby and hit him over the head with it.

'That'll teach you to touch my sister,' he shouted, falling to the side of the man. The young man lay unconscious. Blood began to flow from the side of his head. Bart waited for him to move, but he didn't. He appeared lifeless. Bart quickly checked for a pulse; he couldn't find one. Bart began to panic. He hadn't hit him *that* hard, had he? He couldn't have. He fell back on the ground in a wave of horror. What had he just done! His mind raced. *What to do? What to do?* He was thinking of fleeing the scene when his brother Augustus arrived at his side.

'What the *hell* have you done?' he said.

'I… I wasn't thinking. He attacked Ariadne.'

'You better call the police.'

'I can't… I'll go to jail. What should I do Augie? Help me!'

'I don't know.'

Augustus allowed a few minutes to pass between them before he told Bart to go to the garden shed and get a shovel and bury him deep in the woods.

Bart looked horrified. But he didn't protest for very long.

'Do you recognise him?' Bart asked.

'I'm not sure,' he replied.

Bart thought for a moment. *If he worked at the Manor, we simply say he left to continue his travels or work elsewhere. That will work.* Bart ran back towards the Manor to find a shovel. In the garden shed he also found a large plastic bag in which to wrap the body. He didn't like the thought of this man lying in a dirty shallow grave. *What if the ground starts to smell or rot, or woodland animals dig him up?* he thought. *The smart thing to do is cover him in plastic.*

Bart returned to the woods with his supplies and began digging the grave. It was harder than he thought. He was sweating profusely.

About an hour later, George arrived.

'Fuck… What the hell are you doing?' he yelled.

Bart jumped back in shock, startled by George's arrival. The body was already wrapped in the plastic bag and resting by the half-dug grave. Bart reacted quickly.

'He's dead, George… You killed him.'

'What? I… I didn't hit him that hard.'

'He must have hit his head on something when he fell back. This is really bad, George.'

'Fuck… I didn't mean to. I'll… I'll explain everything to the police. I was protecting Ariadne.'

Bart jumped up out of the grave. 'You can't call the police. I can't have my family involved in this. Besides we've all been drinking and smoking too much shit tonight. Do you want me to get thrown out of Oxford? Look, I'll take care of it. Go home George, and act like everything is all right. If anyone asks, we've been together outside all night. My friends will back me up. I'll talk to Ariadne and Augustus.'

'He knows too?'

'Yes. But he said he'll keep your secret.'

George didn't know what to do, it was all happening too fast. He felt sick.

'Go on, George,' Bart ordered. 'Get out of here, I'll take care of everything. Just keep your mouth shut.'

George did what he was told. He couldn't believe what was happening. What would his parents say if they found out? His hands were shaking as he walked back to the gardener's cottage his family rented. He couldn't believe he'd ruined his life all because of a single punch. George stopped more than once on his way home to throw up. He knew in the pit of his stomach he had just made the biggest mistake of his life.

Bart continued digging the stranger's grave by a large oak tree. He finally heaved the body into the grave and filled it with the upturned soil. Then he covered the area with some layers of grass and woodland debris. He finished a little after five in the morning. As he walked back to the Manor the sun began its rise on a new day. He entered through the servant's entrance and went up to his room where he showered and washed his clothes before falling exhausted into bed.

It was never spoken of again. Well, not for a while anyway.

The Goodes could never let a good opportunity pass them by.

Augustus heard someone cry out and headed towards the sound. He first thought it was a couple of guests making out, but then he saw George charge up to them. Augustus quickly squatted behind a bush as he watched George fight with the man then pick the woman up—*wait, is that Ariadne?*—and carry her back to the house.

Still crouched behind the bush, Augustus watched the drunk man, the one who attacked Ariadne, begin to wake. Augustus recognised him from earlier in the day. He had been loitering around. But when he started to stir, another man appeared on the scene and walked up to Ariadne's attacker.

The drunk lashed out and hit the young man hard, knocking him down unconscious. Then, he staggered out of the woods. He had no intention of hanging around for the police to arrive.

Augustus watched Bart arrive on the scene. Acting so self-righteous. The young man mumbled something to Bart, but he couldn't make out what was said. He watched as Bart fought with the man. He continued watching after Bart hit the man unconscious with a rock. Seeing his brother's distress, Augustus made his move.

Augustus remembered what his father once told him, "If you can't get what you want legitimately, then get it by any means necessary."

Augustus II rose from his hiding place and walked up to Bart and offered him some advice. Bart thanked him and ran off towards the Manor. On his return, Augustus watched his brother bury the man and found it even more comical when Bart blamed George for his death. The cunning prick.

It went without saying, Augustus hated Bart, who was smarter and more charismatic and loved by all who knew him, at home and at Oxford.

But Bart wasn't the heir, *Augustus* was.

Augustus remained by the body while Bart ran back to the Manor to find a shovel. He walked up to the young man. Looking down at him, he knew he had Bart over a barrel. The thought made him smile.

Augustus walked the long way back to the Manor to avoid being seen, smirking to himself all the while *I'll have the last laugh. Bart will pay for this one day.* But only when it suited him.

He would enjoy telling Bart he killed the wrong guy.

Saturday, night of Bart's death

Ariadne took a stroll across the estate gardens, she was having a restless night and needed to clear her head. She decided to walk to the Manor and see if George was still awake. She promised Bartie transparency. But she had to speak with George first.

Once she walked through the clearing, she saw a light on at the Hall, in the library.

Ariadne entered through the back door, using the spare key. She walked past George's office and private rooms. But there was no sign of him. She headed to the library and entered.

Someone was sitting in Bart's chair. She instinctively thought it was George and walked up to him. Ariadne's legs nearly gave out from under her when she came face to face with the brother she believed dead.

She couldn't believe he was just sitting there. She wanted to run up to him and hug him. Then throttle him. Then hug him again. *What is happening!*

Then she felt a deep betrayal. He was just looking up at her. He wasn't even happy to see her. He just looked mortified.

Anger gripped her. He had deceived everyone. The selfish bastard. The will reading, the game, everything was a hoax. She couldn't understand why he would do it. But then she did. It was sport to him. Damn him.

'You bastard,' she snapped.

Bart strained against the pain. His body was rigid, and he was hot with a fever. Pain was shooting from every muscle in his body.

'Help me!' Bart strained against the pain. 'Call an ambulance.'

Ariadne ignored his pleas. She wanted answers.

'Why the hell did you do it? To me of all people? All this time, you've lied to me,' she demanded.

'Not now!'

'Yes, now!'

Bart's pain was getting worse by the minute. He was becoming delirious. He hadn't been able to get out of the chair to call an ambulance. He was fearful. His muscles began to spasm. *How the hell did she find out?* he thought. *It could only have been Augustus. The bastard told her.*

There was no time to argue. He was sick, he needed help. The only option was for Bart to tell Ariadne the truth. He could always pay recompense to George.

'I was protecting the family. I had to make George believe he'd done it. Otherwise, he would have gone to the police.'

'What!'

Bart gritted his teeth and strained against the pain, 'He came around after George took you back to the Manor. I hit him with a rock. I panicked and buried him. Augustus saw me, he told Felicity. I'll make it right with George, I promise. *Now, please help me.*'

Ariadne took a step back. She couldn't believe what she'd just heard.

'I was talking about you pretending to be dead. Playing this stupid game. Oh my God! All these years, you've lied to us.'

Bart turned pale. He felt sick. He needed a doctor.

'I'm sorry.'

'George has been living in hell since that night. All those years… and you simply watched him suffer.'

'It was me or him. Now call an ambulance.'

Rage grew up inside Ariadne. Thirty years of lies and deception had built up into a fiery anger which couldn't be controlled. Ariadne screamed. Seeing a letter opener on the side table, she grabbed it, and without warning, thrust it into Bart's chest.

Ariadne stepped back quickly as blood gushed from the wound. She panted and gasped at what she had just done, as her rage subsided and reality set in. Bart choked and gulped as he tried to inhale for a full minute before he died. Ariadne stood still, traumatised, her hands were covering her mouth. Specks of blood were now on her face. She couldn't undo what she had just done. She began to panic. She wiped the letter opener with her tracksuit top. All the while, Laurel and Hardy sat quietly by their master. Watching everything Ariadne did.

Self-preservation set in. She didn't have time for emotion now.

She left the way she came in. Wiped the door handle to the library and the back door. Then she remembered that the security cameras would have been activated when she entered the Hall. She found the control box inside George's office and turned them off before leaving. She walked quickly back to Rose Cottage and climbed the stairs quietly as not to wake Eleanor. She hid her clothes; she would burn them when she was alone. Tomorrow Bartie was arriving. She stayed awake all night waiting for the police to arrive.

Morning arrived, and the police hadn't banged down her door. Overnight any guilty feelings she had were overcome by the anger she felt towards Bart for a lifetime of lies. She cared for Bart, all the while, he ridiculed her about her anxiety which he caused. And ruining George's life in the process.

When Eleanor woke and Bartie arrived, she delayed their arrival at the Hall by insisting Bartie have a proper breakfast.

On their arrival at the Hall, Ariadne heard one of the dogs howling.

They entered the library…

About the Author

This is my fourth self-published book, which I have enjoyed writing immensely. I'm currently writing my second Sofia Faraday murder mystery.

I have always loved Agatha Christie and many other great fictional crime writers.

My first novel, *A River of Fortune*, won an honourable mention at the 2021 Readers' Favorite Book Awards for Adult Fiction—Adventure.

My second novel, *The Interlopers*, won first prize for a children's fiction book age 8 to 12 category for the 2022 Readers' Choice Book Awards.

Carousel